Praise for Xander

"So much excitement!! So much drama!!! So much love and friendship!! Xander was packed full of everything that makes an addictive book. I was hooked in chapter one and now the withdrawals begin as I wait for the next amazing read from Patricia A. Rasey."

—*Trudy, GoodReads*

" Xander gets an AMAZINGLY WRITTEN FIVE SHOOTING STARS! Its full of passion, danger, action, and a wild crazy love that is all around dream worthy."

— *Marie, Marie's Tempting Reads*

" Xander is the most emotional of the SoS books so far... I went through a rollercoaster of emotions with India as her determination and devotion left me in tears at times."

— *Michelle, Goodreads*

"The book is a page turner and had me sucked in halfway through the first chapter - it's just that good."

— *Christina, Goodreads*

Other Books by Patricia A. Rasey:
Viper: Sons of Sangue (#1)
Hawk: Sons of Sangue (#2)
Gypsy: Sons of Sangue (#3)
Rogue: Sons of Sangue (#4)
Draven: Sons of Sangue (#4.5)
Preacher: Sons of Sangue (special edition)
Love You to Pieces
Deadly Obsession
The Hour Before Dawn
Kiss of Deceit
Eyes of Betrayal
Façade

Novellas:
Spirit Me Away
Heat Wave
Fear the Dark
Sanitarium

Xander
Sons of Sangue

Patricia A. Rasey

Patricia A. Rasey

Copyright © 2017 by Patricia A. Rasey.

All rights reserved. No part of this publication may be reproduced, distributed or transmitted in any form or by any means, including photocopying, recording, or other electronic or mechanical methods, without the prior written permission of the publisher, except in the case of brief quotations embodied in critical reviews and certain other noncommercial uses permitted by copyright law. For permission requests, write to the publisher, addressed "Attention: Permissions Coordinator," at the address below.

Patricia A. Rasey
patricia@patriciarasey.com
www.PatriciaRasey.com

Publisher's Note: This is a work of fiction. Names, characters, places, and incidents are a product of the author's imagination. Locales and public names are sometimes used for atmospheric purposes. Any resemblance to actual people, living or dead, or to businesses, companies, events, institutions, or locales is completely coincidental.

Book Layout ©2013 BookDesignTemplates.com

Ordering Information:
Quantity sales. Special discounts are available on quantity purchases by corporations, associations, and others. For details, contact the email address above.

Xander: Sons of Sangue / Patricia A. Rasey – 1st ed.
ISBN-13: 978-0-9903325-7-2

Dedication

*To those of you who helped me get through this story, you know who you are.
It's been a roller coaster ride of emotions.
Life happens, thank you for being there!*

In Loving Memory

*To my mother, Arlene Miller.
Rest with the angels!
Love you, Mom.
Gone but never forgotten!*

Acknowledgements

Thank you to my cover artist, Frauke Spanuth, from Croco Designs for creating the Sons of Sangue covers, and making Xander one of the best.

*Thank you to my editor, Trace Edward Zaber.
You rock, man!!*

CHAPTER ONE

"YOU GOT SOMETHING OF MINE, ASSHOLE."

Rage itched up Alexander "Xander" Dumitru's spine. No one spoke to him with such blatant disrespect, especially someone who apparently didn't have the courage to do so face-to-face. Heat pooled in his eyes, threatening to turn the ocular organs into twin obsidian pools.

"I want it back," the caller hissed.

The voice on the other end of the blocked call wasn't familiar, rendering Alexander clueless as to what the hell was going on. If he possessed whatever the caller accused him of taking, then he was damn well going to keep it.

"Who the fuck are you calling 'asshole'?"

The caller chuckled, the sound thick with menace. "If I don't get back what belongs to me, that will be *dead* asshole."

Fangs punched through his gums. He didn't bother to hold his vampire DNA at bay. The motherfucker was lucky Alexander was on the other end of the cell and not standing scant inches from him. He'd take great pleasure in draining the craven fuck with little regard.

"I'd say you must have a huge set of balls, but then that would require you having the nerve to call me 'asshole' to my face."

"Consider yourself forewarned," the man said, Alexander hearing the smile in his final words.

The call ended.

"Son of a bitch." Alexander stared at his own reflection in the Gorilla Glass before tossing the cell to the scarred bar.

After grabbing the tumbler of Sprite he had been sipping before the phone rang, he tossed it back, feeling the carbonation burn a path down his esophagus. His gaze went to the bottle of Gentleman Jack sitting half empty on the bar. For the most part, he didn't partake in whiskey. It reminded him too much of his alcoholic parents and how it had torn apart his family. But right now, he'd certainly welcome the buzz, no matter how temporary. Damn his vampire blood for not allowing him a good drunk.

If the idiot on the phone wanted whatever he thought Alexander possessed, then it was only a matter of time before the gutless recreant showed his face.

He ran a hand down his slightly whiskered jaw, his gaze sweeping the dark, empty living area of the clubhouse. Grigore "Wolf" Lupei and Ryder Kelley, the other two residents of the Sons of Sangue clubhouse, had gone to bed a little over an hour ago. He had meant to follow suit, bunking on the sofa since his room was otherwise occupied. Alexander needed to get his head screwed on straight and figure out what the hell he was going to do with the clubhouse's new occupant.

India Jackson.

The black-haired, dark-skinned, leggy beauty had walked into the clubhouse a couple of months ago, pregnant, with nowhere to turn. And his stupid ass had invited her to stay. Kaleb "Hawk" Tepes, the Sons of Sangue club president, had damn near blown a gasket. But what kind of a man would he be to turn her away when she had been in dire need of a friend?

A smart one.

Hell, he still had no clue to the identity of the baby's father. The thought gave Alexander pause. Could the caller have been speaking of India? If that were the case, then he definitely wasn't giving her back. The asswipe, whoever he was, had wanted her to abort the baby, India having expounded as much when she had first moved in. So, in Alexander's eyes, he didn't deserve to have her back. He'd have to go through Alexander first.

Alexander poured himself the other half of the lemon-lime soda, then set the empty silver and green can beside the phone on the bar. He took a sip, then leaned his forearms on the wood and folded his hands around the glass. His gaze traveled to the window, catching sight of a small red flare.

What the fuck?

Righting himself, he skirted the bar and headed through the living area to see exactly what the fuck was going on. The explosion popped his ears milliseconds before the blast wave of air and fire threw him against the bar, knocking the wind from him and snapping bones, flipping him over the counter where he landed in a heap on the floor behind it. The smell of burnt hair, flesh, and wood wafted to his nose.

Alexander groaned.

He tried to suck in much-needed oxygen, only to cough up toxic fumes. Smoke hung thick in the air, obstructing his view. The electricity flickered, then died. He struggled to stand and regain his balance. He could barely hear the thundering of feet headed in his direction over the ringing in his ears. Hacking up more black smoke, he spit on the wood floor.

His equilibrium had him stumbling, grabbing the countertop to steady himself. He'd likely ruptured an eardrum from the force of the blast. Grigore and Ryder skidded to a halt, just shy of what remained of the living area. Ryder snatched the fire extinguisher from the hook on the wall, aimed, and spread nitrogen-laced foam over the area, putting out the remaining flames.

The sofa on which Alexander normally slept was little more than burnt wood and steel. Had he gone to sleep an hour earlier when his MC brothers had, he'd be part of the burned rubble. Alexander ran a smoke-blackened hand through his hair, sending soot airborne.

"What the fuck?" Grigore looked about the room, his jaw slackened. "You all right, man?"

"Other than a few broken bones, never been better," Alexander grumbled, sarcasm dripping from his words. "And no, I didn't get the license plate number of the truck that just drove through the fucking place."

"Truck?"

"Seriously? I was being a fucking smart ass, man. I didn't see a truck."

India stepped up beside him, her footfalls so light he hadn't detected them. She finished shoving her long arms into her robe and tightly cinched the belt around her waist. Thankfully, she had been in his bed and didn't appear hurt.

Her full, deep brown lips rounded. Her gaze swept the room. Rubbing her hands up and down her slender, terry-cloth-covered arms, she asked, "What happened?"

"You okay?" He dare not touch her. Having her underfoot was one thing, but allowing himself to care on a deeper level was an entirely different matter.

"I'm fine." Her gaze left Ryder and Grigore and what was left of the room, and looked up at him. "Everyone else?"

"All accounted for." Alexander rubbed a hand over his nape, his gaze traveling back to his temporary bed. "Good thing I was too keyed up to sleep."

India worried her lower lip but said nothing in response. Nothing needed to be said. He'd been lucky. And if he was placing bets on the guilty party, Alexander had his money on the unknown caller. It was too damn coincidental that the bomb had gone off following the disconnected call.

He needed to find out who he'd pissed off and what the fuck he wanted ASAP.

"Ryder and I'll take a look outside, Xander." Razor-sharp fangs protruded from beneath Grigore's upper lip. "You call Hawk. Let him know what the fuck happened. We need to get this tidied up and quick. We're like sitting ducks, man. We need to get this shit contained."

India laid her hand on Grigore's forearm, reminding Alexander of a time when she had openly flirted with the big ox in front of him. It had been the last time he had used India as a donor or looked upon her as anything other than a friend. Even then, that had been pushing the term until she had asked for his shelter.

"Shouldn't we be calling the police?" she asked.

Grigore smiled at her naivety. Other than Kane "Viper" Tepes's mate, Cara Brahnam—a detective for the Sheriff's Office—the Sons of Sangue had their own form of law. They took care of their own, meted out justice when need be. Whoever the fuck had bombed the clubhouse might want to get on his knees and say his prayers, because if any of the three of them got a hold of the bastard, they'd take him out.

No second chances.

"We take care of our own, *gattina*." Alexander wasn't sure why he had called her "kitten." It had slipped easily enough off his tongue and he wasn't about to examine the stupidity of using the term of endearment where she was concerned. Thankfully, Grigore and Ryder let it pass without comment. "I'll call Hawk."

Grigore and Ryder exited via the door and became visible through the gigantic hole in the clubhouse wall seconds later. He turned to India. "You know of anybody who might benefit from one of us biting it?"

Her dark brown gaze widened. She took in a sharp breath. "You think I had something to do with this?"

He tipped up her chin with his knuckle, forcing her to look at him. He'd easily spot a lie. "I got a phone call just before the blast, *gattina*. The caller said I had something of his and he wanted it back. I'm thinking he was referencing you. You know who that might be?"

"It can't be me."

"You said the baby daddy doesn't want anything to do with your unborn child. I'm thinking maybe he's changed his mind."

She shook her head vigorously, sending her long black braid draping across her shoulder. "It can't be, Xander."

Alexander released her chin and gripped her shoulders. He was having a devil of a time keeping his anger at bay. No one played him for a fool. "Then explain it to me. Because from where I stand, it makes perfect sense. Who is the baby daddy, India? If you want to continue to be under my protection, I need to know what I'm up against."

"Spike."

His heart stuttered. *Fuck!* Kaleb would blow another gasket. "The Devils's Spike?"

"Yes. But don't you see?" She placed her palm against his bare chest, just above his heart. Her touch seared his flesh more thoroughly than the firebomb had moments ago. "He's dead, Xander. Rogue killed him in the café a couple of months back. Dead men can't talk, let alone bomb a place."

"Then you haven't heard." He dropped his hold on her and stepped back, a grimace on his lips.

"Heard?"

"Spike is very much alive, *gattina*. He rose from the dead about a month ago."

Her lips parted as she sucked in air. "That's not possible. The café burnt, along with everyone in it."

India stumbled back a step before Alexander directed her onto a barstool he righted from the blast. Her shock appeared genuine. She looked about as happy with the news as the rest of the Sons when Draven Smith and his mate, Brea, had returned from Mexico. Apparently, Spike had turned up at Brea's godfather's, Raúl Trevino Caballero's, beach house. Draven had left Spike dying at his feet when he went to rescue Brea from her godfather. And for a second time, Spike had cheated the Grim Reaper, disappearing with the Sons of Sangue nemesis, Raúl.

"You don't look too happy about the news." Alexander couldn't help the menace from creeping into his snide remark.

Seriously? Spike?

Could she have stooped any lower? And here he thought her flirting with Grigore had been a low blow. Spike was a miscreant and the thought of him fucking India turned Alexander's stomach sour.

"Happy? Please tell me this is some sort of a cruel joke." Her eyes darted about the clubhouse as if she were afraid her very thought of him might conjure him up. "Rogue killed him."

"Rogue *thought* he had. When we got there and torched the café, somehow Spike had managed to slip by us." Alexander pulled a bottle of water from the refrigerator and twisted off the cap, handing it to India. "We had no clue until he turned up south, a guest of Raúl's. But I don't think that's the worst of it."

India took a long pull from the bottle, then wiped her trembling fingers across her lips. "Please ... what could possibly be worse than having the father of my unborn baby turn up alive?"

"You slept with him, *gattina*."

"Don't remind me." A shiver shook her shoulders. "A definite faux pas on my part."

Alexander raised a brow. She had made the decision. "If you think so lowly of him, then why the hell did you crawl into the sack with him? Or was it rape? I'll fucking kill him. Just say the word."

"He didn't rape me. It was bad judgment on my part."

Alexander chuckled. "Bad judgment is Wolf, *gattina*. Spike?"

"Are you kidding me? Wolf wouldn't have anything to do with me. We were friends, Xander. Nothing more. Besides, I wouldn't have done that to you." She looked at the water bottle clutched in her hands. "I used him to make you jealous. When that backfired, I earned your hate. Spike came along… I don't know, he treated me as though I mattered. But once I got pregnant, his demeanor changed, he became violent. I thought he might hurt me or the baby. That's when I came here."

Alexander tilted up her chin. "You thought I would protect you from him?"

She lowered her gaze, unable to look him in the eye. He couldn't say he blamed her. She had used Alexander to hide out from the man with whom she had chosen to make her bed. Christ! He couldn't wipe that picture from his brain. He had been played for a fool.

India squared her shoulders and lifted her gaze. "I needed your protection. I thought he might come after me. When Rogue said he had killed Tank and Spike, it was then I felt free from the burden of my past."

"Now you know he's alive."

"You mentioned it gets worse. What could possibly trump his rise from the grave?"

Alexander dropped his hold on her and stepped out of reach. His gaze went to the large hole in the front of the clubhouse, where Grigore and Ryder rummaged through the rubble.

"The fact that it's a damn good possibility he's now a vampire."

CHAPTER TWO

India gasped, one of her hands covering her abdomen out of natural instinct. Even if she had yet to birth the child, she was already feeling maternal.

Spike?

Was all kinds of wrong for her and the child.

Risen from the ashes?

One of her worst nightmares come to life. *Strike that.* Her *worst* nightmare. She had made a colossal mistake by taking up with him. She might not regret the result, but she trembled with fear and loathing over her baby ever calling the mean son of a bitch "daddy."

Their affair had been brief. When Spike had come to visit Draven at the Blood 'n' Rave, they had met by accident. She had been looking for Draven when she had found the two huddled in conversation. Spike had all but tripped over her, making her feel beautiful. Something of which her ego was in dire need, given Alexander's rebuff.

She had fallen for Spike's pretty words ... every single one of his pickup lines.

India had found him oddly sexy, a bad boy, the exact opposite of Alexander, who never appeared ruffled. A man of few words, Alexander seemed as though he allowed very little to get beneath his skin. India had developed a bad habit of comparing all men to him, men who stood little chance of measuring up. Due to Alexander's rejection, she had turned to Spike, looking to salve her wounds.

Spike had seduced her into his bed with his pretty lies. Though their affair had been short-lived at best, she hadn't come away unscathed. When she had first followed him to California on his suggestion, it had been exciting, impulsive. Things quickly escalated, taking an ugly turn toward abuse. India had been too damn scared to walk away. In truth, she was afraid of what Spike might do if she did leave. The straw that finally broke the camel's back was when India told him of her pregnancy. He'd slapped her hard enough to knock her to the floor, bruising her cheek. He swore if she didn't get an abortion, he'd cut the baby from her belly himself.

India didn't doubt for a moment the validity of his statement, yet had kept that part of the tale from Alexander.

Her heart beat heavy and she had trouble catching her breath.

How could she have ever shared a bed with a man capable of such violence?

Apparently, she had worn blinders, wanting to believe he was the man she'd followed on a whim, the man who had promised her a fairy tale.

India had quickly packed what little clothes she had taken with her and headed north, sneaking out in the dead of the night while Spike remained passed out from one of his drunken binges. She couldn't return to Draven, knowing he was in deep with the Devils, still selling drugs behind the

Sons' back after they had forbidden him the racket. At the time, she hadn't known about Draven's undercover work for the DEA. Nor did she know Anton "Rogue" Balan was also enlisted to bring down the Devils and the La Paz cartel. Even so, she did her best to secrete away when they were present, not wanting them to report back to Alexander. Although it hadn't started out that way, her relationship with Spike had become more of an embarrassment than a means to make Alexander jealous.

Having nowhere else to turn, India had sought out Alexander, calling upon his sense of honor. On her own, she had no protection from Spike should he decide to come after her. Alexander had thankfully taken her in, making her feel safe for the first time in weeks. With the news Anton had killed Spike at the diner, a weight had been lifted from her chest and she had been able to breathe easier. She'd never have to tell anyone who had fathered her baby, taking that secret to her grave.

Except now, Spike had resurfaced, surviving his brush with death.

Please don't let the son of a bitch have nine lives.

The thought had her teetering on her stool, blackness threatening to consume her. Alexander gripped her elbow, his concerned gaze on hers. Sucking in clean oxygen wasn't going to be an option, not with the smoking rubble. She stifled a cough with the back of her hand, needing to exit the clubhouse to get some fresh air. Surely the fumes weren't good for her or the baby.

India wet her lips with her tongue. "I should probably walk outside. I can barely catch a breath in here."

"You should." Alexander palmed her chin, his concern touching her in ways his hand could not. "But first, I need confirmation from Wolf and Ryder it's safe for you to be outside in the open. I'm not about to take a chance with you. Sit tight for a bit longer."

He pulled a towel from a drawer, then wet it before handing it to her. "Put this over your mouth and nose. Breathe through the cloth. It'll help."

India did as instructed, taking a few deep breaths through the wet rag. "How is it possible for Spike to not only be alive but have vampire genes?"

Dropping his hold on her, he stepped back and rubbed his nape. His vampire DNA, though certainly intimidating and alarming, was also sexy as hell, fangs and all. "Draven watched him being riddled with bullets, left him to die. But when he went after Brea and Raúl, Brea's godfather and the La Paz kingpin that Viper and Hawk have been gunning for, somehow Raúl backtracked and took Spike with him. When Draven and Brea returned to the lower level of the beach home, both Raúl and Spike were missing."

"Leaving seven lives too many," India grumbled beneath her breath. "That doesn't explain the fangs."

"Come to find out, Raúl's a bloodsucker. Brea's godfather took some of Ion's blood years ago while he held him captive."

"Viper's son? Before he died?"

"Somehow the son of a bitch was able to keep it from the Sons all this time. But yes ... unfortunately a full-fledged vamp. From the Tepes's bloodline to boot."

"And Spike?"

"If Draven was correct and Spike was on his way to see the Grim Reaper, the only way he made it out of there was the La Paz kingpin sharing his DNA."

"Well, if that isn't just wonderful." India grimaced, shifting in her seat. "You believe he set the bomb?"

Alexander narrowed his gaze. "I do."

"Meaning you also believe he's coming after me."

"I wish I could tell you otherwise, *gattina*. But, yes, that's my belief."

If Alexander expected her to fall to pieces over the news, he had another thing coming. India had started this mess, and she'd damn well find a way out of it. She'd fight Spike with everything she had. He wasn't getting his hands on her unborn child, even if she had to kill the bastard herself. Spike would never get the chance to be a daddy to her child should he decide to as long as she drew breath.

"Tell me what I need to do."

He raised one dark brow. "Excuse me? *You* aren't doing anything."

"I'm pregnant, Xander. Not an invalid."

"If you value that baby's life, you'll damn well let me and the Sons take care of Spike. You'll stay the hell out of it."

Heat rose up her neck. She'd been taking care of herself for far too long to allow someone else to take over. Sure, she had come to Alexander for protection, but she wasn't about to lie down and play dead.

Ryder walked back into the clubhouse, stopping the argument from leaving her lips.

"All's clear, Xander. Looks like whoever set the bomb is gone. Hell, for that matter, he could've used a remote and had set it from a distance."

"Fucking coward." Alexander looked at India. "Ryder, take her outside to get some fresh air. Don't fucking let her leave your sight for even a second. I need to call Hawk, inform him about this fucking mess. We'll need to call a church meeting … STAT."

"Got it." Ryder held out his hand to India, which she took if for nothing more than her need for fresh air.

She'd speak to Alexander in private later about his need to boss her around. India wasn't going to embarrass him in front of his MC brothers, but she'd be damned if she allowed him to be a dictator. She had a mind of her own and she'd damn well use it.

"No one will get past me and get to her, Xander," Ryder said. "You have my word."

BOBBY "PREACHER" BOURASSA strode into the meeting room of the clubhouse, filling the doorway. Alexander couldn't believe the sheer size of the man. He was definitely a welcomed addition to the Sons of Sangue. The man was a beast. The beard reaching his chest was pretty impressive, too. Good call on Anton, secretary of the Sons, wanting to bring the ex-minister onboard. They had already lost a few good men. The Sons could stand to increase their numbers. Bobby was a good start.

Anton stood and shook Bobby's hand, then bumped shoulders. The two men had been close ever since Anton brought the ex-Devil to Oregon and opened his house to him. "Good to see you, man."

Bobby looked at Alexander, using his thumb to indicate the living area behind him. "Rogue says Spike's the cause of half the wall missing out there? If I find that little fucker, I'll put his lights out for good. He should've never been made P over the Devils. He doesn't have the balls Tank did. Fucking 'yes man' is what he was."

"I can't believe he escaped the café," Anton said, grabbing a bottle of Jack and pouring a couple of tumblers full, handing one to Bobby. "I thought for sure he had choked out. I crushed his windpipe, for crying out loud. Fucker must have sold his soul to walk out of that inferno."

"He was probably long gone before we even torched the place, Rogue," Alexander said. "He's alive at no fault of yours. Son of a bitch does have a fucking death wish, though."

"It would be my pleasure to take him out," Bobby repeated his offer. "Only thing that kept him alive when I was in the Devils was Tank. He's walking on borrowed time, no doubt about it."

"You best get to him before I do then." Kaleb strode into the room. "Spike wants war? He came to the right place. We'll put it to a vote as soon as everyone gets here that any Devil spotted on our side of the border is a dead Devil. It's time to show them what messing with the Sons will get you … a fucking early grave."

"Hear, hear," Grigore spoke up from his seated position at the back of the table, his face half hidden in the shadows. "The only thing a Devil is good for is holding up the dirt from six feet under."

"Not all of them are bad." Anton took his seat at the table. "You won't get a unanimous vote, Hawk. I won't agree to take them all out."

Kaleb snorted. "It figures you'd argue."

"What the hell is that supposed to mean?" One of Anton's blond brows rose. "You weren't the one who spent time in their camp. I agree with you on most accounts where they're concerned. There aren't that many worth a damn, but there are a few I'd go to bat for."

"Then each Devil's demise will be decided case-by-case," Kane chimed in as he walked through the door. "But the guy who blew a hole through our clubhouse? He's a dead man. I don't give a fuck who he is."

"Glad we agree, brother." Kaleb clapped Kane on the shoulder. "Now, where the hell is everyone else?"

Bobby picked up the bottle of Jack and thrust it at Kaleb, stopping just shy of hitting the president in the chest. Alexander contained his chuckle, knowing it wouldn't be well-received. Bobby's action wasn't exactly disrespectful. After all, the bottle never made contact.

"Have a drink, P. It might help take off the edge." Bobby's deep voice rumbled from deep in his chest, gaining everyone's attention. The man's presence alone demanded respect. Alexander could see why Anton liked him. "I'm sure the rest of the Sons will be by shortly."

Alexander detected the humor in Anton's gaze, though his lips remained a straight line. Kaleb had always been a bit high-strung. It was going to be fun watching how he handled Bobby. Position or no in the Sons, he wasn't about to take crap from anyone. Kaleb, on the other hand, demanded respect from all members. He had yet to earn Bobby's.

The rest of the men began filling the room over the next fifteen minutes, each taking a seat around the table, while others stood. The prospects remained outside the meeting room doors, being given the orders to secure the clubhouse. No one got by without an official invite or wearing the Sons of Sangue rockers.

No patch, no entry.

"What's the plan, P?" Grayson "Gypsy" Gabor's normal bright blue eyes were edged in black, telling of his agitated state and the fact his vampire DNA lay close to the surface. "I say we ride. We hunt down Spike and his crew, take them all out."

"Hold on, Gypsy." Anton leaned back in his chair and crossed his arms over his chest. "We have no proof of their guilt at this point."

"You go soft on those bastards, Rogue? They mess with your head while you were playing undercover?"

Alexander, true to his quiet nature, watched as egos and tempers began to flair. Rather than add to the chaos, he sat back and watched, preferring to let others speak. Unless, of course, he felt the need to add his two cents. Which as of now, he didn't. Grayson and Anton had at one time been best friends. Ever since Anton and Grayson had a falling out, over a woman no less, their friendship had been strained. Following Anton's undercover work, though, their friendship had been on the mend. Grayson's comment proved it hadn't yet one-hundred-percent healed.

"Seriously, Gypsy? We going to go there?" Anton shook his head and laughed. "You're right, I spent a good deal of time with those bastards, trying to help out the case for the DEA because Viper's mate, Cara, had asked me to. Like it or not, some of the Devils are good men. My only point was to slow down, figure out who is at fault and take the bastard down. From what we learned from Draven and Brea, and the phone call Xander received, I'd say the evidence points to Spike. I give you my blessing, bro. Take his ass out. Just be careful. Apparently, he doesn't want to die and it appears Raúl Trevino Caballero has taken a liking to him."

"I'll gladly see him dead." Grayson narrowed his gaze at Anton. "And any other Devil who happens to get in the way…"

"Point taken, Gypsy." Kaleb knocked the gavel against the table and gained everyone's attention. "As much as I'd like to admit otherwise, Rogue has a point. We don't need to be taking out the innocent, even if they do wear Devil patches. Let's be smart about this and find out who the hell is guilty. We find them and we deal out justice. If that means taking a few Devils captive, see who we can get to sing, then we will. Spike, on the other hand, doesn't deserve our hospitality."

"I agree." Kane pushed off the back wall and stepped forward. "From everything Xander has said, I believe wholeheartedly Spike is behind the rubble out there. No one leaves here tonight until we get this shit contained. We need to make sure our club is secure."

Kaleb leaned forward, bracing his hands on the table. "While the rest of us are here cleaning this shit up and rebuilding the front of our clubhouse, I want Xander, Rogue, and Preacher scouting for Spike. No one knows Spike better than Rogue and Preacher. Xander apparently has pissed off Spike by holding onto something the asswipe wants. The three of you, go find the fuck. Bring him in. If he gives you any trouble at all, you have my permission to kill him."

"Don't forget," Kane brought up, "it's very likely he's sporting fangs. Go for the kill. Don't take any chances. He won't fight fair."

"Are we agreed then?" Kaleb asked. Low murmurs filled the room, rising in decibels as the energy increased. "Then let's put it to a vote. I motion we take out Spike and any Devil that gets in the way. Do I get a second?"

"I second the motion," Grayson, the Sons' vice president, said.

Once the vote traveled the table, not a single nay had been voiced. Kaleb hit the strike plate again. "It's done. Are there any other matters we need to bring to the table before we contain this shit?"

Alexander cleared his throat. "Since I'll be on the road, as Road Captain, I'd like to request that someone keep an eye out for India. If I'm right and Spike is behind this, then it's India he wants. I can't leave her unprotected."

"Wolf—" Kaleb began before Alexander cut him off.

"No offense. Not Wolf."

Grigore chuckled in the back of the room, knowing damn well why Alexander didn't want him in charge of India. Alexander might not be laying claim to the long-legged beauty, but he'd be damned if he put her in Grigore's care.

"I'd prefer she stays with Viper and Cara."

Kaleb turned and looked at his twin. "Do you mind?"

"The farmhouse is big enough." Kane shoved his hands into his pockets. "She's more than welcome to stay with us. When Cara's at the Sheriff's Office, I could send for a prospect—"

Alexander shook his head. "One of us needs to be with her at all times. I don't want her alone for a minute. If he's a vampire, we can't trust this to a prospect."

Kane nodded. "We'll take care of her, Xander. Spike won't get his filthy paws anywhere near her."

"Someone want to explain to me why there's a huge fucking hole out there?" Vlad Tepes, primordial and the Tepes's great-grandfather, strode into the room, slamming the door closed behind him. "Who the hell did you guys piss off this time?"

Anger and supremacy radiated from him, and he wore it like a boss. A happy Vlad was alarming enough to deal with. A pissed-off one was some scary-ass shit. Long, razor-sharp fangs protruded well past his upper lip, laying claim to his many years of vampirism. His black, marble-like eyes glanced around the room, taking in each man sitting at the table before landing on his oldest living descendants, Kane and Kaleb. Long, ink-black hair flowed past his broad shoulders, framing his tanned face. As big and brawny as Bobby and Anton were, they didn't compare to the primordial.

One of his jet-black brows raised. "Not to mention, someone want to explain to me why there are two undeserving asswipes out there wearing fangs from my DNA?"

Alexander hadn't a clue the primordial was back in Oregon, normally living on his own island off the coast of Belize. But then again, Vlad had a habit of showing up when he was least expected. He supposed Kaleb was the reason he now stood in the meeting room. The club P no doubt called his great-grandfather, a few times over, when Draven and Brea had come back to town with the news of her godfather and his vampire genetics. Vlad was rightfully pissed to see his lineage expand into the Devils and the La Paz cartel. No telling how many new vampires those two might spawn.

The situation needed to be fucking contained.

"WE HAVE A BIT OF A situation, Grandfather."

Vlad moved around the floor soundlessly, as if he merely floated. The skill certainly could be used to sneak up on his enemies, and no doubt the art had been honed over time. There was no one more powerful than his great-grandfather, Kane thought. Vlad was a primordial and the original vampire, his brother Mircea being the second eldest. Vlad continued to keep his brother in captivity on his private island near Belize for his recent shenanigans.

"I hadn't mentioned it to the rest of the Sons, but it's certainly something the three of us need to further explore," Kane continued. "The impossible has happened."

Vlad's chuckle was deep. "Dramatic much, my boy? Nothing is impossible."

"A woman changing a human into a vampire was supposed to be." Kaleb stepped up to the table now vacated by the rest of the Sons. "And yet, it's happened."

"What the hell are you talking about?" Vlad's humor fled. "What female was able to change a human?"

"Brea Gotti." Kane walked around the table and sat on the corner, crossing his arms over his chest. "She came back with the barkeep from the Blood 'n' Rave, now mated."

The twins had no doubt piqued the ancient vampire's interest. "Go on."

Kaleb took in a deep breath. "Brea Gotti is the goddaughter of Raúl Trevino Caballero, kingpin of the La Paz cartel, who as you know now sports fangs. Her late father was a mobster, ran the family business. He and Raúl were quite close. Anyway, we didn't know anything about Brea until recently. Apparently, one of my men, Joseph Sala, had kept her as a mate in secret, telling none of us due to her connection to the kingpin, knowing full well we wanted the man dead. He didn't want us using Brea for our gain."

"Kinky told her to go to Draven should there be trouble," Kane said, "since the Sons of Sangue didn't know about her. When he was assassinated by one of Raúl's men, she sought the barkeep out." Kane tapped the table with his forefinger. "That led them on the chase south where they encountered her godfather, who was already a vampire. Long story short, Draven took it upon himself to bite her, thinking by turning himself he'd better be able to protect her. When he did so, he had no idea women didn't possess the DNA type that was needed to turn humans."

Kaleb took over the story. "A woman cannot turn a human into a vampire with her blood. Only the men carry that trait, or so you've said over the years. Of which was backed up by history. And yet, somehow she did. Draven turned from ingesting her blood. Do you have any idea how that could happen?"

Vlad frowned. "It's never happened before that I'm aware of. Trust me, Rosalee would have had an army of miscreants had she been able to. She tried and failed years ago. Other than who Brea's father was, do we know anything more about this woman? Her roots?"

Kane shook his head. "We know nothing."

"That's where we start. Have the others questioned the anomaly?"

"Not yet, Grandfather." Kaleb righted himself, straightening his spine. "I'm surprised they haven't. Maybe they've talked amongst themselves, but no one has yet asked. We thought it best to keep it quiet until we know more."

"There's something else, now that we're talking oddities." Kane ran a hand across his whiskered jaw. "Ryder Kelley."

"What about him?" Kaleb asked.

"When he was turned, his change happened in a little over a day. Most humans can take up to a week," Kane continued. "You don't find that odd?"

Kaleb shrugged. "Now that you mention it, I guess I never really thought it was something we needed to concern ourselves with. Not everyone's DNA reacts the same."

"Maybe we need to check his roots as well, Hawk, see where he comes from. It might not be anything, but then again we won't know unless we look further into it."

Vlad slapped his hand on Kane's shoulder. "I trust the two of you will figure it out. In the meantime, when I get back to my island, I'll question my brother, see if Mircea has ever heard of this. Raúl and Spike, though, need to be the priority. We don't need these two bumbleheads running around the countryside and turning humans into vampires."

Kaleb chuckled. "Let's hope their egos won't allow it."

"What do you mean?"

"Think about it, Viper. They're going to luxuriate in the power that comes with being a vampire. They won't want their men to revolt against them, but rather hold it over their heads and rule with fear."

"With those two, I think you might be correct, Hawk."

Vlad squared his shoulders and straightened to his six-foot-six height. His black hair fell past his shoulders, complementing his equally black eyes. The man's fierce presence commanded attention and instilled fear. Anyone would be a fool to cross him, including his coward of a brother.

"Great, then I trust the two of you will get to the bottom of these peculiarities. I'll be curious to see who's in their family trees. There's an answer, we just need to find it." Vlad's jaw hardened. "But meanwhile, it's well past time for Raúl and Spike to take their last breath."

CHAPTER THREE

India stepped from the shower and dried herself, feeling much better knowing the smell of the explosion and burnt wood no longer clung to her like a second skin. She piled the terry cloth towel above her head, before stepping into a pair of white lace panties and a matching bra. She glanced at her reflection sideways in the long mirror attached to the back of the bathroom door. Her hand smoothed over her slightly protruding belly. Most might not notice the subtle change, but India could tell the difference. Her normal trim frame had begun to fill out, giving her curves where before she had none.

She couldn't help but wonder what she'd look like in another few months, or what Alexander might think when she began to waddle into a room. Tears sprung to her eyes at the very thought of him and what might have been.

A shiver passed down her spine.

Thank goodness, no one had been injured in the blast.

More importantly, Alexander had not been fused to the burnt metal and steel frame of the sofa. Had he been lying there at the time of the explosion, even his vampire DNA wouldn't have protected him from becoming ash. The very thought of him being killed because of her set her stomach roiling.

Her gaze traveled to the granite countertop of the vanity where she left her Ruger SR9. India had begun carrying following her flight from Spike, fearing he'd eventually come for her and their child. Her fears had been put to rest when Anton announced he had single-handedly killed four of the Devils, Spike included. Now that he had resurrected, she'd taken up the habit once again. She'd not be caught unaware, regardless that she was surrounded by vampires capable of protecting her.

Before leaving the clubhouse following the explosion, she had retrieved her gun from Alexander's bedside table where she had kept it. India had no qualms about pulling the trigger. If Spike thought to steal her away in the dead of the night or while the others were otherwise pre-occupied, then he had another thing coming.

Stepping into a pair of black form-fitting jeans, India pulled them over her hips and fastened them before shrugging into an oversized burgundy fleece, crew neck sweater. She ran her hands up and down her biceps in an attempt to warm what had gone cold since finding out Spike was among the living. India couldn't shake the feeling that Alexander might have been correct.

Spike had been the caller and he was no doubt staking his claim.

Well, fuck him and his demand. India wasn't about to be Spike's victim. Not again. Her Ruger would make damn sure of it. He might have fangs, but her aim was dead-on. She'd take him out, vampire DNA or no. He'd never hit another woman again … more specifically, he'd never hit *her* again.

And God willing, he'd never lay one finger on her child.

"India?" Cara Brahnam called from the other side of the door. "I'm making a pot of coffee. Would you like a cup?"

She gripped the brass knob and opened the door, using her free hand to tuck the gun into the back waistband of her jeans. "Actually, I'd prefer hot tea if you have some. I've never been much of a coffee drinker. Otherwise, water would be fine."

Cara's blonde hair had been piled loosely atop her head in a messy knot, her face makeup-free. Kane Tepes's pretty mate didn't need cosmetics. She was gorgeous and fierce at the same time. India admired the woman for her dedication to her job. Being with Kane, as a member of the Sons of Sangue, was in exact opposition to being a detective, and yet she managed to keep the two separated. She had actually stood up to the MC and convinced them she wouldn't allow it to be a conflict of interest.

"Let me look for the tea." Cara headed for the small kitchen of her and Kane's farmhouse. She rooted through her cupboards. "You'll have to excuse me. We don't keep a lot of food or staples here. Not since Kane and I don't need the sustenance. But Suzi's on her way over. If I can't find any, I'll give her a… Bingo!"

She held up a box of black tea bags. "This work?"

"Perfect." India pulled her gun from her pants and placed it on the countertop. "I can't thank you enough for opening your home to me. I promise not to be underfoot. I used to waitress at the Blood 'n' Rave before I went to California. I'm sure Draven would give me my job back. I'll compensate you for the inconvenience."

"Nonsense. The Sons are family. We help each other." Cara's gaze landed on the black gun, standing out in contrast against the silver-flecked white countertop. "You know how to use that?"

"Well enough. If Xander is correct and Spike is still out there demanding my return, then I can't be too careful." India sat on a barstool next to the breakfast nook. "I refuse to be his punching bag again."

"He hit you?" Her blonde brow arched, an edge to her tone. "Not that I'm surprised."

"Yes. We dated briefly, if that's what you want to call it. When he beat me the last time, I left and never looked back. To be honest, I was more than thrilled to hear Rogue had taken his life."

India heard a car door slam about the time Cara's nostrils flared, her gaze going briefly to the door. "Suzi's here."

"You have somewhere I can lay Stefan?" Suzi Stevens asked, walking through the front door with her son snuggled against her shoulder. "Little guy passed out on the way over."

Cara pointed toward the living area. "Use the other spare room."

Suzi, Kaleb Tepes's mate, returned shortly to the kitchen, shrugging off her coat. She sat on the wooden barstool beside India. "What did I miss? Hawk said someone blew up the clubhouse."

India tugged the terry cloth towel from her head, shaking out her hair and finger combing it. "Not entirely, but there's a huge hole in the side facing the parking lot. Doesn't appear anyone will be sleeping there for a few nights. Alexander asked that I stay here for a bit."

"You can stay until the clubhouse is rebuilt."

"You'll be safe here." Suzi smiled, her hand indicating the Ruger on the counter. "Cara carries a big gun."

"That's not mine." Cara chuckled. "Apparently, India carries a big gun, too."

India shrugged, pulling her hair over her left shoulder. "It's mine. I'm hoping I won't have to use it. But if Spike does show his face, I will aim to kill."

"Good girl. Don't take any chances. Aim for the heart or between the eyes. Only way to kill him is to stop his heart from taking another beat." Cara placed a kettle of water on the stove and turned the knob. Yellow and blue flames popped on beneath the pot. "You want coffee, Suzi?"

"Sure." She turned her concern to India. "What makes you think he might come looking for you?"

India supposed she owed them the truth. After all, Alexander had put her into their care. It was only a matter of time before she could no longer hide beneath baggy clothes. "Spike is my baby's sperm donor."

Cara's jaw dropped, not bothering to hide her shock. "You're pregnant?"

"No shit? Xander know?" Suzi asked.

"He knew I was pregnant." India nodded. "With Spike dead, I thought the identity of the father was mine to keep. Following the explosion, I came clean about it being Spike."

"Son of a bitch is like the fucking Terminator. He won't go down and stay down. He keeps rising from the dead." Cara grabbed the steaming kettle, filling a tea cup with hot water and a steeping bag before pouring mugs full of coffee for Suzi and her. "I sure as hell hope he can't walk on water or turn water into wine."

Suzi snorted. "Bad comparison."

"Couldn't help myself." Cara laughed, then sobered just as quickly. "Seriously, India, we have your back. You're safe with us, even if the piece of crap has fangs."

India dipped her tea bag up and down into the steaming water. "You can't know how much that means to me."

"You're one of us." Suzi patted her forearm. "We take care of our own. I'd like to see Spike try to get past us. I don't think he has the balls."

"No, but Raúl Trevino Caballero certainly does," Cara pointed out. "*Him* we have to take seriously. He was hard to kill as a human, what with his freaking army of assassins. Add fangs and we have a huge problem on our hands. He'll be gunning for us, no doubt about it. And if Spike is hanging out with the kingpin, you need to take this shit serious, India.

Don't go anywhere without one of us. Even with your Ruger, you won't be safe."

"What about finding a job?"

"You won't need one."

"Even though you all are kind enough to give me a place to stay, I refuse to allow it to go by without compensation."

"I won't take your money."

India shook her head. "I refuse to freeload off your hospitality. If nothing else, I'll need food, which you don't require. You'll not pay for something you don't call for."

"Fine. I understand, believe me. Kane and I argued over me remaining with the Sheriff's Office. Suzi still works part time at the nursing home. If nothing else, it gives us an excuse to get away from our mates for a few hours," Cara jested with a wink. "Ask Draven for your job back, but you best run it by Alexander first."

No reason at all Cara and Suzi wouldn't want to spend what free time they had in the company of their hot-as-sin mates and in their beds. If she were only as blessed to be able to say the same. She had dreamed of as much with Alexander. But now that he knew she had slept with Spike and conceived his baby, that wasn't likely ever to happen. She had screwed herself when she followed Spike to California. Alexander might be offering her his friendship, but it would be a cold day in hell before he offered her his bed with him in it.

"If you insist on going to work, then someone will have to shadow you." Suzi took a sip of coffee. "I'm not sure Xander will agree to it, knowing Spike is most likely the guilty party for the hole in the front of the clubhouse."

India took a sip of her tea. Even though she wished Alexander was completely off base, she couldn't pose a single argument. Her gaze traveled to the Ruger on the counter. No, Spike was coming after her, she felt it to the marrow of her bones. She wasn't going down without a fight. If it meant not having to look over her shoulder the rest of her days, then she would gladly put a bullet between the son of a bitch's eyes. There would be no chance in hell he'd rise from the dead again. Not this time.

India would *not* be a victim.

And she'd be damned before she'd allow him to raise the unborn child that he wanted to cut from her belly.

Spike didn't know it, but he was already a dead man.

ALEXANDER FOLLOWED KANE through the back door of the farmhouse. Stepping into the kitchen, his gaze immediately landed on India, glad she hadn't been injured in the earlier blast. Hell, he would've never forgiven himself. Alexander had made it his job to protect her, and protect her he would. He was drawn to her like lube to a motorcycle chain. Maybe not the world's best analogy, but the truth nonetheless. She was gorgeous from the top of her straight, raven-black hair, to the tips of her red polished toenails. The dyed red streaks in her hair he found sexy as hell. Wise or not, he wanted her, there was no doubt about it. Just the sight of her had him tamping down his rising desire.

Down, boy.

The last thing he needed was a full-blown erection in the company of his MC brothers. Bad enough they'd smell his desire if he didn't get a handle on his craving.

What the fuck had she seen in Spike?

That was reason enough for him to keep his dick to himself. The man was lower than slime. He damn near grumbled his discontent aloud at the idea someone like India had been attracted to the drug-toting psychopath. Alexander knew women had a penchant for "bad boys," but Spike took that term to a whole new level.

India lifted her gaze from her teacup, looking at him longer than what might be deemed mild curiosity, before returning her attention to the women and whatever they had been conversing about. Just as well. The less they said to each other, the less chance messy emotions would get in the way. Alexander didn't have room in his life for all the drama. He had agreed to protect her, be there as a friend, and nothing more.

Regardless of what his dick had to say about it.

Which he had become damn good at ignoring over the past couple of months.

"Where's my boy?" Kaleb asked as he entered the kitchen behind them. He strode over to Suzi and embraced her from behind, kissing the crook of her neck. "Everyone here okay?"

Suzi snuggled her back against his chest. "Stefan's in one of the spare bedrooms, fast asleep. He wanted to wait up for you, but he passed out on the way over."

"Nothing to worry about, Hawk," Cara replied to his second question. Kane draped an arm across her shoulders, tucking her safely into his side. "Suzi and I wouldn't have let anything happen to India."

"Don't underestimate Spike, Cara," Kaleb said. "He's lethal."

"I have no doubt about that." She smiled at her brother-in-law. "But so am I."

Kane tightened his hold on his mate. "Hawk is right, Cara. The man is not only deadly, but he has no fear. Crazy people do crazy things. And now that he likely has fangs, none of us should take him lightly."

"Not to mention he has the cartel's backing." Alexander shoved his hands into his pockets to keep from reaching out to India. He needed confirmation she was all right following all of the turmoil over the past few hours. "You okay?"

"I'm fine. Cara's been a fantastic hostess."

Her fresh, lilac scent carried to his nose, mixing with his stench from the bombing. Hell, he needed to shower away the malodor. "Glad you were able to scrub up."

"You're welcome to use our bathroom as well, Xander. There are extra towels in the cabinet just inside the door."

"Thanks, Cara." Alexander rocked back on his heels, continuing to hold himself at bay. "I brought a change of clothes. Viper had offered the use of your hot water."

"It's because you fucking stink, Xander." Kane laughed, before addressing his mate. "I've also invited him to stay until the clubhouse has been rebuilt."

India's gaze raised from her teacup again. Something troubled her, he could see it in her expression. Suddenly, she seemed leery, apprehensive. Not at all comfortable in his company as she had been before the blast. India had made a mistake, a damn stupid one, but a lapse in judgment nonetheless. Was she truly afraid of how he'd now view her, knowing she had fucked Spike?

His gaze dropped to her full lips before darting to the living room. "I'll sleep on the sofa, if you don't mind. India can use the spare bedroom."

"We have a third bedroom, Xander. You're welcome to use it."

"Thanks, Cara, but I'd feel better resting outside the door to India's room, where I can keep a better eye on her. Now that we know how far Spike will go to get her back, I'd prefer to keep her close."

"Speaking of..." Suzi looked over her shoulder at Kaleb. "Where are Ryder and Wolf going to stay? We have a spare room if they need it."

"Ryder and Wolf will be staying on site, *piccolo diavolo*."

"You can't be serious?"

"We need to keep the site secured. And since their rooms weren't compromised by the blast, there's no reason they can't stay in the clubhouse. They may not have electricity for a few days, but it's nothing they can't work around."

"Hawk's correct." Kane skirted the counter, grabbed himself a mug, and poured a cup of coffee. "We can't take chances. Not only are Ryder and Wolf keeping an eye on the clubhouse, several others are taking shifts, including the prospects. Spike might lay low for a while following tonight's theatrics, but it won't be long before he resurfaces. You don't blow a place with no motive. Until we find out what his plan is, we need to keep everything secured and our eyes wide open."

"That includes seeing to the protection of the three of you," Kaleb said. "We aren't taking chances. When you're not with us, then you, as well as the other mates and girlfriends, should gather here. Safety in numbers. Until we are one-hundred percent positive, we can't take chances with any of you. I told Gypsy, Rogue, and Preacher this could be the safe house for all of you. We'll keep one of us here with you at all times."

"What about the S.O.? I could get them involved, bring in Joe Hernandez and a couple of the deputies to keep an eye on things."

"Hell no, Cara." Kaleb lips thinned. "No offense, but we take care of our own. Leave the Sheriff's Office out of it."

"You don't want me to forewarn them of impending trouble? Spike already bombed the clubhouse. He isn't likely going to come in quietly. No one was harmed this time. But what about his next attack? That could put the citizens of this county at risk. Not to mention, we'd have another set of eyes."

He shook his head. "This is Sons' business."

"If it's all the same to you, Hawk," Alexander said, gaining Kaleb's attention from Cara, fending off a brewing confrontation, "I'll volunteer to stay with the women."

No way in hell was he entrusting India's care to anyone else. Not that he didn't trust his brethren or their vampire mates. But if anything should happen, he'd have no one other than himself to blame. Alexander would keep her safe, or die trying. He wasn't about to go down without a fight.

"I agree with Xander." Kane leaned his forearms on the counter and cupped his mug between his hands. "Since India's the one Spike is seeming to target, then she should be in his charge. I'm with Kaleb on making sure it's one of us here. Rogue's woman has yet to be mated, so I'm sure he'll feel safer having one of the Sons here. It's not that I don't trust the S.O., Cara. But they aren't vampires."

"I'm sure Preacher will feel the same." Kaleb placed his hands on Suzi's shoulders, still standing at her back. "His mate, Tena, is newly turned. She won't be as strong as the rest of us."

"Did I hear you're needing a guard for the women?" Vlad Tepes filled the doorway, a large smile curving his lips. "Who better than a primordial for the job?"

"Grandpa." Cara's grin split her face as she ran into his arms, his large biceps damn near swallowing her in his embrace. "Kane never told me you were here. When did you arrive in Pleasant?"

Vlad released Cara, giving her a quick kiss on her forehead before setting her back. "A few minutes before the boys all met at the clubhouse, or what the hell is left of the place."

"And your pain-in-the-ass brother, Mircea? You didn't leave him unguarded?"

Draping an arm across Cara's shoulders, he strode into the room where the others were still gathered around the breakfast nook. "Oh, trust me, Kane, I'd never be foolish enough to trust his sorry ass to stay put. On the contrary, he's heavily guarded. And even if he manages to break out of the cell I placed him in, my men know to contact me immediately. I saved him from death once, and there won't be a second time. I've been more than generous with him."

"You can say that again," Kane grumbled. "You should've let me take his life when I had the chance."

"His life is not yours to take. If Mircea loses his head, it will be by *my* hand. And trust me, if it comes to that, there will be no regrets. Now, enough about my brother"—he placed his large hands on the counter—"do I get the job guarding the women?"

"Only if you want me by your side." Alexander leaned a shoulder against the wall and crossed his arms over his chest. "India isn't leaving my side."

CHAPTER FOUR

"A LITTLE NEANDERTHAL, DON'T YOU THINK?"

Alexander opened his eyes and looked at her from where he reclined on the sofa, arms crossed behind his head. Moonlight spilled into the room, casting a beam across his chest and face, probably making it hard to sleep. Kaleb and Suzi had taken Stefan, heading to their home, while the others were on their way to the Blood 'n' Rave, no doubt looking for a few donor necks to tap.

With the exception of Vlad, of course.

The scary-as-fuck vampire was out there somewhere, preferring his life of solitude over partying it up at Draven's nightclub. He had promised to keep an eye on the women, and India bet he was not one to break his word. Knowing Vlad and Alexander was making sure she stayed safe and far from Spike's reach was certainly a comfort. But even so, she had stowed her Ruger beneath her pillow.

"Excuse me? A Neanderthal?" Alexander's deep voice jolted her from her musing, stirring parts of her that had no right thinking about him.

"Telling Vlad that you weren't leaving my side." She braced a shoulder against the bedroom doorjamb and crossed her arms beneath her breasts, drawing Alexander's gaze downward.

Seemingly unabashed, he glanced up without apology. "You came to me, *gattina*. You asked for my help and I don't take my duty lightly."

"Glad to hear that." She studied his handsome face in the dim lighting. A five-o'clock shadow darkened his cheeks and chin, making her wonder what the whiskers might feel like against her more sensitive flesh. "I think."

One of his dark brows arched. "You think?"

India smiled, though not feeling joviality. "I'm worried about you."

Moonbeams accentuated his chest and abs, glinting off the dog tags he wore about his neck. Her gaze couldn't help following the happy trail down to where it disappeared into the top of his jeans, sitting low on his hips. Her desire for him had never diminished. She still recalled what it felt like to be in his arms while he fed from the crook of her neck.

"Stop."

His sudden softly spoken command startled her from her reflections.

"What? Worrying about you?"

"No." He chuckled, amusement turning up his lips, lips she craved to taste. "Whatever you're thinking that has me scenting your desire. I'm only human. *Scratch that.* The vampire side of me is the one taking notice."

She drew her lower lip between her teeth. "Have you ever found me attractive, Xander?"

He rubbed his jaw. The soft, sexy sound of his whiskers teasing her longing. "I don't play games, India. That's the first thing you should know about me. I offered you my friendship throughout your pregnancy. That includes my protection. Don't make the mistake of thinking it entails anything more."

"Wow, you really know how to flatter a girl."

"Not my intention. But my honesty is."

India considered what he said, trying her damnedest not to be offended. She learned long ago not to get up her hopes up where he was concerned. Alexander seemed to be alone most times when not in the company of his brethren. She couldn't recall seeing him with another woman, other than to feed. Her hand went to the red vial of blood hanging at the crook of her neck, marking her as part of the donor society Draven Smith ran at the Blood 'n' Rave. Although Alexander had requested she stop wearing it while pregnant, she hadn't relented. The necklace reminded her of why she remained a donor. *Him*. But she'd be damned if she told him that.

"What's with you anyway?" she asked.

"I don't know what you're getting at."

"You don't seem to date women. You're never with one other than to feed. According to my friends at the Rave, none of them have ever done more than offer you sustenance."

He tipped back his head and laughed, the sound deep and rich. She hadn't meant to humor him. On the contrary, she had hoped to goad him into the opposite response. Something … anything that showed he might be interested in her more than as a friend.

"Do you prefer men? Is that it? I'm mean it's okay if you do."

Alexander stood and closed the gap between them with lightning speed, causing her to squeal. He leaned down, his breath fanning her cheeks, her neck, as his nose ghosted her flesh. Her breath stuck in her throat; her pulse hammered in her ears. Her center was slick and wet. Lord, there was no denying she wanted this man. His tongue darted out, licking the sensitive spot beneath her ear, so lightly she wasn't one-hundred percent positive he had touched her at all.

Gripping her shoulders, he set her away from him, all traces of humor vanishing. His dark eyes had gone black as night, telling her he was but a hairbreadth away from unleashing the vampire. If he'd only give in to his desire…

"Make no mistake, *gattina*, I'm anything but gay."

"Do you not like sex?"

His amusement returned. "Of course, I do. I just prefer to be discreet. Who I fuck is no one's business. I've probably mastered the art of hypnotism more than any of my brothers."

His confession left her gaping. Did he seriously make everyone forget they'd had sex? "Why would you do that? Did we…? Did you make *me* forget?"

"Trust me, *gattina*, if we fucked, you'd remember."

"You really don't have a problem with your ego, do you?"

Alexander turned his back on her and returned to the sofa. He lay down, arms behind his head and seemingly dismissed her.

Seriously? "Xander."

"What?" His eyes remained shut.

"Why would I remember? Why not hypnotize me?"

"Because there wouldn't have been a need, *gattina*. You're a donor."

Again, his confession took her by surprise. "You never fucked a donor?"

He opened his eyes and looked at her. "Why the inquisition?"

She shrugged, not wanting to hear that he had, but needing the truth nonetheless. It shouldn't bother her if he had slept with one of them. After all, it was another *service* the donors sometimes supplied for the Sons, even though India had held out for Alexander. That was, until Spike.

"Did you fuck a donor?"

He closed his eyes again. "I'm not saying I haven't, but too much fucking drama. Although it's frowned upon, I prefer to take my desires elsewhere. You women can be so fucking catty."

India grinned. The thought of him having sex outside her circle pleased her. Definitely less drama.

"Huh."

He opened one eye and peeked at her. "Are we done?"

Her smile widened. "We are."

She turned, walked into the bedroom and shut the door, leaning against the cool wood. It seemed there wouldn't be any competition with any of the other donors. Maybe there was hope yet.

DAMN, THE WOMAN BEWITCHED him. Alexander had spent the last few hours tossing and turning on the less-than-comfortable sofa, trying to get some shuteye. His raging hard-on had other ideas. Maybe if he had gotten up and taken a cold shower, sleep wouldn't have eluded him.

He hadn't missed her interest when they had met a few years back at the Rave, nor did he now. And to be honest, he shared in the attraction. He'd have to be fucking blind not to be tempted by the long-legged beauty. Her skin reminded him of warm chocolate, smooth and silky. She had a cute, pert little nose that turned up on the end, centered above a set of kissable, bow-shaped lips. Lips he had wanted to devour from the first time he'd seen her. And although he had used her as a donor for a short period, he had managed to remain the gentleman by keeping his hands to himself.

Not that he didn't want to fuck her.

Hell, he still wanted to in the worst way, the evidence now plaguing his too-tight jeans. But Alexander liked to keep his sustenance separate from his sexual appetite. Much less messy. Piss off one donor and it became a pack mentality. Enraging those who provided your nourishment didn't even border on a bad idea. It was out-and-out stupidity. Alexander had made the mistake alongside his MC brothers a time or two, then had to work damn hard to get back in their good graces. Not that they'd withhold nutriment. No, they had "making your life a living hell" down to an art form.

When Grigore had flirted with India at the Rave, Alexander had turned his back on the beautiful donor. He hadn't bothered to stick around to see if India had reciprocated the vamp's advances, instead hightailing it from the club. He no longer used her as a donor, which in all honesty was more out of self-preservation. His emotions were getting muddled up, wanting to spend far more time with the donor than need be.

Alexander had been infatuated from the get-go.

Taking the coward's way out, he blamed her for not brushing off Grigore's advances. Hell, Grigore flirted with all the donors. Alexander was well aware of the big guy's reputation. But it was easier to walk away and use Grigore as an excuse, to hide from his own emotional entanglement. His parents' relationship had set a bad example. From an early age, he had found it easier to detach himself from his feelings ... had, in fact, become damn good at it.

By the age of eighteen, he had joined the military, quickly rising in the ranks. In the end, Alexander bore a tattooed cross on the side of his neck as a reminder for each of the three men he'd lost on his final mission, blown up in a tragic accident of which he had been the lone survivor. Self-hatred ate at him to the point of recklessness. He left the military, became reclusive. Food no longer appealed to him. And before long, he was unable to keep anything down. He had lost a lot of weight, looked as if he were knocking on death's door. Had Kane and Kaleb not stumbled upon him, he might have died, aged without reason.

Alexander was a true blood, born a vampire.

Most true bloods came of age by the time they turned sixteen. Alexander had reached twenty-one before finding out his DNA required human blood, his personal fountain of youth. As the story was recounted to him by his mother's sister, his parents had found him dumped in a wastebasket at a rest stop. Alexander had always felt a bit off, not quite like the other kids. He blamed it on his upbringing and his lack of a loving home life.

The Tepes twins had found him weak and in need of sustenance at the Blood 'n' Rave, leaning on the bar for support. They scented his vampirism, knew what he was when he had no clue, and took him under their wings, easing him into the vampire lifestyle. Alexander was indebted to the brothers. They were the closest thing he had to a real family. Since becoming a Sons of Sangue, he had found a real home.

It was no wonder he was fucked up in the relationship department. Hell, his birth parents hadn't wanted him and the ones who plucked him from the trash can had been slaves to the bottle. Finding answers about his lineage or why his biological parents felt the need to dump him was never going to happen.

Now, Kane and Cara's scent caught Alexander's attention, rousing him from his past, long before they entered the farmhouse. The hinges creaked, just before the wooden screen slapped against the frame. Kane tossed his motorcycle keys on the counter, then patted Cara on the ass before she headed up the stairs.

"You still up?" he asked.

Alexander sat, scrubbing a hand over his whiskered jaw. "Can't sleep."

Kane's gaze flitted to the closed bedroom door. "India asleep?"

"I suppose." He shrugged, standing and heading for the kitchen. "I haven't heard from her in a couple of hours."

"You know you could have come with us to feed. The old man would've kept an eye on her. He's likely out there doing just that anyway." Kane grabbed a fresh bottle of Gentleman Jack from a shelf above the refrigerator. He tore the paper seal, then twisted off the cap and took a swig from the bottle. Wiping the back of one hand over his mouth, he held out the bottle to Alexander with the other hand. "Drink?"

"You know I don't like that shit."

Kane chuckled. "Yeah, but I've also seen you partake when the occasion called for it. You look like you could use a drink."

"Truthfully, I could probably use the whole damn bottle." He grabbed a glass and instead filled it with water from the dispenser on the refrigerator door. "What am I doing, man?"

"You like her?"

"More than I should."

"Then go after her, Xander. Take it from me, having a mate isn't a bad thing."

"Even if she'd want me for a mate, I'm not good for her."

"Spike isn't good for her." Kane laughed. "She could do a hell of a lot worse than you, bro. What're you scared of anyway? She looks pretty damn hot, from where I stand."

Alexander took a long pull from the glass of water, then set it down, staring into the bottom. Kane was right, she certainly could do a hell of a lot worse—already had, for that matter. But a mate? He wasn't mate material. Her pretty face and killer body didn't change that fact.

"I'm not going to act on what my dick wants, Viper. Nor am I prepared to offer her more." He sighed. "Besides, man, she's pregnant. That makes her all kinds of off-limits."

"You believe Hawk waited nine months to have sex with Suzi? You're an idiot if you think so."

That may very well be, but he was also a gentleman. "Suzi was pregnant with Hawk's baby, dumb ass. India's having Spike's kid. Jesus, what was she thinking?"

"Don't know. Can't say I haven't wondered the same thing." Kane took another swig from the bottle of whiskey before recapping it and setting it on the shelf. "According to Cara, India regrets it. She made a mistake, Xander. We all make them."

He ran a hand down the crosses on his neck. *Ain't that the fucking truth.* "Can't argue with that. But I offered her my friendship, Viper. I don't care how damn hot she is, I'm not prepared to offer her more."

Kane's lips thinned. "You keep telling yourself that, Xander. It's time to let the past go. Stop judging everyone because of the shitbags you had for parents. You aren't them."

"Christ, Viper, I don't even know who the hell sired me. What blood runs through my veins? I was dumped off. The last three people who depended on me blew up."

"Not your fault. You had no idea you were walking into a booby trap."

"I should have known. It was my job to protect them."

"It was war, bro."

"Even so, I'm better off being on my own. I don't do relationships."

Kane tapped the counter. "You keep telling yourself that. Whatever gets you through the night. I'm off to bed with what gets *me* through the night … my mate. Think about it, Xander. You don't have to be alone."

He watched Kane's retreat as he climbed the stairs to the woman who warmed his bed. It wasn't that Alexander didn't also want a woman who could chase away the edge of loneliness and abandonment. Alexander knew from an early age he'd never allow his happiness to be governed by a woman. Nor was it in him to reciprocate.

His gaze landed on the closed bedroom door.

Fuck! He headed for the sofa and lay down, staring at the ceiling. One arm went behind his head, while his free hand encompassed the dog tags around his neck. If he stayed on his own, then he damn well couldn't let anyone down. Nothing changed the fact he wasn't fucking relationship material.

CHAPTER FIVE

The rubber tires of the V-Rod Muscle Harley Davidson took the curves of Highway 101 at ninety miles per hour with ease. The views as they passed Dinosaur Caves Park were stunning, to say the least, with the ocean crashing against the shore just yards from the highway. But Alexander didn't have time to reflect on the scenery while heading south along the coast of California, nor did he have the liberty to enjoy the sunshine. The sooner they arrived at Hades' Nest, the quicker he could get back on the road to Oregon. Not that he worried about India's safety with the old guy keeping an eye on her. Hell, it would take complete idiocy to try to steal India away while she was in the company of Vlad.

Maybe he ought to be the one worrying about her sharing time with the primordial.

That is, if he were the jealous type … which he wasn't.

Not at all.

Then why the fuck was he hell-bent on getting back to Oregon in record time?

Alexander pulled down on the rubber handle grip, hoping to nudge his fellow riders into increasing the speed along the straightaway. As Road Captain of the Sons of Sangue, he followed Grayson, VP, and Anton, Secretary, as protocol and his obligation to his club called for. He hadn't been happy that Kaleb had ordered him among those to head south, to flesh out Spike. Not that he didn't want to kick his ass first-hand, but the idea of leaving India for a moment, even in the capable hands of Vlad, left a sour taste in his mouth. If anything happened to her, he wouldn't forgive himself.

Hell, he had yet to absolve himself of the deaths of his three comrades. Alexander had led them right into the booby trap. Christ, he couldn't have known what was about to transpire, but nonetheless the blame lay on his shoulders. Those men had counted on him, just as India now did. He wasn't about to let her down.

About an hour and fifteen minutes later, they turned off Shoreline Drive in Santa Barbara onto a public lot of Leadbetter Beach. Grayson parked his bike and kicked down the side stand, followed by Anton and Alexander, pulling into adjacent spots.

After cutting the engine, Alexander took off his skullcap and laid it across his lap. "Why are we stopping? We're wasting precious time."

Anton stepped over the seat of his bike and looked at his wristwatch. "We have another hour or so before sundown. Spike ain't about to crawl out of his hole until that happens."

"Says you." Alexander couldn't help the grumble that tumbled from his lips.

Neither had to worry about the safety of a woman. While Grayson was mated, Anton had a steady old lady living with him. He didn't doubt for a minute Anton's commitment. Anton was giving Kimber time to adjust, allowing her to decide the when and where of her turning. The librarian was completely taken by Anton, any fool with a pair of eyes could see as much. Alexander was clueless as to why she hadn't taken the next step. Just like a woman, full of fucking drama.

Anton chuckled, not at all put off by Alexander's surly mood. "You forget I know Spike better than both of you. He doesn't crawl out of his hole before the moon rises. And even then, it can be well into the night."

"Let's hope he shows his ugly mug earlier."

"Don't get your panties in a knot, Xander. There isn't one of us who wouldn't rather be home." Grayson dusted his hands on his tan dungarees. "I'd prefer to be hanging at the beach house with my old lady and son, rather than chasing this piece of shit halfway down the coast. But he started a war. You don't take on the Sons without repercussions."

"What makes you think he even returned here, Gypsy? He could still be in Oregon."

"Maybe." Anton sat sideways on his bike, kicking his booted feet out to the side and crossing them at the ankles. "A rat always returns to his hole. Spike's arrogance will have him returning with what he'll think is his bragging rights for bombing our clubhouse, no doubt thinking he got away with it."

Alexander shrugged. "Then maybe again he figures we'll come here looking for him. Spike still doesn't have what he came for. That's India. I have to believe he isn't leaving Oregon without her."

Grayson smiled. "Let him try. I'd pay to watch that. Grandpa would eat him for supper."

A chuckle rumbled up from Anton's gut. "I wish he was here to hear you say that, Gypsy. As I recall, he ordered you once not to call him that again."

"I'm not stupid." Grayson winked.

"Now what?" Alexander crossed his arms over his chest. "We wait?"

Anton raised one dark blond brow. "You got a better idea? I'm too recognizable down here, even without my dyed black hair. Any of the Devils see me, we'll have a huge fight on our hands. I'd rather sneak in under the cover of night, tackle Spike, and maybe another Devil or two. Less messy that way. I'm sure we could take the lot of them, but remember, Spike is now a vampire. We have no idea how many of his disciples he turned."

Which was the reason they had left behind their Sons of Sangue cuts. No sense announcing their arrival in Devil territory. Alexander knew timing was everything, but that didn't mean he didn't want this mission done and over with. The sooner the better. With any luck, he'd be able to return to Oregon and stop worrying about India.

Alexander shoved his hands into his jean pockets. "Let's just hope he's here. I'd love to get a handle on this situation and damn quick. The longer he's alive, the more damage he can do."

"Little fuck has a date with death."

"You can say that again, Gypsy." Alexander pulled his keys from the ignition and pocketed them, then headed for the beach.

Enough of the small talk.

He was in no mood for babbling when it wasn't about to get them anywhere. They could sit here all night and hash out the reasons for waiting for the moon to rise, but it wasn't going to move time. Alexander had a huge chip on his shoulder. Taking it out on his brothers wasn't going to knock the damn thing off. Taking out Spike with his bare hands—now that might go a long way in improving his mood.

Reaching the shore, Alexander stopped just shy of the incoming waves touching the soles of his leather boots. His gaze cut across the darkening horizon, approximately three miles of beautiful ocean stretching before him. He had lived near the coast much of his life. The tranquility of the waves crashing against the beach was as soothing a sound as one could get. He'd never tire of simply standing on the beach. This was home, whether in California or further up the coast in Oregon.

His stint in the military was the longest duration he had ever spent away from the ocean. At one time, he thought to make the military a lifelong career, having no reason to return. And even though he always felt as if he were a bit different from those enlisted, he still had a sense of belonging. That was until the night the four of them happened upon the bomb, leaving him the sole survivor. He was honorably discharged shortly thereafter when he returned to Oregon. Lord, he had been filled with self-hate and pity. He certainly hadn't been good company to be around and had become pretty much a loner.

Had it not been for Kane and Kaleb, he might have tried to end his pain once and for all. But the joke would've been on him. He was a true blood. Born that way, yet having no fucking clue who had sired him. Unless he had managed to instantly stop his heart, his DNA would've healed his efforts.

The Sons of Sangue had given him a home, pulling him from despair. But he still liked his solitary existence. No one to disappoint, no one to answer to other than his brethren.

Alexander picked up a few pebbles, skimming them across the water surface. What the fuck was he doing? Even if the three of them managed to find Spike and end his sorry existence once and for all, India would still be there … in his bed. The threat of Spike would be eliminated. She would no longer need his protection, and still his promise to see her through her pregnancy hung over his head.

When he told her he'd be there as a friend, he hadn't once considered how hard it would be to resist her, pregnancy be damned. Every night that he lay his head on the sofa, his fucking dick reminded him of his attraction and how easily he could make her his. Thankfully he required little sleep, because India was driving him to the brink of madness, knowing she was off limits to him. The pregnancy alone demanded it.

It wasn't his kid, for crying out loud.

He needed his fucking head examined.

"Want to talk about it?" Grayson came to stand beside him.

Alexander had been so deep in thought he hadn't heard the other man's approach. Of course, being a vampire, Grayson could move almost soundlessly.

"Not much to talk about."

Grayson chuckled. "You're kidding me, right? Bro, I've been there. Hell, my old lady even manipulated the situation to get what she wanted. We worked through our shit, and you know what? She's the best damn thing to happen to me. I may not have thought so at the time. But Tamera and Lucian, they're my whole life. Don't miss out on something good because you're being so damn stubborn you can't see what's right in front of your face. I almost lost the love of my life because I was filled with hate."

"You're a bigger man than I am. I'm not sure I could have forgiven Tamera for trickery."

"She was young and dumb. No doubt about it. She made a mistake, bro." Grayson shrugged. "Who hasn't made them? I'm just glad I saw through all that shit. She's my better half and my life's richer with her in it."

"I'm happy for you, Gypsy." Alexander turned to look at him. "I really am. But I'm not sure what all this has to do with me."

Grayson's smile might as well have called Alexander a dumbass. And maybe he was. "India's one of the good ones, bro. Don't be so blind that you can't see it."

"She's having Spike's kid."

He nodded slowly. "She made a mistake, Xander."

"So why should that matter to me?"

"That girl is infatuated with you."

Alexander turned his attention back to the horizon. He knew as much. He had smelled her desire, another fault of his vampire DNA, a time too many. But that didn't equate love, not that he wanted her adoration. Hell, no. If there was no way her emotions wouldn't get involved, he wouldn't mind taking advantage of that longing. After all, he was a man. And a damn horny one to boot. No way in hell, though, was he going to allow her to think it could be anything other than it was.

"That may be, but the feeling isn't mutual."

Grayson shook his head, a smile splitting his short-cut beard. "You keep telling yourself that, bro."

"What the hell is that supposed to mean?"

"It means you're no different than me."

Anton walked up, sticking his cell phone into the pocket of his pants. "Looks like Spike's been in the house."

Alexander welcomed the interruption. Maybe because Grayson was getting too close to the truth … a truth for which he had no room in his life. Regardless how it had turned out for Grayson.

Tamera Cantrell might have been a little schemer to get what she wanted to start with, but she had been duped by the greatest bitch of all, Rosalee. Thank goodness, Vlad had finally realized her conniving ways and ended her underhandedness. After causing her own son's death, being a thorn in Kane and Cara's side, not to mention scheming against Grayson, if Rosalee hadn't gotten what she deserved at Vlad's hand, Grayson would have done the deed. In the end, Tamera proved to be the best thing for Grayson.

"Who was on the phone, Rogue?" Grayson asked.

"Preacher. He put some feelers out with a few of his old Devil MC brothers. Turns out, some of them are less than thrilled with Spike and have no loyalty toward him as club P. Apparently, he arrived back in Santa Barbara around noon, but they couldn't say for sure if he was still in town. Said he's been hanging around a lot of the LaPaz cartel soldiers."

Somehow, the asswipe going the way of the cartel wouldn't surprise Alexander. "They think he's joining up with Raúl's crew?"

"Preacher didn't say. I'm sure they weren't willing to give him too much information considering he flipped sides. He's a Sons of Sangue brother. Even if they don't care for Spike, they consider Preacher a rival."

"If he's at odds with his men, then there's a good chance he won't show up at Hade's Nest tonight." Alexander rubbed the tension from his neck. How many fucking days would they be stuck here? "What's the plan if he doesn't?"

"We stay put." Grayson, being club VP, made the call. "We'll stay a few days if we have to. I didn't make the drive down the coast to pussy out and head north. We find him and we take him out."

"If any of the cartel soldiers get in the way?" Anton asked.

"We take them the fuck down, too.

CHAPTER SIX

India might have chuckled had the entire situation not been so dreadful. *Spike alive?* She needed to talk to Draven Smith, hear it from his lips that he saw the miscreant, living and breathing, in Mexico. She hoped to prove Draven wrong ... *needed* to prove him wrong. Maybe he had thought he saw Spike when instead it was another Devil MC member.

Okay, I prefer optimism.

She headed for Florence, on her way to the Blood 'n' Rave, with Vlad Tepes stuffed into the passenger seat of her habanero orange Volkswagen Beetle. A sixties-style white and yellow daisy was pasted in the center of her hood. He damn near swallowed her black seat. His knees were jammed against the glove box, the seat back as far as it could go. He couldn't be comfortable. Hell, he could barely move, and yet he politely rode beside her without a single complaint. While she could have gone alone to see the owner of the bar and head of the donor society, Vlad had insisted on accompanying her.

Alexander, Anton, and Grayson were in Santa Barbara, hoping to intercept Spike, leaving India in Vlad's care, who had yet to leave her side. Apparently, the big guy took his job very seriously. When she had mentioned she wanted to talk to Draven about the events that took place in Mexico, Vlad had been quick to offer his company. She was sure the elder vampire had better things to do than babysit her, and yet here he sat, crammed into a car three times too small for someone of his breadth.

With Alexander a state away, should Spike still be in the area, he posed a real threat to her and her unborn baby. Not that she couldn't take care of herself, but India was happy to have the big guy along for the ride nonetheless. Spike would have to be a few bricks shy of a full load if he thought to take on one of the oldest living vampires, if not the oldest. And even though Vlad had to be older than dirt, he still looked as if he weren't a day older than thirty. Had it not been for her serious crush on Alexander, she might consider the older vamp. After all, he was seriously hot. Vlad could hold his own against any of the younger guys.

Her thoughts returned to Alexander and how he'd looked stretched out on the sofa the night before, with the moonlight accentuating his well-toned muscles. Contours she'd love to follow with her tongue. Talk about all kinds of sexy. At one time, India had held hope he'd look at her as more than a donor. When she'd thought to make him jealous more than a year ago with Grigore, her actions had backfired. Alexander had since avoided her, no longer using her to feed. Now? Sure, he had offered to be there for her—*as a friend*—but there were times India swore he looked at her with blatant interest. It was those times she held out for. She wouldn't be pregnant forever. India planned to use the time they'd spend together to get Alexander to see her as someone other than a friend, someone he wouldn't want to do without.

"We're here." India pulled into the nearly empty parking lot. Coming to a stop, she cut the engine. "You going to need help getting out of my car?"

For the first time in the twenty-minute drive, Vlad smiled. "You may want to get a can opener."

"I'll see what I can do." She laughed, surprised by his sense of humor. "You going in?"

"I'll stay out here. I'm going to sweep the perimeter. If trouble shows up, I'd prefer to see it arrive rather than be on the blindside. You go on in." He grabbed the handle and opened the door. "When you're ready to leave, just call out for me. I'll hear you."

India acknowledged his directive with a nod, then alighted from the car and headed for the entrance. Rhett, the Rave's big lovable bouncer, opened the steel-framed glass door and greeted her. Since she hadn't been back in a while, it was good seeing him. He enveloped her in his big arms, his embrace gentle for a man of his size.

"Draven in?" she asked.

"He's by the bar with his old lady."

"Thanks," she said, breezing past him.

"India?" She turned back to look at him. "Good seeing you."

She allowed her smile to be her thank you, then headed for the back of the nightclub, where she spotted Draven with a woman she had never met nor seen before. She was shorter and smaller in stature than India. Where she was dark, the woman was light, pale even. Draven's gaze alighted on her as she made her way past the dance floor and skirted the tables surrounding it. Celldweller filtered through the speakers, but at a much lower volume than if the nightclub was in full swing. A few patrons sat about, drinking fruity drinks and pitchers of beer, but for the most part, they were alone.

The woman next to Draven rose as India stepped up to the bar. She held out her hand and smiled warmly. "I'm Brea Gotti, Draven's mate. He tells me you're one of the donors."

India liked the woman on sight. The fact she didn't wait for Draven to introduce them spoke volumes for her outgoing personality. She might be small in stature, but India bet she made up for it in spunk.

"I'm India Jackson. Nice meeting you, Brea."

"What can I do for you?" Draven braced his hands on the bar. "Something to drink?"

"Just water. Thank you."

He used the filtered hose, pushed a button, and drew her a glass. "Anything else I can get for you?"

India shook her head, taking the offered water. She took a sip, then set it on the bar top. "My job back?"

Draven laughed. "No way, India. I like my balls right where they are, thank you. You get permission from Xander to return to work, I'll gladly hire you back."

"Word got around, huh?"

"Xander made it quite clear to everyone that you're off limits for the time being."

India blew out a steady stream of air through her pursed lips. Alexander wasn't leaving anything to chance. "I need to ask you some questions, Draven ... about Spike."

Brea sat on her stool resting her slender arm along the bar, seeking out Draven's hand and intertwining fingers with him. There was no mistaking the compassion in her blue eyes.

India returned her gaze to Draven. "I was told you saw him in Mexico."

"Not sure if you consider it good news or not, but it's true. He was alive ... though maybe not well when I last saw him."

India sat heavily onto a stool of her own, no longer able to support the weight of the news she prayed had been incorrect. "You're positive it wasn't another member of the MC?"

"I worked closely with Tank and Spike through the years, India." He paused, his lips thinning. "Before and after I stopped selling X. It was Spike. I'm not mistaken."

"You said 'maybe not well.' What did you mean?"

"The shape I witnessed him in, he wasn't walking out of the beach house alive. Raúl had to have carried his sorry ass. I'm sure you've heard Raúl's now a vampire."

India nodded, looking at Brea. Alexander had earlier briefed her on Brea being the kingpin's goddaughter. "I'm sorry. All of this must be very hard on you. I didn't mean to come in here and cause you grief."

Brea smiled. "Sweetie, trouble has found me all my life. You get that with a last name like mine. Raúl's my godfather and at one time I loved him. Now? He needs to be stopped at any cost, no matter our history."

"Spike's alive." Draven skirted the bar and came to stand beside Brea, draping an arm across her shoulders. "I'm sure of it. Why else would Raúl bother carrying his nearly dead ass out of there? It's my guess the kingpin shared his vampire DNA."

"You haven't seen or heard from him following your trip to Mexico?"

"No. Nor have we heard from Raúl. Why the concern?"

India supposed she owed them the truth. Sooner or later it would come out anyway. "I'm pregnant."

Brea's breath caught before she quickly masked her surprise. She reached for one of India's hands and squeezed her fingers. "Congratulations," she said with a tender smile.

India released the other woman's hand. "Thank you, Brea."

"Is that why you told me you needed time away from your job?"

"I should have been more upfront with you, Draven. You've been nothing but a good friend to me. I made some bad choices. When I learned I was pregnant, I came back and went to Alexander for help."

"Xander? As in Dumitru?" His forehead furrowed. "He's not exactly the most approachable. Hawk told me you had been staying at the clubhouse but didn't elaborate. Why not go to the baby's father?"

"Because the father was no longer in my life." India tugged her lower lip between her teeth. "And later he turned out to be dead, or at least that was my hope."

"Spike?" Brea gasped.

India nodded, tipping her head toward her hands that she wrung in her lap, unable to look at the censure certain to be in their eyes. Her secret was supposed to be hers to keep. Unfortunately, Spike had to have nine lives. Heat traveled up her neck and warmed her cheeks. Not her proudest moment. In her defense, she hadn't realized his true personality until after it was too late.

"Fuck me! Seriously?" Draven scratched the whiskers on his cheek. "Wow. Can't say I saw that coming. No wonder you're less than thrilled with the news he's alive. Shit! That's got to suck."

"Tell me about it." India drew in a deep breath. "Now because of me, the Sons had a hole blown in their clubhouse. Preacher and some of the other Sons are taking turns playing babysitter to the women, while Vlad's keeping me company."

One of Draven's brows rose. "Vlad's here?"

"I invited him to come in, but he preferred to keep an eye on things from the outside."

"I'll be damned. I thought the primordial rarely left his island."

"Raúl being a vampire isn't setting well with him. He's going to want to deal with the cartel kingpin." India glanced at Brea. "Again, I'm sorry."

A sad smile crossed Brea's lips, telling India she wasn't completely unaffected by the turn of events. "As I said, he needs to be stopped."

Draven pulled her closer to his side and kissed the top of her head. "Vlad will have to get in line. There are a lot of people who want to see Raúl brought down, Brea and I included. I only wish we could've finished the job in Mexico. We aren't done looking for him by a long shot. The man is a threat that needs to be taken out. I would be more than happy to do it."

Brea looked up at him. "Not in your dreams. I'm not about to lose you to his madness. We talked about this, Draven. The Sons, and now Vlad, are more than capable of taking care of him. You are too newly turned. You aren't strong enough on your own."

"If your godfather even thinks to come after you, Brea, I won't stand down. I won't cower."

She took in a shuddering breath, then looked back at India. "Damn stubborn man."

"They all are." India patted the Ruger tucked into her waistband. "As with Spike, if he comes anywhere near me, I'm shooting to kill, consequences be damned."

"Be careful, India." Brea placed a hand on India's knee. "You may be packing a gun, but he'll be packing friends. He most likely has the cartel's soldiers on his side. You need to stick like glue to Vlad or Alexander."

"Spike's a coward, India," Draven said. "He won't come alone, not knowing the Sons will be gunning for him."

She nodded, knowing Draven and Brea were correct. Spike wouldn't be stupid enough to take on the Sons of Sangue by himself. He had rarely traveled alone when she was with him. Now that he had friends in high places, he'd be more dangerous than ever.

"I've taken up enough of your time. It's safe to say, we all need to be careful."

Brea stood and pulled her into a brief hug. "You ever need to talk, feel free to stop back."

"Thank you, Brea." India looked at Draven. "Thanks to both of you for not judging me."

"This isn't your fault," Brea told her. "No more than Raúl being my godfather is mine."

Draven placed a hand on her shoulder. "Take care of yourself, India. You're always welcome here."

She turned and left, heading for the front of the club, the weight on her shoulder heavier than when she had arrived. Spike was truly alive. Tears sprung to her eyes, but she refused to allow them to fall. This was trouble of her own making. She wouldn't fall to despair or her own cowardice.

Rhett opened the door at her approach. "Take care of yourself, India. I miss seeing you around here."

She smiled up at him. "I'll be back, Rhett. Thank you," she said, then passed through the exit and headed for her VW Bug.

Her gaze took in the surrounding area, wondering where Vlad had taken himself to. Before India could utter his name, she walked into a solid chest, causing her to squeal.

The primordial gripped her arms to keep her from falling over and smiled down at her. "Ready?"

"Where the hell did you come from?" India placed her hand over her sternum, drawing a shuddering breath. "You scared the bejesus out of me."

"Better than scaring the babe from your tummy. Let's get you back to my grandson's."

India pointed her key fob at her VW and unlocked the doors. "See anything?"

"If you are referring to Spike, not even a scent."

Didn't that just figure. Once a snake, always a snake. The slithery bastard was going to continue to slip through their fingers. She hoped Alexander, Anton, and Grayson had better luck. Hopefully, they'd come back bearing news that Spike's final days were no longer numbered and he had no more lives left to use.

CHAPTER SEVEN

ALEXANDER PULLED HIS BIKE TO A STOP, KICKING DOWN THE side stand and cutting the engine. After taking off his helmet, he tucked it under his arm and stepped over the seat of his bike. Kane's farmhouse glowed with warm light as the din of conversation filtered through the opened windows. Vehicles and motorcycles littered the drive. Suddenly, he wished he had followed Anton or Grayson to their homes by the coast.

His mood wasn't exactly conducive to partying.

Repairs on the clubhouse wouldn't be done soon enough for his liking. Not that he didn't care for his MC brothers and their mates, but there were times he preferred his own space to hang. Okay, most times. Especially after a long, hot ride. The only thing Alexander was interested in was a hot shower, then a quick trip to the Blood 'n' Rave to secure nourishment.

Their trip south hadn't produced Spike. Which could be a big part of the reason for his current temperament. He had spent a day and a half on the road with nothing to show for it. He had hoped at the least they would've procured Spike's whereabouts. Instead, they talked to several Devils who either threatened to beat their ass—*they could've tried*—if they didn't immediately turn their bikes around and head out of

Devil's territory, or those who actually shared their extreme dislike for their fearless leader.

Spike apparently had more enemies than just those north of the California border. Hell, half his fucking crew couldn't stand him. After Bobby had called Anton with the news Spike had been spotted in California, sometime following the sighting he had hightailed it out of the state, maybe even out of the country and possibly back to Mexico to hide among the cartel slugs. Just like his yellow belly cowardice ass to tuck tail and run.

What did he expect stirring the hornets' nest by blowing a hole in the Sons of Sangue clubhouse?

The soft trill of familiar laughter wafted to his ears, sending an arrow of desire straight to his groin. The one person he needed to avoid at all costs, especially since his body required sustenance. And yet, the sound of her giggles drew him to the house like a junkie to heroin. He couldn't help but wonder the cause of her amusement. It would do him little good to turn around now anyway. If they hadn't heard the sound of his Harley, then the vampires in the house had already scented his return.

He stepped into the back of the house, through the utility room, stopping just shy of the kitchen with a clear shot to the living area. Conversation came to a halt as their attention turned to him. He sought out only one set of warm brown eyes. India held his gaze for a moment, then looked away. She quickly returned her attention to Cara and Suzi, continuing whatever they had been talking about before he arrived.

He supposed it was better she chose to ignore him. If he got too close, he might be tempted to feed from her. Damn, his hunger anyway … **both of them.**

Kane rose from beside Cara and headed in his direction. "So, the little son of a bitch gave you guys the slip?"

Kaleb and Grigore were quick to join them in the kitchen. Kane grabbed a bottle of whiskey, setting it on the breakfast bar. Rather than use a glass, the men passed around the bottle. Alexander allowed it to go by. Instead, he walked to the sink, grabbed a glass from the cupboard, and poured himself a tumbler of water. His pipes were dry from the road. The water might help the scratchy throat but it would do little to salve the hunger gnawing at his gut.

Bringing the glass to his lips, he peered into the living area, catching India's gaze on him once again. She might try damn hard to feign disinterest, but she wasn't fooling him.

"Xander?"

He turned and looked at Kane. "What?"

"Have you been listening?" He clapped Alexander's shoulder. "What the hell has you preoccupied?"

"Sorry." Christ, she already had him by the balls. He couldn't afford the distraction. "Just thinking about heading for the Rave. I could use a little artery tap."

"India—"

"Fuck you, Wolf. She's pregnant."

"Guilty much?" The big guy chuckled. "I was only going to say she made a trip there herself today."

"What the fuck? Someone go with her?"

"Relax, Xander," Kaleb said. "Vlad tagged along. We've been keeping a close eye out for all the women, especially India. If Spike wants her back, he has to go through us—not to mention Grandpa—to get her."

"You really do want him to kick your ass, don't you, Hawk? He hates that term." Kane laughed. "I think I'd enjoy watching him do it, too."

Kaleb laid his arm across his twin's shoulder. "Relax. The old guy loves me. Besides, he is our grandfather."

"Not that he wants to be reminded by the nickname. Only when it comes from the girls' lips he doesn't seem to mind." Kane shook his head, then looked at Grigore. "How's everything coming along at the clubhouse?"

"I wouldn't mind knowing that myself," Alexander grumbled.

"We had the structure inspected, and believe it or not, it's sound. Now that we got the green light, Ryder and I will begin rebuilding the wall tomorrow."

"Electricity?"

"We have a guy coming out tomorrow, Xander. I think by nightfall, it won't be perfect, but you and India can move back in."

"Any remaining fumes?" Alexander asked Grigore. "If that place is still toxic, I can't let a pregnant woman move back in."

Grigore shrugged. "It's aired out. Could use a little TLC, but otherwise, she'll be fine."

Cara walked into the kitchen. "I can head over there tomorrow. It's the weekend and I don't have anything better to do. I'll give the place a good scrubbing."

"I'll help," Suzi called from the living room. "If we all pitch in, the place will be as good as new in no time. I'll call Tamera and Kimber. Kimber can enlist Tena."

"A couple of us can go furniture shopping." Cara took the bottle of Jack from Kane and poured a couple of rock glasses full of the amber liquid over ice for her and Suzi. "We'll have that place back to new in no time. The guys can work on getting the wall finished and painted."

"I'm going to have a security system installed." Kaleb stepped away from Kane. "If anyone gets even near our clubhouse when we're not there, we'll know about it."

"Good idea, Hawk. We can take care of the work here, but we also need to keep proactive where Spike's concerned."

"I'll go to Mexico, Viper," Alexander said. "I agree, just because we didn't find him in Santa Barbara, doesn't mean we should give up the hunt."

Kaleb rubbed the whiskers on his chin. "You know, I'm thinking you should stay here with India. If we're correct, Spike called you because you're playing protector. We can send Rogue and Preacher south. They know Spike's habits better than anyone since they spent time in the Devil's camp. With you at the clubhouse with India, and if they don't find him, maybe we can draw him back into our territory."

"Hawk has a good point," Kane agreed. "We need you here with India. We'll send Rogue and Preacher south. The rest of us will work on putting our clubhouse back together and get you guys settled."

"I'll drink to that." Grigore chuckled before tipping back the bottle and taking a healthy swig. He wiped the back of his hand across his whiskers. "Now how about you and I go find some arteries to tap, Xander? I could use a cute little donor or two right about now."

Alexander's gaze went to India. There wasn't a single donor who pleased his palate more than the smooth smoky flavor of her blood. Even having not fed on her in quite some time, he still craved her quintessence.

He shook loose the craving for a taste of her and turned to Grigore. There were plenty of donors who would do. "Let's hit the road."

"You like him."

It was a statement, not a question. India glanced away. "We're friends, Suzi."

The short-haired brunette laughed, bringing back her gaze. "It's written all over your face when you look at him."

Not that India could deny the fact. No, she feared it was much worse. Lord, she would be dumber than a box of rocks if she allowed herself to fall for Alexander Dumitru, and yet that's exactly what she was afraid she was doing. Hindsight, moving in with him might not have been in her best interest a couple of months ago. What started out as using Alexander as a way of protection from Spike and the Devils, resulted in her feelings for the vampire growing. In the end, he'd no doubt break her heart.

He had earned the moniker "GQ" from his MC brothers and rightly so. Alexander could have stepped right off the cover of the magazine. The Sons had made wisecracks when he had shorn his longer locks for a closer crop. But India had liked the new look, making his already handsome appearance more noticeable.

And damn her hide for noticing.

There were times she caught a glimpse of hunger and desire in his eyes when he glanced her way, while other times he acted like an overprotective older brother. Her current situation wasn't helping. She couldn't even offer to feed him due to her pregnancy for fear what it would do to the unborn child. Which left Alexander, and the rest of the men, heading off to the Blood 'n' Rave to find cute little donors willing to offer up their blood as nourishment and whatever else might conspire between two consenting adults.

Not that Kane or Kaleb would think of getting anything on the side, or the other mated Sons, for that matter. Mating was for life. Female donors were nothing more than a way of nourishment for those already mated.

Grigore and Alexander, on the other hand, were completely open to getting a little side action. Neither were mated. So, if things escalated while they fed from their chosen donor of the night, then sex was a natural extension of the process.

India took in a deep breath and let it out slowly through her pursed lips. Not that there was a damn thing she could or would do about it. Alexander had a right to be with who he wanted. Vampires were sexual beings. But that didn't mean she was thrilled with the idea of him with another donor. On the contrary, she wanted to go territorial over anyone who even thought to look at the man.

Which only proved that she had it bad for the vampire.

India ran a finger along the condensation gathering on her glass of milk. "Regardless of what I might think of Xander, Suzi, we really are just friends. Even before I found myself pregnant from sleeping with his enemy. He rarely paid me any attention."

"Well," Cara said and chuckled, "Suzi and I can tell you for certain Xander may act like you don't affect him. But we know better."

India looked up from her glass. "Has he said something to Viper or Hawk?"

"Those boys don't have loose lips. They'd never gossip about the guys in the MC." Suzi rolled her eyes. "But the fact is, we're vampires."

"And because of that, we can scent his desire," Cara added. "Xander can deny his attraction all he wants. But when he's in the same room with you, there's lust emanating from that boy. Regardless of what he says, he more than knows you're around."

"Can you smell anyone's desire?"

Suzi chuckled and Cara nodded.

"Wonderful. Well if that isn't embarrassing."

Suzi patted her knee. "No worries. We've all been there. Xander may not like the idea of desiring you, but he does."

India couldn't help but wonder why he treated her with indifference. "Regardless of what his libido is telling him, Xander made it pretty clear that we weren't going to be anything other than friends."

"Give yourself another six or seven months of being around him. Once you're no longer carrying another man's baby, I'm betting that all changes."

"Especially Spike's kid." Cara winced. "Sorry, India, but you have to see where Xander might have an issue with that."

Cara's words rang true. India couldn't even pose a good argument. Spike might have been bad-boy cute, but in the end, he was reprehensible. She had been an idiot in the nth degree to follow him to Santa Barbara. And once she was there, his true self emerged. He had scared the bejesus out of her. Fright had made her stay until the final blow when he had beat her for the last time, making her fear for her unborn child's life.

She sighed. "I won't even bother to disagree. I made a huge mistake and was secretly relieved when Rogue had said he was dead. Just my damn dumb luck he had to rise from the dead."

"Now he has the Sons pissed off." Suzi grinned. "Not to mention he's on Grandpa's bad side. Vlad may not show his face, but I can sense his presence. He's out there keeping an eye out on us. Spike even tries to get by him, it will be off with his head to an early grave."

"I'm sure the primordial vampire has better things to do than babysit me all day."

"No worries, India. He'd be here anyway. Brea's godfather brought him to town in the first place. He's not taking it kindly that the cartel kingpin is sporting fangs—"

Cara paused, sniffing at the air. India knew they could easily scent another vampire in the area. Her lips turned up. "Looks like we have company. Tena Holt, Preacher's mate, is here and I'm betting she brought along Kimber James. Wonder when the hell Rogue is going to make her a mate already?"

"Whenever Kimber stops being such a chickenshit." Tena walked through the kitchen and into the living room. "Who started this party without us?"

"You know you're always welcome here." Cara stood, giving Tena and Kimber a brief hug. "We thought you might be coming by."

"Preacher and Rogue followed us to make sure we arrived without incident. Per P's instructions, they're heading south to see if they can rustle up Spike." Tena briefly embraced Suzi, then glanced at India. "I don't believe we've met."

India stood, clasping her hands in front of her. "I'm India Jackson."

"Donor?" Kimber had obviously noted the necklace hanging from India's neck.

"Yes, but on temporary leave." She placed a hand over her slightly protruding abdomen. "I've been temporarily living at the clubhouse with Xander."

"The baby's not Xander's." Tena would obviously know a vampire could only get another vampire pregnant. "Who's the lucky father?"

India's cheeks heated. "The same man your men are now chasing."

"Jesus, Spike?"

"Tena," Kimber chastised. "You're being rude."

The pixie-haired blonde smiled. "Sorry, I'm not known for my tact. It doesn't help I'm mated to Preacher. I'm used to him saying it like it is."

"It's okay, Tena." India smiled. "I wish it wasn't true, too, but I made a mistake. A huge one at that."

"We all make them." Tena waved off her comment, then looked at the long-haired brunette. "So, back to the question at hand. Cara wants to know when you're finally going to become Rogue's mate?"

"You certainly didn't wait long." Kimber chuckled. It was evident by their banter the two were good friends. "I'm secure with being Anton's girlfriend … for now. Besides, we don't have to use condoms."

"TMI," Suzi joined in, laughing. "You girls get settled and I'll open a couple bottles of wine. Grape juice for India."

India retook her seat and watched as the girls caught up with each other, feeling a bit of an outsider. While she had lived with Alexander for the last couple of months, she had yet to actually mingle with the mates until now. Alexander seemed set on keeping her from them. Most likely because once the baby was born, she'd be gone. Alexander would no doubt move on.

Cara and Suzi returned to the living room, carrying four glasses of wine and a glass of grape juice. After passing around the glasses, they retook their seats. The door to the spare room opened and little Stefan stumbled out, rubbing his eyes. He crawled onto Suzi's lap.

"My little man can't sleep?" Suzi asked, earning her a quick shake of his head as he cuddled in her arms. "Speaking of little ones, Tamera coming by? I haven't seen cute little Luke lately."

"Since Gypsy's still home, I believe they're at the beach house. Hawk and Viper wanted us all in one place when they weren't around." Cara took a sip of the dark red wine. "It's easier for Vlad to keep an eye on us when we're together. So I'm guessing it's a slumber party since Preacher and Rogue are headed to Mexico? We have another spare room."

"Tena and I can bunk in the same room, although I really don't see why it's necessary." Kimber shrugged. "From what I gathered from Rogue, India is the one in danger. I didn't understand why at the time, but then I didn't know she was carrying his child. Our men aren't very forthcoming, are they?"

"Not at all," Tena said. "Speaking of, where are the rest of the guys?"

"The Blood 'n' Rave." Cara stood and headed for the kitchen, bringing back the open bottle of wine. "Anyone?"

India sipped her grape juice, not adding to the conversation. It wasn't that she didn't like the women, but rather the opposite. She found she could easily be friends with them. Her time, however, would be short-lived with the Sons and their mates. Before long, she'd be back to her life as a donor ... if she decided to return to the society at all.

"I'm a bit tired. If you don't mind, since Stefan is no longer needing my room, I might turn in."

"Are you okay?" Suzi asked, concern in her gaze.

"I'm fine, just feeling a little exhausted."

"It was nice meeting you," Kimber said, with Tena nodding in agreement. "We'll see you in the morning?"

"Sure." India smiled. "Good night, all."

Walking into the spare room and closing the door behind her, she allowed the tears to fall. Damn her emotional side. Another thing for which to thank her pregnancy. Surely that was it and not the fact she would have loved to become a part of the gathering outside her door. Not as a donor, but as Alexander's mate.

She had no right wanting what she couldn't have. Her presence had brought nothing but inconvenience and impending danger to the lovely mates sitting beyond the door. India took in a shuddering breath. She had caused enough problems for the Sons and their mates.

She padded across the wood flooring and sat upon the bed. If she stayed, she feared Spike wouldn't give up until he got what he came for ... her. How much more damage would he cause?

Too much.

She needed to formulate a plan, then get on the road. If she left the west coast and Alexander behind, maybe Spike would tire of the hunt and let her go. India laid her head on the pillow and pulled the covers up to her neck, snuggling into the warmth of what was left behind from baby Stefan. If for nothing else, she needed to go before her mistakes not only brought harm to the MC and their mates, but their children as well.

Tomorrow would be soon enough to strategize. Giving Alexander the slip was not going to be easy. India was pretty sure he wouldn't just let her walk out, not after he gave his word to protect her. She yawned. Yep, tomorrow would be soon enough.

The din of conversation quickly claimed her and lulled her to sleep.

CHAPTER EIGHT

ALEXANDER LICKED THE TWIN HOLES CLOSED ON THE SOFT pale flesh and set Cathy from him. She was cute, curvy in all the right places, and adorable in her black framed glasses. The blonde smiled, said nothing and patted his knee, before quietly leaving the room. It was his reason for frequently feeding from her. No drama. She had no ulterior motives as she wasn't here to land a Sons of Sangue member. Not to mention, she made good company by the bar when he just wanted to hang. She was fun and easy to be around, just like his MC brothers.

And even though Cathy had a crush on the bar's owner, Draven, she never became creepy or weird about it. It was probably her rationale for becoming a donor in the first place. It meant more time in his presence and a reason to hang at the Rave. And when Draven had come home with a mate in tow, she had been gracious, happy for him. Her and Brea even seemed to hit it off and had become fast friends.

Padding across the dark burgundy carpeting to the glass and chrome bar cart on wheels, Alexander grabbed and twisted open a bottle of water, taking a swig. He thought of India, knowing she had deep-seated feelings for him. And although he might have reciprocated a time ago, that boat had sailed. He rubbed his neck and grumbled beneath his breath.

At least he thought it had. Then she had to go and move in upon his insistence, stirring up feelings he'd rather not explore.

He couldn't help wondering if she would be as courteous if he came home with a mate. Somehow, he doubted it.

A smile crossed his face. She'd probably go all wildcat on the poor woman, leaving Alexander to play ringleader. And even though the thought of her potential jealousy should bother him, her presence in his home was starting to grow on him. He'd never voice as much, of course. He couldn't afford to get all tangled up with any woman. Alexander had no room in his life for romance.

He'd let that to his mated brethren.

Taking the stairs from Draven's second-story room, he headed down to the bar where he'd no doubt find his MC brothers hanging and knocking back whiskeys. Exactly where he needed to keep his focus, on his MC and the growing problem with Spike and the cartel. He had no doubt that Spike's union with Raúl Trevino Caballero would spell all kinds of bad for the Sons.

Techno dance music gained in volume as he descended the stairs, the bass thumping his chest. Shit he couldn't stand, let alone put a name to. The kids on the dance floor seemed to love it, so he supposed it was the reason Draven's DJ kept the stuff spinning. He'd rather hear bands like Nine Inch Nails or Celldweller, something a little more hardcore. Pushing aside the curtains, he stepped onto the tiled flooring. Neon lights streaked about the club, while the ravers hopped and swayed to the music. Alexander preferred the back bar area where the music was at least muted and the traffic was thin. A larger bar near the front of the club served most of the patrons.

Alexander spotted Kane and Kaleb sitting on barstools chatting with Draven and Brea. Grigore was nowhere to be found. He sat beside the club P. Draven grabbed a clean glass, filled it with ice, then used the bar gun to pour Alexander a lemon-lime soda. He slid the filled glass across the bar to him.

He nodded his thanks, then picked up the tumbler and sipped the carbonated soda, loving the feel of the fizz. Funny, but he always had. Alexander was sure it was a reminder of his childhood when he sat at the bar while his mother drank herself into a stupor.

He set the glass on the bar. "Where's Wolf?"

"Not his keeper." Kaleb chuckled. "Probably getting a piece of ass."

"You're a jackass, Hawk." Kane shook his head, a grin splitting his face. "Ask you and you think everyone's getting laid. Last I saw Wolf he was heading for the door."

"He left?"

"Hell if I know. He didn't say a word." Kane took a sip from his whiskey. "We all went to find donors. Hawk and I met here. If Wolf was leaving, he never said a word to us."

"Any news on Spike's whereabouts?"

Kaleb rotated in his chair, resting an elbow on the bar. "Preacher called, said him and Rogue had just crossed over the border into California. They won't hit the Mexican border for another thirteen hours or so."

Kane looked at Brea. "Any contact from your godfather?"

Her smile didn't quite reach her eyes. "Not since Draven and I were in Mexico. I doubt he'll contact me, now that I know he's a vampire."

Draven chuckled. "You seriously think the old man is going to give up on you that easily? He wanted you in his bed, sweetheart. I'm betting that hasn't changed. He may go underground for a while, lay low, but I'm thinking he'll be back for you."

"Or you," she reminded him. "If you think he still wants me, then just like Kinky, he won't be above going through you to get to me."

"You guys are both correct. Just like Spike, we need to keep a close eye on you and India. I'm betting Raúl is used to getting what he wants. These two men aren't to be taken lightly." Alexander rapped his knuckles twice on the bar. "We've got Vlad keeping a close eye on India and the women when we aren't there. Maybe you should consider staying at the house as well."

"While I appreciate your concern, I don't think it's me my godfather will want to kill. Draven will be who he's gunning for."

"You're probably right, Brea." Kane grabbed the bottle of Gentleman Jack and poured himself a couple more fingers of whiskey. "But that doesn't mean he won't want to try and steal you away, like I'm sure is Spike's plan for India. We have a real shitstorm coming. We all need to be on our toes."

"Viper's correct," Kaleb added. "None of us can afford to let our guard down."

"Speaking of India," Alexander said, "I think I should get back to the house, give Vlad a break from the ladies."

"You sure you want to head over there?" Kaleb laughed. "I just got a call from Suzi—looks like it's a real slumber party over there. Tena and Kimber are spending the night since Preacher and Rogue are heading for Mexico."

"Wonderful." Alexander scrubbed a hand through his short hair. "How soon is the clubhouse going to be ready?"

Kane grimaced. "Not soon enough for my liking either."

"Tell Wolf I'll catch up with him tomorrow. I plan on helping out."

"Will do, Xander. I think we're all going over to help out in some capacity." Kane laid a hand on his shoulder. "We need to get this shit contained. I'm falling behind over at K&K Motorcycles. I have a couple of new customs ordered I need to get working on. I can't have all my guys out working on the clubhouse and not the bikes."

"I can't agree with you more, Viper." Alexander stood, finished off his soda and set the glass on the bar. "All of these women hanging there is starting to give me hives."

He headed for the entrance to the club, hearing his brothers laugh at his parting comment. Sad part, he was only half joking. He had never been a huge fan of having the women around and having them all gathered in one place was enough to give him a serious case of anxiety.

The bedroom door opened, leaving a shaft of light into the darkness. India caught Alexander's silhouette as he peered in. No doubt checking to see if she was fast asleep. Truth of it, she had awakened about an hour after sleep had claimed her. The women had stayed up well past when she had retired. Not that they meant to keep her from getting rest, but it was hard not to hear them just beyond her door. The party had died down about a half hour ago, but sleep continued to elude her.

India had never been much of a partier and had tuckered out. She had quickly washed up in the adjoining Jack and Jill bathroom, thinking that she couldn't wait for her head to hit the pillow and let exhaustion claim her. But once aroused from her sleep, her eyes had remained wide open and her thoughts refused to quit. The reason now stood in her doorway.

"You're awake?" Alexander whispered, stepping further into the room.

"I am. You may come in if you'd like."

"I probably shouldn't. I just wanted to check on you. Make sure you were okay."

"Vlad kept an eye on the house. I don't think Spike, or anyone for that matter, would want to cross him." India scooted to a sitting position on the mattress and turned on the bedside lamp. Soft light filled the room, bathing his handsome face with a warm glow. "Is anyone else yet awake?"

"A couple of the women moved into the kitchen, apparently to entertain Viper. Hawk, Suzi, and Stefan hit the road."

"Wouldn't you rather be entertaining the women with Viper?"

A smile crossed his face, one that could easily steal her heart if he hadn't already. "I think you know me better than that."

"Close the door and come sit." She patted the bed beside her. "I won't bite, I promise."

"You want the company?" His gaze was skeptical. "Cara told me you were tired."

"I slept a little."

"You need your rest," Alexander said, though he closed the door and approached the bed anyway. "I'll lie with you for a bit—maybe it will help you fall back asleep."

Like that would happen. Quite the opposite, in fact. Just knowing he would be beside her kicked up her libido. And now that she knew vampires could scent desire, Alexander would know his effect on her as well.

"I'm sorry," she said.

"For?"

"Cara and Suzi informed me earlier that vampires could detect desire."

He chuckled. The mattress dipped beneath his weight as he sat. Placing one of his arms across her shoulders, he pulled her against his side and kissed the top of her head.

"*Gattina*, I've known you've desired me for some time. Scenting it on you now is no different."

She placed her hands over her heating face and groaned. "This is embarrassing. And so not fair."

Alexander pulled down her hands, then tipped her chin so she looked up at him. "How is it not fair?"

"Because you obviously know how I feel about you. I don't have the faintest idea if you like me or hate me."

He placed a second kiss on her forehead. "If you were to look at the front of my jeans right now, *gattina*, I think you might get an idea."

Lord, she would not look—she would *not*—and yet, her gaze drifted downward to the large bulge in the front of his jeans. Her face heated even further. Hell, her whole body likely blushed.

"Make no mistake, I more than know you're around."

India snuggled into his side and laid her cheek against his chest. "Aren't we a pair."

"What do you mean?"

"For months, I tried to catch your attention to no avail. Now that I find myself pregnant with Spike's kid, you notice me."

He shrugged, another chuckle rising from his gut. "I can't help myself. Pregnant women are sexy as hell."

She slapped his T-shirt-covered chest. "You won't think so in about five months when I'm all fat and waddling."

"I'll likely still think you're sexy."

India thought about his admission and wondered again why he treated her more like a little sister. "Xander?"

"Yes, *gattina*?"

"Why do you treat me as if I have the plague?" She tipped back her head and looked up at him. "Am I really so distasteful?"

He used his palm to smooth back the long black hair from her forehead. "You've never been distasteful, India. Quite the opposite. I thought we already established I desire you."

"Then why?"

"Wolf—"

"No." She shook her head. "You don't get to use that as an excuse. I tried to make you jealous with Wolf. It was one night, Xander. And it obviously backfired. We never did anything. Had I truly wanted him, I would've continued my flirtation past that night."

One of his dark brows rose. "And Spike?"

She whispered, "Was a mistake."

"I get that." His answering chuckle sounded humorless. "For certain, you had to know that once you went with Spike, that you and I weren't going to happen. He's the fucking enemy, India."

"I came to terms with you and I not happening long before I left, Xander." India pulled herself from his embrace. "Do you hate women in general? Or is it just me?"

His dark gaze held hers for a long time, so long she feared she'd pissed him off and he wasn't going to bother with a reply. His jaw hardened, his cheeks heavily shadowed from his day's growth of whiskers. Lord, if the situation was any different, she might have crawled on his lap and demanded he put to use the erection in his pants. But they couldn't go back and change the past if she wanted.

"I don't hate you, *gattina*." He scrubbed his jaw with his free hand, the scratching sound of whiskers filling the otherwise quiet room. "If I did, I wouldn't be here, nor would I have offered you my friendship through this pregnancy."

"Would you have offered had you known the baby was Spike's?"

Again, he went quiet. He glanced away, staring at the far wall and took in a deep breath before returning his attention. "I can't say for sure, but I doubt I would've turned you away. You looked like you needed a friend. I'm not a complete asshole."

"So where do we go from here?" India laid her head onto his chest. His arm tightened around her. "Spike won't stop coming for me. I shouldn't have involved you or the Sons. He blew up part of your clubhouse."

"I'm counting on him not giving up, *gattina*. He may have gone into hiding, the chickenshit that he is. But he'll surface, and when he does, I'll be there. He won't hurt you again. I won't allow it."

CHAPTER NINE

India looked up at him in hero worship. Hell, he was no one's hero, the dog tags resting against his breast living proof. Oh, he intended on following through with his promise to her. He'd make damn sure Spike never laid his filthy hands on her again. The scum would die. He'd never take India from him.

From him?

As if Alexander were laying claim. Christ, he was getting tangled up in his emotions, something he'd vowed not to do. He ought to walk away before things got messy, turn her over to the capable hands of Grigore—no, not Grigore—then Ryder. Alexander hardened his jaw. *Fuck!* Maybe Vlad. Hell. To. The. No. Women seemed far too easily charmed by the primordial.

"Xander?"

He returned his focus on India, feeling her warm gaze on him, everywhere. As if she had taken her hand and stroked his chest and abdomen, rather than just laying it upon his T-shirt. Had she not been carrying another man's baby, he might be tempted to toss aside all past hurts and bury himself balls-deep into the dark beauty. No one took a hold of his balls the way India did when she entered a room. His cock more than knew she was around.

Every. Damn. Time.

He shook his head. Yep, he wanted to fuck her in the worst way. But as long as she was pregnant, that wasn't going to happen because she was off-limits. He'd respect her body and her person. Once she gave birth, maybe he'd consider exploring this thing between them. No, not maybe—for certain, there was no denying it.

Mate?

Absolutely not. Nope. No can do.

But that didn't mean he couldn't enjoy the company of and be faithful to one woman for a bit of time. Having a donor as a fuck buddy? Something he normally stayed away from, since the last thing he wanted to do was bite the hand that fed him. No pun intended. Now that he had spent a considerable amount of time in India's company, yeah, he could see dating her for a spell.

"What can I do for you, *gattina*?"

"Will you forgive me?"

He scrubbed his whiskered jaw again, more than one kind of frustration itching up his spine. "There's nothing to forgive. You may have been foolish, but your actions are your own. They have no bearing on me."

"But they do. You and all of your MC. I have brought the Devils—more specifically, Spike—to your doorstep. He may have only blown a hole in the front of your clubhouse this time, but hard telling where he'll stop. Maybe not until someone dies. The Sons have seen enough death."

Alexander couldn't argue with her. Too many of his brothers had been killed in the past couple of years, men he had respected and loved. "Spike will be the one to meet his maker. He doesn't stand a chance against the Sons."

"He won't fight fair." She absently traced a finger along the design on his T-shirt. Hell, *she* wasn't fighting fair. His erection plagued him unbearably. "I don't want to be the reason you lose another MC member. You lost Kinky not that long ago."

Alexander thought of his late MC brother, Joseph Sala, gunned down in front of the Blood 'n' Rave. The vampire hadn't stood a chance. The gunman had aimed for the T-zone of his face, killing him instantly. No doubt the man had been a professional. Alexander had been disturbed and angered later to learn the details of Joseph's relationship with his then-mate Brea Gotti. Hell, he hadn't wanted to believe Joseph had been cruel enough to screw another donor while his mate had to watch the man she loved callously take another.

He wasn't sure how he would have handled the situation Joseph had been in, mating with a woman when he clearly wasn't ready. He could understand how Joseph must have felt trapped. Nevertheless, his actions had been uncalled for. Joseph had made his decision to mate with Brea, regardless of whether he had been ready, and kept that alliance from the rest of his MC brothers. Following his death, Brea had met Draven. They both seemed thrilled to have found one another. Alexander was certainly happy for the barkeep.

Deep down, Draven was a good guy. Brea would help keep the newly turned vampire on the straight and narrow.

"Kinky's blood is on the cartel's hands. They'll be served justice."

"I don't doubt that." She palmed his cheek. He resisted the urge to lean into the warmth. "I don't want your death to be on *my* hands."

"I'll be fine, *gattina*."

"You can't promise that. Spike bombed the clubhouse—what if you had been lying on that sofa as you did every other night? You can't tell me Spike didn't set the bomb there on purpose."

"Maybe."

Alexander couldn't dispute her theory. Had it been any other night, he would have been ash, right along with that damn sofa. Spike could have been easily staking out the clubhouse and hoping Alexander would've been lying there like any other night when the explosion happened. How Alexander had missed Spike's vampire scent, though, he was unsure. Spike's phone call right before the blast was to no doubt make sure Alexander was awake for the fireworks. Thankfully, he had been up late that evening and hadn't been able to sleep.

"Look, India," he said, tucking her hair behind one of her ears as he looked into the deep chocolate pools of her gaze, "he didn't accomplish what he set out to do. Now, he's on the run. He might have blindsided us once, but it won't happen again. It's only a matter of time before we catch up to him.

And when we do, we'll deal out our own form of judgment. We won't need the law."

A tear slipped from her lashes. Alexander thumbed away the wetness. "Look at all of the trouble I've caused you. I deserve Spike. Not you."

"Christ, India. Don't even say that. No one but the Grim Reaper deserves that piece of shit. If Rogue and Preacher don't find him and take him out, I guarantee I will."

More tears fell as she slowly shook her head. "I can't let you do that, Xander. I'll leave first."

His brows creased. "Do you have so little faith in me?"

Her bow-shaped lips rounded, but she said nothing.

"You'll do no such thing. If you even think to go back to Spike, you'll make your bed, *gattina*. You'll no longer be welcomed here." He tipped her chin, forcing her to look him in the eye, to see the seriousness of his declaration. He'd spot the lie the minute it left her lips. "Do I make myself clear?"

The thought of her back in the arms of Spike chilled his blood. Christ, she'd be putting her own life and that of the baby in danger.

"I would never."

"Then where do you think you could go that would offer you more protection than I can give you? Or the Sons of Sangue, for that matter?"

"If I were to leave—"

"Enough!" Lord, he wanted to shake some sense into her, turn her over his knee. Alexander grit his teeth at the image his last thought conjured up. "You will remain with me. Do I make myself clear?"

Her gaze darkened. "You're ordering me?"

"No, India." He narrowed his own gaze, anger heating his spine. "You will always have a choice. My demand was fueled by my anger. But if you choose to leave, you will be leaving my offered protection. You won't get that back. No second chance. So, choose wisely."

Her pink tongue darted out, wetting her lips. The heat from his spine now pooled in his groin. Only he could go from angry to horny in less than a second's time. She was definitely his biggest temptation and weakness. Never had he come across a female who could grab him by the balls the way India did. If only she wasn't pregnant. Hell, if only he could get her to grab his balls. Christ, it would take even less time to toss her on her back and bury himself to the hilt.

Alexander released a deep sigh. It looked like his palm was going to be getting all the action tonight.

"I only wanted to protect you."

One of his brows inched upward. "Do I look as if I need a woman's protection?"

"A bomb—"

"We've already established that. Are you trying to unman me?"

She rolled her eyes. "*Men*. It's always a power play with you guys, sizing up each other's dicks."

Alexander wasn't sure what he expected her to say, but her comment left him chuckling. Certainly, his cock was more impressive than Spike's. And damn himself for wanting to prove it. But he knew what she meant. It was a metaphor, and not about the actual size of the appendage in his pants, which was impressively large at the moment, though he could do little about it. Maybe he ought to make his excuses and go yank one off in the adjoining bathroom. He couldn't help but wonder how embarrassed she'd be to know she was the reason he needed the release.

"Quite honestly, I'm betting I'm more suited at giving you pleasure than your man Spike."

"Seriously?" She pushed away from him and sat up, crossing her arms beneath her breasts and drawing his gaze downward. Her fingers gestured from him to her warm gaze. "You're such a guy. Eyes up here."

"I am a guy." His chuckle deepened. "A guy who just happens to appreciate a nice pair of tits."

"One-track mind." She smiled and shook her head. "First of all, I'm not trying to unman you. I care what happens to you. I never said I didn't think you couldn't beat Spike in a fair fight. But he *doesn't* fight fair, Xander. He never will. He's a scumbag, not worth the oxygen he draws."

"And yet you slept with him."

"I did. Several times, in fact. How long are you going to beat me up over that?"

The heat rose from his spine, up his neck, and into his cheeks. He knew he was being an ass. After all, he had turned his back on her first, months ago, before she ever hooked up with the dirtbag.

"Please don't go into detail. It's bad enough knowing you slept with him more than once."

"You *are* naive."

"No, just not a masochist."

"What's that supposed to mean?"

"The idea of you sleeping with him once turns my stomach, India. Add on Lord knows how many times"—he shuddered—"and I just want to kill something with my bare hands, preferably Spike."

"Why, Xander?" Her gaze hardened. "You. Didn't. Want. Me."

"I wish that were true," he whispered.

Gripping her chin, he pulled her forward, slanting his lips over her fuller ones. He waited for her reaction, thought for sure she'd slap his face for taking the liberties. Instead, her hands smoothed up his T-shirt and around his nape, anchoring him. He drew her lower lip between his teeth, lightly biting down. His fangs punched through his gums, nicking her lips. His tongue darted out, soothing away the sting for her, and tasting the smoky flavor of her blood.

Lord, it was his undoing.

Alexander suckled her lip, sipping the morsel of blood, though denying his fangs further access. India moaned, giving him admittance. Deepening the kiss, he pushed his tongue past her lips and teeth, sweeping the soft flesh of her mouth, tangling his tongue with hers.

His groin ached and his hold on her tightened.

India moaned, spurring him forward when he knew damn well he should pull away. Nothing tasted as sweet. Gripping her long black hair at the nape, he tilted her head, giving him better access. Her breasts pressed against his chest, her nipples now taut. Kissing her was wrong on so many levels. She didn't belong to him.

I belong to no one.

She carried another man's child, for crying out loud. For that alone, he should walk away, be the bigger man. But damn, he could go on kissing her until tomorrow. Alexander moved from her mouth, kissing a path down her neck to the sensitive spot beneath her ear. Her pulse beat heavily against his lips and it was all he could do to keep from sinking his fangs deep into her artery. Instead, he pulled on her earlobe, again nicking the flesh and allowing himself another taste.

Pure torture.

India's lips parted on another moan as she leaned into him, offering herself. The scent of her desire told him she was in just as deep as he was, that she wanted this … him.

If only their situation was different…

"Christ, *gattina*. We can't," he whispered into her ear. He quickly licked the small wound and leaned back, setting her away from him. He wiped a hand down his mouth, willing his fangs to retreat. "As much as I want to fuck you right now, it can't happen."

India raised a brow. "It was just a kiss, Xander."

He chuckled. "You keep telling yourself that. Remember, I can scent your desire. I think you were just as invested as I was."

Her cheeks reddened. "That may be, but neither of us would have allowed it to go further."

"Now you're the one being naive, India. Had we kept going and I hadn't backed off, I would have fucked you and you *wouldn't* have stopped me.

CHAPTER TEN

India swept up the dirt with a broom and dust pan, emptying the filth into the large black receptacle. A surgical mask covered her nose to keep her from breathing in debris. Fresh boards had replaced the charred ones from the explosion, nailed into place on the wall. All hands were on deck and the noise was damn near deafening. She was glad to see the work being completed, meaning she no longer had to inconvenience Kane and Cara. Although she was touched they had opened their farmhouse to her, India was content to return to Alexander's room.

A sense of home washed over her.

Releasing a deep sigh, India knew it was foolhardy to start thinking of this place as home, earning her nothing but heartache in the end. No matter her desires, if Alexander didn't share them, she'd be sent packing in the end.

The spot where the sofa had been drew her gaze, causing a shudder to pass down her spine and raising the hair on her arms. Alexander could have easily died in the explosion. Thankfully, nothing more than the furnishing and structure had been damaged. India wasn't sure she could have lived with herself if she had been the cause of Alexander's death.

Grayson and Kaleb were busy replacing the flooring with new hardwood, while Kane, Ryder, and Grigore worked on the structure. At this rate, the clubhouse would be good as new in little time. Cara and Suzi had taken Stefan and headed for the store to pick out new furnishings, leaving her with Kimber, Tena, and Tamera. Tena's friend Chad had also come by to lend a helping hand.

He was proving to be quite the comedian as he kept an eye on little Lucian. The baby was getting more animated as he tried to grab everything in sight and take it to his mouth. And since the clubhouse was far from clean, Chad had offered to hold him while the women continued to tidy up. At the moment, Lucian was sucking on his tiny fist while Chad cooed adorably at him.

India couldn't help but think about the baby growing in her stomach and how her life was about to change. Babies required work, *a lot of work.* She feared Alexander wanting to move on, expecting her to do the same. Finding a new place to live would have to be on the top of the list when the time drew near, having given up her old apartment when she'd moved south with Spike. Even if India desired to stay, she couldn't ask Alexander to provide further housing for her and the baby until she got on her feet. India had asked that he be with her through the pregnancy and nothing more.

She was a big girl, and once the threat of Spike was gone, she'd damn well stand on her own two feet. The last thing India wanted was Alexander to start thinking of her as a burden, or worse yet, one huge pain in his ass.

Their shared kiss the night before came to mind, warming her.

Alexander had instigated it and had been just as invested in the show of affection, had even admitted as much. And yet he had promptly left the room following their exchange, and was gone from the house before she rose for breakfast. Kane had informed her that he'd be giving her and the rest of the women an escort to the clubhouse. Even now, Alexander was absent from helping with the repairs, having gone to get more wood for the siding.

The truck carrying the purchased lumber had arrived nearly an hour ago.

And yet, Alexander was still MIA.

He no doubt regretted allowing things to go too far. But not India. She wasn't about to forget the kiss or the way he'd looked at her. Damn, if he hadn't made her feel as if she'd never been kissed before.

At least not a kiss of that caliber.

And since he had all but ordered her to stay put, canning her idea to go off on her own, she planned to, for once, follow his directive. If for no other reason than to prove to him he not only wanted but *needed* her in his life. India wasn't ready to give up. His actions were a good indication that he wasn't completely unaffected by her, and India had about six months to convince him this thing between them was worth exploring.

Tamera walked over to India, hand held out for the broom and dust pan. "Why don't you let me sweep? You look like you could use a little rest, maybe help Chad with Lucian if he starts to get fussy. He can be a handful most times. He's definitely Gypsy's son. A chip off the old block, if you will."

India's hand covered her stomach, thinking Tamera might be right. She was a little tired, having not gotten much sleep the night before. India had first met the redhead from when she was a donor at the Rave. At the time, Tamera hadn't been exactly cordial to the rest of the donors, especially if they came within touching distance of Grayson. India wasn't one to hold grudges, though. Lord only knew she had made enough mistakes all on her own. Besides, a small part of her could certainly understand with her wanting to be territorial when it came to Alexander.

India pulled the mask from her face. "Are you sure?"

Though she couldn't argue with needing a break from all the work, India didn't want anyone to think she wasn't holding up her end of the chores either.

Tamera smiled, taking the broom and the dust pan. "Go sit. Or if you prefer, go lay down a bit in Alexander's room. Being pregnant is exhausting enough. Kimber, Tena, and I can handle the cleanup from here. We'll have this place whipped back into shape in no time."

Grayson stood, walked to the bar area and pulled down a couple glasses and a bottle of Gentleman Jack. He winked at Tamera, gave her a quick peck on the cheek, then poured a couple of tumblers full of the amber whiskey. He held one out to Tamera.

She shook her head. "Give that one to Hawk. He could probably use the drink. At the rate you guys are putting in that flooring, this place should be finished by nightfall, then maybe you and I can head for the Rave. I could use a little thirst-quencher of my own."

"You are looking a little paler than usual."

Tamera swatted his shoulder, earning her a chuckle. Grayson kissed her briefly on the lips, then walked away. He handed a tumbler of the amber liquid to Kaleb. The club P laid down his rubber mallet and took the offered glass, swallowing the contents in one gulp. Before long, the two were back at the hardwood again, already over halfway done.

"Do you like being a … well, a…"

"Vampire?" Tamera supplied. "If you mean do I mind drinking blood, not at all. Once you're turned, it just becomes as natural as having a glass of milk. The taste can be quite pleasing with the right donor. As a human, that's hard to understand. Not to mention, the idea of consuming someone else's blood is enough to turn anyone's stomach. But as a vampire? Quite the opposite. It's like having your favorite food and wanting more of it. Besides, it's kind of fun having the extra strength that comes with it, not to mention the other heightened senses. Like now, Gypsy has a big mouth telling Hawk about our late-night romp in the ocean."

"I heard that." He chuckled. "Not a big mouth, just a well-pleased vampire."

Tamera laughed. "See what I mean? As a human, I wouldn't have heard their conversation over the racket. Not to mention detecting his desire. Knowing your man is always one step away from wanting to get you horizontal does a lot for your ego."

"I do suppose." India's face heated. "But as a human, that can be quite embarrassing."

"You mean like when Xander walks into a room." Her teeth flashed white as she smiled. "It's okay, India. We've all been there. Now if we can just get said vampire's head out of his ass, he might see the worth of what's standing in front of him."

"Seriously?" India grimaced. "I feared you all might have thought I was trying to be manipulative."

"Honey, I'm the last person to judge someone. Everyone knows how I teamed up with the vampire bitch from hell to gain immortality." She rolled her green eyes. "I was so taken by Gypsy, I was willing to make a pact with the devil herself. Even though at the time, I had no idea she was playing me. I was damn lucky Gypsy was a forgiving man. I would've loved to have taken Rosalee's life myself had Vlad not done the honors."

"You would've had to have gotten in line," Grayson said.

Tamara laughed again. "Thankfully, it all turned out and my man loves me."

"Damned straight, *il mio dolce rossa*."

"What I'm saying, India, is"—Tamera laid a hand on her shoulder—"no matter the hows and whys, don't give up on Xander just yet. The way he looks at you, I'm betting he cares far more than he's letting on."

"If it makes a difference, I really do care for Xander."

"That's as plain as the nose on your face, honey." Tamera smiled. "You're just wrapped in a few too many complications."

India grimaced. "Namely, Spike."

"And his baby. One step at a time, India. We're all here for you. All you need do is ask."

"Thanks, Tamera." India gave the redhead a brief hug. "You all have been so nice to me, when I don't deserve it. I left ... I took up with a rival MC member. And now it appears he's going to make the Sons' life hell because of me."

Kaleb approached the bar, pouring himself another whiskey, and knocked it back. He slammed the tumbler onto the bar surface. His lips turned up. "I sure in the hell hope so, India. There's nothing more I'd like to do than to go to war with the Devils over a good cause. Getting rid of Spike is about as good a cause as any. You don't worry your pretty head over this. You didn't bring the war to our door step, Spike did. That's on him. When we're through with him, you won't have to worry about him ever again. Regardless of where you sit with Xander. You may not be his mate or his old lady, but you're damn sure under the Sons' protection."

KALEB WOULD LIKELY HAVE his ass. But at the moment, Alexander didn't give two shits what the club P thought. He needed to be far away from the clubhouse and Mexico seemed about as good a choice as any. Following the purchase of the lumber, he had called Anton. It seemed Bobby and he had bunkered down just outside of Ensenada, where Raúl Trevino Caballero kept a vacation home on the beach.

And the last place Draven Smith had seen Spike alive.

They had yet to spot the cartel kingpin or the dumbass Devil. Anton had mentioned seeing a flurry of activity within the compound and could probably use Alexander's help. Hard telling if any of those bastards had been turned, or if just their boss and Spike were vampires. Anton had said they couldn't get close enough to scent out any vampires in the area.

The cell in his pocket vibrated. This stretch of highway was pretty much deserted, so Alexander parked his bike off the road and cut the engine. He pulled his phone from his pocket and swiped his finger across the surface.

"P. What's up?"

"More like, where the fuck are you, Xander?" Kaleb chuckled. "I send you out for lumber and the wood arrives and you go missing. Too much work rebuilding the clubhouse, you decided to ditch us? Or did you finally decide to put in a day's work at K&K Motorcycles?"

Not that he minded the job, but the prospects were handling the motorcycle shop for the time being. Besides, if anything major came up, Kane and Kaleb were within shouting distance. Once the clubhouse was completed, the twins, Grigore, and Ryder could handle the workload at the shop until the three of them returned from Mexico.

"You know the prospects got the shop handled."

"They do. But you're better at the job. Any idea how long you're going to be gone?"

"I'm heading for Mexico, Hawk. I figured Rogue and Preacher could use a little help. Turns out Raúl's little beach house is a flourish of activity."

"You talked to Rogue?"

"I did." Alexander unsnapped his skull cap and laid it across his lap. The sun beating down on him would've been unbearable had it not been for the slight ocean breeze. "He hasn't spotted the kingpin or Spike yet. But he said there is plenty of activity going on. They can't get close enough to sniff out any vampires in the area."

"Why the hell not? Draven and his little mate seemed to get on the inside easily enough."

"And if you recall, they also got caught." Alexander scrubbed the short hair on the back of his head. "Rogue and Preacher are being more cautious. If the two we're looking for aren't in residence, no sense in going in. They're hanging tight until I get there."

"Something else going on you want to tell me about?"

"I'm not sure what you mean, P."

"You know damn straight what—or rather *whom*—I'm referring to. You promised to protect India, and yet there you are, racing down the coast."

Alexander hung his head. It had been a coward move and he knew it. No sense lying about it. "Look, Hawk, I need time. She has plenty of protection around there with the mates, not to mention Vlad hanging in the shadows."

"He's around ... for now. You never know with Grandpop, though, when he might just up and disappear. India isn't in his charge. *You* promised to protect her."

"I did."

"You get out whatever bug you got riding up your ass, get what you need to get done, and hightail your ugly mug back up the coast and finish what you promised to do. She's under the Sons' protection. Make no mistake about it. Anyone even tries to take her, they'll have to deal with one of us. But she's your responsibility. You took her on, Xander. You ain't dropping this in our laps. Going to Mexico—that's an excuse. I'm sure Rogue and Preacher are glad for the help, but they could've handled it on their own and you damn well know it."

He didn't argue. Hell, he couldn't, not when Kaleb had hit the nail on the head. After ordering the lumber, Alexander had fled, not wanting to return to the clubhouse. It was hard enough spending the night in Kane's farmhouse with her just beyond the closed door following that kiss. He wiped a hand down his face. Jesus! That kiss. It had taken all his willpower and then some to walk away. Returning her to the clubhouse? To his bed?

Fuck!

He wasn't sure he had much willpower left. Even with her being pregnant with another man's baby, he wanted India with the force of two colliding locomotives. Staying away until he got a hold on his desire was his only self-preservation.

"Once I assess the situation in Mexico, and I find I'm not needed, I'll head back."

"You get your shit figured out, Xander. We're going up against the cartel soon and I need your head out of your ass. You got me?"

"Loud and clear, boss."

"Good." Alexander heard Suzi's voice in the background. "The furniture's arriving. I got stuff to do so we can get this place back in order. India will be moving in here with Grigore and Ryder to watch over her tonight. You get it together, Xander, then haul your sorry ass back here. Tell Rogue and Preacher to keep me informed. If they find out Raúl and Spike are in Mexico, then the rest of us will meet you down there. No one moves without a plan. I don't want Spike disappearing on us. He needs to answer for his actions."

"Got it, P." Alexander took a deep breath and released it slowly. "And P, tell India I'll be back in a few days. I don't want her worrying needlessly about me."

"Call me when you get to Mexico."

The line went dead.

Alexander sat back on the bike and looked across the horizon. Turbulent waves crashed against the rocky shore, fierce and unsettled like his emotions. He never thought he'd ever feel anything more for a woman than what they could do for him beneath the sheets. Damn, if India wasn't making him feel as if he might want more.

After placing the helmet back onto his head, he started the engine. Regardless if he was beginning to feel even a smidgen of something for India, nothing could happen between them until the baby was born. The way he saw it, he had a long six months ahead of him. And one dead Spike to see to.

CHAPTER ELEVEN

"You bombed their clubhouse?" Raúl Trevino Caballero paced the penthouse suite of the downtown hotel he had secured in Eugene, Oregon.

The view from the top floor was phenomenal. Hanging with the kingpin definitely came with its perks. Spike stood from the rolling cart on which their late supper had been wheeled in. Even though he no longer required food, he still enjoyed a good filet mignon, not to mention the delicious lobster bisque. The restaurant staff was second to none.

Earlier, they had dined on a couple of hotel housekeepers' arteries, followed by a good hard fucking. Raúl had swept their memory of anything other than their cleaning of the rooms and sent them on their way. They might wonder the cause of the ache between their thighs, but they'd have no recollection to the cause.

Damn, I need to learn that hypnotism shit!

The hotel Raúl had chosen was far enough from Pleasant to escape detection by the Sons of Sangue, or anyone else who might be looking for them. Raúl had wanted to personally check in with his capos to see how the soldiers were doing moving his heroin. He had wanted to infiltrate the colleges and schools of Oregon before moving up the coast to Washington. Thanks to the Devils, he had a good stranglehold already on California. Anton Balan and Draven Smith had worked undercover with the DEA, closing down a good share of his profits in Oregon, costing Raúl a small fortune. Their days were numbered and Spike would be only too happy to help the kingpin send them to an early grave.

Raúl was anxious to get his shipments moving again. Time meant money. Had Anton not done Raúl the favor of taking out Tank, Raúl would've personally done the job himself. The Devils' late president had made the mistake of putting his trust in the wrong men. Raúl's misfortune was Spike's gain, as he was now leader of the Devils. Not all the men seemed on board with following his command, but fuck 'em. If any one of them thought to double-cross him, he'd take them out personally ... cartel style.

Man, I live for this shit!

Once they finished with the capos, Raúl planned a trip back to his home base in La Paz, leaving Spike time to deal with his little slut and his baby. Maybe even take out a couple of Sons of Sangue while he was at it ... particularly Alexander Dumitru.

Spike smiled at his handiwork. "I did."

"You want to give me one fucking good reason?"

His eyes rounded. *What the fuck?* The way he saw it, he had been doing the kingpin a favor. "Seriously? After what Anton Balan pulled, ratting out your drug channels to the DEA?"

One of his gray brows arched. "Anton was working to bring down the Devils."

"Which indirectly includes you. Who do you think runs your drugs?"

Raúl stopped pacing and faced Spike, fists perched on his beefy hips. The older man was short and bulky. A fat little troll, if Spike were being honest. But Spike was no fool, the kingpin was not to be underestimated. He had seen the man take out men much larger than himself.

Straightening to his five-foot-five inches of height, the kingpin glared at Spike. "*Pinche idiota!* The Devils are only a small part of my organization. I wouldn't be so quick with the wit if I were you."

Spike knew best when to back the fuck off. Getting cocky with the kingpin would only earn him a one-way trip to hell. "I meant no disrespect."

"I'll take care of the biker all in good time. But higher on my hit list is that bar owner who thinks he can take what's mine. Soon, I'll have his head, then I'll claim my goddaughter."

Spike bit the inside flesh of his mouth to keep from out and out laughing. Even if Raúl managed to take out Draven Smith, there was no way in hell that little mate of his was going anywhere willingly with the kingpin. She might be his goddaughter, but it was pretty obvious when they had last seen her in Mexico, she spared no love for her god-papa.

"I'll ask you one more time, *pendejo*. Why the fuck did you bomb the clubhouse? Don't lie to me. You could care less about the one they call Rogue. You and I both know by killing Tank, he did you a favor."

"Because the Sons have something that belongs to me."

"Which is?"

Spike scratched his nape. Knowing Raúl was after his own woman, maybe he'd not take so unkindly to Spike's reasoning. "India Jackson."

"What is she to you?"

"My bitch."

Raúl's forehead deeply furrowed. "Then why is she with the Sons of Sangue?"

"She's misguided."

"Is she a mate to one of the Sons?"

"No. She went to one of them, Alexander Dumitru, for protection. She thought she could steal my baby from me."

"Your baby? I wasn't aware—"

"She's pregnant with my child."

"*Pinche puta!* Why didn't you say so in the first place?" His eyes blackened and his thick lips turned down. "You will get your bitch and your child, though you'll not be able to take her from the Sons on your own. You'll need a good diversion."

"That's what the bomb was."

Raúl chuckled so hard that tears leaked from the corners of his eyes. When he finally got control of his laughter, he said, "You might've had better luck if you had tried to steal her away. All you managed to do was stir up the hornets' nest. They'll no doubt be looking for you, wanting to take your head."

"So, what do you suggest we do?"

"We? I'm heading to Mexico, *compadre*. This is your mess, a mess I have no time for. You ... you will need to lure her away."

"And how do you suppose I do that?"

His large smile bared his razor-sharp fangs. "I got word not more than an hour ago that her protector, this Alexander, crossed the border into Mexico. While I return home to strengthen my compound, use this time to your advantage. Go get your woman ... soon, I will get mine."

Spike couldn't help but feel a bit sorry for Brea Gotti. Who the hell would want to be mated to this disgusting slob? But then again, he'd sleep with the fat little fucker if it meant he'd get his hands on even a small portion of his rumored billions.

ALEXANDER WIPED THE SWEAT dotting his brow with the back of his forearm as he straddled his motorcycle, looking out across the Pacific Ocean. Few clouds stippled the sky, making the day extremely uncomfortable. Leave it to him to drive south on a sweltering day. Good thing only fictional vampires incinerated in direct sunlight, or he'd have been toast. Due to his DNA, his skin was merely more sensitive to the sun and he'd no doubt wind up with a sunburn somewhere. Thankfully, he'd heal just as quickly. A long-sleeved T-shirt had covered most of his upper body for the biggest share of the ride, but somewhere along the southern California border he had changed into a black tank.

"You look like you're a bit cooked, Xander. Not smart enough to ride it out at night?"

"You don't look like you're faring much better, Preacher. Might help if you chopped off some of that ridiculous beard."

"Ridiculous? Jealous much?"

Alexander laughed. "Seriously? What do you have hiding in there?"

"Only a real man can grow a beard this stellar. Besides, Tena finds it sexy, loves it when it rubs her—"

"Oh hell, I don't need a play-by-play with what you do with that thing." Alexander faked a shiver, then retrieved a do-rag from his saddle bag and tied it around his head to help catch the sweat. "It's hot enough I could fry bacon on my tank."

"Well, if you are inclined to do so"—Bobby chuckled, running a hand down his long beard, smoothing it—"please, don't let me stop you. I'm famished."

Alexander shook his head with a grin. "Little good that would do you. Maybe you ought to be looking up an artery instead."

The ocean breeze smoothed over his flesh, the only reprieve he would get from the heat until the sun's descent in a little over an hour. He glanced at Anton. "Any new developments, Rogue?"

The large blond vampire shrugged. Bobby and Anton both towered over Alexander's six feet as he alighted from his bike. Even so, he'd give them a run for their money any day. Alexander might be shorter, but what he lacked in height, he more than made up for in strength.

"We've seen several of Raúl's soldiers, but no sign of the kingpin or Spike yet. We've had the place under surveillance since we got down here. No one has come or gone without our notice."

"Any scent of vampires?"

"Not that we could detect, Xander," Anton said. "The ocean current doesn't help. Any scent we might've been able to distinguish from this distance likely blew away on the breeze. We'd have to get damn close to the beach house to tell for sure."

"Raúl's amped up security." Bobby pointed to the upper balconies, where soldiers walked the patio with what appeared to be AK 47s or assault rifles of some sort pointed downward in their attempt to keep them camouflaged to passersby. "After Brea and Draven took his beach house by surprise, he's probably not taking chances … not if he's smart."

"Any Devils in the area?"

Bobby shook his head. "Not a one that I've seen. The Devils have no authority in Mexico. They might come south of the border, but they do so without creating a spectacle. We're in La Paz cartel country. Raúl could care less about the Devils MC, other than for running his drugs. He must have some reason for befriending Spike. He's not a man to go outside his circle of trust. He didn't get where he's at by being careless. The question is, what can Spike do for him?"

"Isn't that the million-dollar question. Why the hell save his sorry ass when Brea and Draven were down here?" Alexander rubbed the back of his neck. They stood in the shade of a small wooden deck that had a set of steps leading over the dunes to the ocean. From here, they had a clear view of the house without being seen. "The only thing that bastard is good for is death."

"I couldn't agree with you more," Bobby grumbled. He walked past the edge of shade and peered up, shielding his eyes from the sun with his hand. "I think we might be wasting our time. My gut tells me those bastards are still up north."

The idea Spike could be anywhere near India clenched Alexander's gut in a vice-like grip. Christ, had he made a huge mistake by heading south because he had been too much of a coward to face India following their shared kiss? He had the sudden urge to let Anton and Bobby finish up and head to Oregon. *Like right fucking now.* But doing so would raise more questions than he was ready to answer.

"I think you might be right, Preacher." Anton slapped his hand against the big man's shoulder blade. "But I came down here for a little action, so what do you say we make the trip worth our time?"

"You've lost your marbles, Rogue." Alexander looked back at the beach house. "We may heal from a gunshot wound easily enough, but those assholes are going for a kill shot. They hit us directly in the heart or in the T-zone of the face, we aren't coming back from that. Besides, there are a whole hell of a lot more of them than there are of us."

"Where's your sense of adventure, Xander?" Anton's smile told Alexander he meant to make some noise. *Lord, help them.* "I say we lure a few of them out of Raúl's fortress, let them know we're here. We'll allow one to live—send a message back to the man. What do you say? You in?"

"Hell to the yeah!" Bobby's whiskers turned up with his smile. "Let's party."

Alexander placed his hands on his hips and looked at the sand beneath his boots. "I'm so going to regret this."

Bobby laughed again. "Think of it as much-needed stress relief, Xander. You look like you could use it."

"You got that right. Let's just make it back to Pleasant in one piece. I have a promise to uphold."

Bobby placed his large paw on Alexander's shoulder. "You don't worry yourself. We'll get you back to your little lady."

"She's not mine."

Anton snorted. "Whatever you want to believe, Xander. The rest of us see what the hell is going on."

"You have a lot of room to talk, Rogue. What about Kimber? When are you going to quit dragging your feet and finally make her a mate?"

He shrugged. "Hey, I'm not in denial like you, Xander. I'm waiting for Kimber to give me the green light. Enough about us, let's talk about taking a few of these sons of a bitches out of the drug trade."

"What's the plan?" Bobby stroked his beard again, the smile evident beneath. "I'm ready to fuck up some of these bastards! A few less drug-peddling assholes in the world can hardly be called a loss."

"We wait for the cover of night. The beach will be deserted, then we make just enough of a racket they send a few men out to investigate. They won't risk sending too many and leave the beach house unprotected."

"And until then?" Alexander asked.

"We wait."

Following Anton's suggestion, the three of them settled in for the sun to set. An hour didn't seem like a long time, unless you needed to be somewhere else. Then it felt like a fucking eternity. Alexander sat in the sand with his back to a deck post and closed his eyes, praying for the time to quickly pass. His legs stretched out before him, boots crossed at the ankles. He was done with small talk. He'd leave that to Anton and Bobby.

Let the wait begin.

THE SUN SET WITHOUT A moment of rest. Alexander swore Bobby and Anton were no better than a pair of chatty women. It was surprising his ears hadn't bled from the abuse, he thought with a twisted smile.

The time had come to finally put their plan into action. Bobby had volunteered to be the diversion. He'd lure a few of the foot soldiers from the house, then lead them back to their secluded spot by the dunes. Alexander could hardly wait, ready to kick some serious cocksuckers' asses so that he could head back north. Leaving India had been a bad decision. His anxiety increased with each passing minute, even if Spike would be all kinds of stupid to cross Vlad Tepes.

Besides, India wasn't Vlad's problem.

She's mine.

The thought made him pause. At what point had he started to think of India as more than just a problem and more of a possession? Christ, the thought of her in the hands of another man lit a fire deep in his gut. If Spike even thought to—

"Let's rock and roll," Bobby interrupted his thoughts, then ducked beneath the overhang of the deck, bringing Alexander's focus back to the plan.

Bobby stumbled down the beach, wearing a pair of board shorts and a white wife-beater, looking very much like the drunk he portrayed. He had pulled the garb from his bike saddlebag. His biceps bulged and his thighs were as big as tree stumps. Even if he were inebriated, a man would have to be thick in the head to tangle with him.

By dumb luck, Bobby found an abandoned bottle of whiskey near the shore, out of the line of sight from the beach house. He bent to retrieve it and carried it in his fist, continuing on. The two soldiers nesting on the top balcony facing the ocean took notice straight away. They hadn't raised their rifles, but their gazes appeared fixed on the man staggering down the beach. From the men's vantage point, he no doubt looked like a drunken fool aimlessly wandering the beach. Either way, they didn't let down their guard, nor did they leave their position. One of them raised his wrist and appeared to speak into it. Likely some type of communication device.

If the rest of the house were unaware of Bobby's presence before, Alexander bet they were taking notice now. Even though Bobby appeared to be nothing more than a civilian with a little too much to drink, the sheer size of him would garner attention.

Alexander wasn't quite sure what Bobby had in mind to lure a few of the men from the fortress until he saw the whiskey bottle sail toward the large bay window. The alarm screeched, shattering the quietude the minute the bottle struck glass. The bottle imploded but the window stayed intact. No doubt the windows had been constructed with bulletproof glass. Raúl's ego and sizable pocketbook had in all probability fully safeguarded his house. Porch lights from surrounding dwellings lit up, lending a soft warm glow to the beach.

So much for stealth mode.

Bobby didn't wait for gunfire to erupt; he paused long enough for the backdoor to swing open and took off running down the beach. Sand kicked up from his feet as he ran at the pace a human might if the hounds of hell were nipping at their heels. To any normal person pissing off the cartel, that might be true. But for the three of them, it was going to be one hell of a soiree. The spectators from the neighboring houses quickly returned inside once they spotted the La Paz cartel soldiers taking chase, shutting off their porch lights and once again dousing the night in blackness.

The two soldiers on the top balcony stayed their position, keeping an eye on Bobby until he ducked beneath the shelter of the deck. Apparently, the men didn't consider Bobby much of a threat, leaving their rifles at their side, jabbing each other with their elbows, laughing and taunting the fools taking chase.

Alexander and Anton quickly leapt the dunes to the ocean side, not wanting witnesses from the neighboring homes to the carnage about to go down. Once the men pursuing had sighted Bobby again, he quickly followed suit and vaulted the deck effortlessly, landing with a soft thud in the sand. As the soldiers drew near, their footfalls slowed, laughing and exchanging words in Spanish, telling Alexander the fools didn't feel threatened in the least. On the contrary, they probably thought they were about to teach Bobby a lesson. Truth of it? Bobby could easily take on the four of them without getting so much as a scratch.

The sound of their boots striking wood carried across the breeze, rising above the roar of the waves crashing against the beach. The first man cleared the deck, a large smile pasted on his thin, dark lips as he spotted Bobby standing in the middle of the beach, fists on his hips. The clown had yet to realize they were no longer facing a besotted fool but a menacing lethal vampire. His facial changes weren't as evident in the dark of the night. No light illuminated this side of the beach other than that of the moon, peeking out from beneath the partially clouded sky.

The last of the men cleared the steps and stood beside the first. The shortest of the four said something in Spanish, causing them all to guffaw before the largest descended from his perch and approached Bobby.

"You, *papanatas*, have barked up the wrong tree." The man's white teeth shown bright in the partial moonlight. "Do you know whose house you threw your bottle at? Only a drunken *papanatas* would be so *estúpido*."

"The only fool on this beach … I'm looking at." Bobby's voice was thick with fangs. He used his fingers in a forward motion to taunt the man. "If you think you can take me—"

The soldier launched himself at Bobby, tackling him to the ground. Bobby back-flipped, taking the soldier with him. Now straddling the large man's waist, Bobby gripped his neck and squeezed. The man choked, his fingers clawing at Bobby's vice-like hold to no avail. When Bobby bared his fangs, the man's screams died in his throat, barely audible above the breeze.

Anton reached up, grabbed an ankle in each hand, yanking two of the men from the deck, dropping them to the sand like rag dolls. Their guns clattered to the deck, rendering them less than useless. Without a weapon, they stood no chance against Anton. He was more than capable of taking them out in a blink of an eye. Their blood-curdling screams died quickly as he twisted one head quickly, snapping his neck. The second didn't stand a chance once Anton bared his fangs as well.

Before the fourth man could get a bead on Anton's back, Alexander leapt from the sand, landing silently on the wooden deck beside him, fangs bared. He stripped the man of his weapon, then gripped him about the throat and leapt to the sand below before anyone from the beach house could see the scuffle. He heard the soft pop of flesh and fangs sinking into arteries behind him, but his black gaze stayed on his man, not giving him the chance to flee. The shorter man gasped for air as his fingers clawed at Alexander's large hand circling his neck. The man sputtered, gasping for air, but not a word uttered past his opened mouth. Widened eyes took in Alexander's vampire features and long, thick fangs. He tried his damnedest to buck Alexander from straddling his waist, all to no avail.

Alexander wanted this done so the trio could get back on the road north. No more fucking around. Apprehension continued to claw up his spine at the thought of India falling into the hands of Spike.

"Which one lives?" Alexander growled, his gaze not leaving his prey.

The man coughed, his breath faltering in Alexander's tight grip. His flailing increased, his attempts for naught. Not waiting for an answer, Alexander let go of the man's neck and jerked his head to the side, sinking his fangs gum-deep into the artery. The man's coppery blood flowed over his tongue, fueling him for the ride home. The only thing that stopped him from drinking him dry was the bloodied hand that landed on his shoulder.

"Leave him." Alexander released his fangs and glared at Anton, angry for being denied the kill.

Alexander sealed the wounds with the pad of his tongue, holding onto the man's weakened body. Three dead men lay sprawled out, blood seeping into the sand beside them.

"What about them?"

"Bobby will take care of them, food for the sharks."

"And this one?"

The man's eyes widened, telling Alexander he clearly understood the nightmare unfolding around him and that his next breath hinged on their decision. Three very real vampires stood in a circle around him, discussing his fate while his comrades lay dead just feet away.

"We'll hypnotize him to forget everything. Tell him to let the others know that the Sons of Sangue are far from done."

Alexander looked back at the short dark-skinned man, saw that his wide eyes were now trained on his obsidian ones. "Hear me now, asshole."

The man nodded. His eyes glassed over, telling Alexander he had been a breeze to hypnotize.

"You'll remember nothing. You have no idea what happened to your comrades or where they went. But you do know that they died at the hands of Sons of Sangue. Tell your boss we'll be coming for him."

CHAPTER TWELVE

"Xander, Rogue, and Preacher are headed back," Kane said. "Xander called, said they were about an hour out. That was about forty-five minutes ago. Nasty storm coming in, so I hope they make it back before it hits. We're expecting some high winds. Won't be ideal riding weather." Kane took a seat on the newly delivered sofa, plopping his booted heels on the industrial style coffee table the girls had picked out. He liked their taste. The work was almost completed on the clubhouse and he had to say it looked damn good. "Any news pertaining to Brea or Ryder yet?"

Kaleb shook his head. "Lightning is working on it. He has a knack for digging into this kind of stuff. Great with computers. But so far, he hasn't gotten any leads to either of their lineages. Although Brea's family does have a pretty colorful past."

Kane smirked. "With her surname, I wouldn't think otherwise."

"It's time for me to head out, pay Mircea a visit. See if my brother has any ideas." Vlad stood from his chair and stretched, the bones in his neck cracking as he tipped his head from side to side. "I swear I'm getting older by the minute. These bones aren't getting any younger."

"You don't look a day over thirty-five." Kane chuckled. "You're in better shape than most twenty-year-olds."

"This sedentary crap isn't for me. I trust Alexander can keep an eye on his problem. India is a lovely child, but I'm no one's babysitter. Besides, her car is no bigger than a peanut."

"You rode in her car?" Kaleb raised one brow.

"I did, and let me tell you, it wasn't the most pleasant ride, regardless of the company. I had to keep an eye out, make sure Spike or any of his fucking lackeys didn't try to make a move while Alexander was out of town." Vlad smiled, edging up his lips. "I can think of much better ways to spend my time with women."

"Too much information, Gramps." Kaleb rolled his eyes and shook his head. "I can't say I blame you, though. We'll make sure she's taken care of until Xander gets back. She's in his room. How much trouble can she get into? We may need to come up with a better plan, though, move her from the clubhouse. She's not safe here, not as long as Spike knows her location."

"You're correct." Vlad ran a hand through his thick, long hair. "I'll leave it to the two of you. I'm sure you'll get her someplace safe. The idiot would be a fool to try something so soon, not while you have your guard up. Have Lightning continue to look into Ryder and Brea's backgrounds. Ryder might have been an anomaly, the vampire DNA changing him very quickly. But Brea? She did the impossible. Only male vampires can change a human. So, what the hell was different about Brea's makeup that Draven biting her caused his change?"

"You got me," Kane said. "Damn curious is what it is."

"I trust you know how to get a hold of me."

Kane and Kaleb nodded. Vlad turned and quit the room, leaving the twins alone. The room felt much larger without their grandfather in it.

"Won't likely see him again for a while."

"Not unless he has news about Brea." Kane stood and walked to the window, looking out across the parking lot.

The gray storm clouds were rolling in, and unless Alexander, Anton, and Bobby made a quick entrance, they were about to get wet. One fat drop of rain splattered against the window as if laying proof. He turned, crossed his arms over his chest and leaned against the sill.

"So, what do we do with India?"

INDIA UNLOCKED THE WINDOW and pushed it open, loving the smell of oncoming showers. It reminded her of her childhood, dancing about in the rain, splashing through the puddles. Oh, to be a child again. Adulthood wasn't always happy-go-lucky and sometimes not nearly as fun.

A strong breeze blew through the window and lifted the tendrils of hair that had escaped her ponytail, brushing them feather-light across her cheek. The weather station had reported the oncoming storm could be severe at times, producing wind gusts of up to thirty miles per hour.

Earlier, Kane had mentioned the men were on their way home from Mexico, due to arrive shortly. She certainly hoped Alexander made it back before the storm hit. She couldn't help but be concerned over him being on the road with no protection from the elements. A large crack of lighting made her startle.

Stepping away from the window, India took a deep breath to calm her frazzled nerves and made her way to the dresser. Maybe she'd busy herself while she waited. After grabbing a brush and bare minerals, she dusted a light coat over her cheeks and nose, smoothing out her complexion, then finished up with a little blush and a light coat of mascara. She didn't want to come across as too enthusiastic over his return. After all, he had been the one to leave without so much as a word.

A shiver ran down her spine. India shrugged it off, nothing more than the cool breeze. Drawing her lower lip between her teeth, she glanced back in the mirror for a last-minute check on her appearance.

Her reflection was no longer alone.

Before she could utter a peep, a foul-smelling rag covered her nose and mouth. India clawed and yanked at his forearms, trying damn hard to free herself to no avail.

The man was far stronger, more so than any human.

Vampire strength.

"Hello, India." Spike's evil grin mocked her in the mirror. "Stupid of you to leave open a window, don't you think?"

She shook her head, trying hard to dislodge the rag from her mouth and nose, not wanting to breathe in the chemicals. Her gaze flitted to the door. She'd never be able to outmaneuver him or break away. If only Kane or Kaleb would hear or scent something ... anything.

"Viper and Hawk haven't a clue, doll face. Thanks to the storm and the wind blowing my scent east."

Unable to hold her breath a moment longer, she sucked in air, her lungs needing oxygen. She fought against his hold and tried for what seemed like several minutes to dislodge the rag. Her arms and legs began to numb. Her vision blackened around the edges.

The last thing she heard was Spike's, "Say goodnight," before unconsciousness claimed her.

RAIN SOAKED HIS LONG-SLEEVED T-shirt, plastering it to his chest. His jeans clung to him like a second skin. Moisture gathered in spots he'd rather not think about. If he didn't get a dry set of clothes soon, he'd be chafed for days. Alexander could think of little else as he walked through the clubhouse door. Well, that and the damnable woman who had been occupying his thoughts for weeks.

The last fifteen minutes had been the ride from hell. Wind gusts made it difficult to keep his cycle on the road while rain pelted his face and goggles, making it hard to see, let alone keep the bike upright. Water dripped from his clothes and pooled at his feet. Anton and Bobby fared no better.

"Best mop that up, boys." Kane plopped his feet to the wooden flooring and stood. "The women won't be happy to see their newly finished floors soaked by the likes of you three."

Kaleb raised a brow on his approach. "Since when do the women claim the clubhouse, Viper?"

"They were the ones to clean it. Just saying." Kane laughed as he walked over to the linen closet and grabbed three towels, tossing them each one. "Bet you're glad to be finally indoors. No sense asking how the ride went."

Bobby wiped his face and beard first, before heading the towel south. "Fucking rain stings like a bitch."

"At least you have all that hair covering the lower half of your face," Alexander grumbled.

"What's a matter, GQ, worried about messing up your pretty-boy looks? Or jealous you're not old enough to grow a proper beard?" Anton grinned and shook his head. Water droplets flew from his hair, further wetting the floor. "You two need to toughen it up."

"What the fuck, Rogue?" Bobby threw his towel at Anton's head. "I wasn't whining like a bitch."

Alexander didn't take the bait, just rolled his eyes and ignored Anton's taunt altogether. Turning to Kane, he asked, "Where's India?"

"In your room."

Alexander dropped the towel to his feet, soaking up the remaining water, then headed for the closed door. Whether he wanted to admit as much or not, he couldn't wait to lay eyes on her. He still felt like a complete jackass for leaving the way he did. A real man—or vampire, in his case—would've stayed and owned up to his actions. After all, it was just a fucking kiss. Though one he wouldn't mind repeating, and one he couldn't kick out of his thoughts no matter how hard he tried. Hell, he didn't even give a rat's ass to the jeers following in his wake as he headed down the hall.

Alexander had one purpose—to make up for being a class-A jerk.

His knock on the door went unanswered. "India?"

Certainly, she wouldn't have already retired. He tested the knob, finding it unlocked. Opening the door a crack, a cool breeze brushed over his skin and raised the hairs at his nape. Why the hell would she have left the window cracked during the storm?

"India?" he called a second time, still receiving no answer.

Shoving the door the rest of the way open, he strode into the cool, damp room, finding the bed made and the room empty. Rain struck the wood window casing, soaking the carpeting beneath. Alexander noted a large gash running the length of the screen.

What the fuck? He pulled the window closed and returned to the door in three large strides. "Viper! Hawk!"

The twins skidded to a halt just shy of entering the room.

"What the hell happened?"

"What's going on, Xander?" Kane peered around his shoulder. "It's been a pretty quiet day."

"Then where the hell is she?"

Kaleb looked over Kane's shoulder. "She never left this room, Xander. We would've noticed. We've been right outside this door all day, for fuck's sake."

Kaleb pushed past Kane and Alexander. His gaze swept the room before landing on the makeup brush lying in front of the dresser. He bent to retrieve it, turning it over in his palm.

"The screen was cut." Alexander nodded at the closed window. "Damn thing was wide open. Is it possible someone got to her, took her without notice? And where the hell was Vlad?"

"Son of a bitch," Kaleb grumbled, jamming a hand through his hair. "Gramps headed home. Had some things he wanted to question Mircea about. We didn't think ... with you on your way back—"

Heat rose up Alexander's spine. He couldn't blame Kane or Kaleb for losing India. Hell, no. That was on him. Had he been here, he wouldn't have granted her permission to leave his sight. Instead, he had allowed his emotions to get tangled up and ran off like a coward, leaving her accessible. Spike had already proven ballsy by blowing a hole in the front of the clubhouse while three of the Sons of Sangue were in attendance. Why the hell not just crawl through a window and take what the hell he wanted?

"If it was Spike, then the storm likely masked his scent." Alexander paced the room. "The blame is on me. I left her. She wasn't your responsibility."

"We'll find her. There are five of us that can track them. Any idea where to start, where he might take her?"

"No clue, Viper. He wasn't in Mexico. All we know is he made an appearance with the Devils in Santa Barbara before disappearing. He could be anywhere. Tracking him by scent won't be easy, not with this storm."

Alexander gritted his teeth to deter the fangs from punching through his gums. Anger would do him no good. He needed his head about him and couldn't allow himself to be ruled by the fury building inside him. If Spike had so much as touched a hair on her head, he'd rue the day he took her away from him.

Of course, it wasn't like India was his possession, but damn himself for thinking the only place she belonged was by his side. Hell, he couldn't say he'd be ready to let her go even after the baby was born.

That kiss.

Had it been anything other than a knock-your-socks-off type of kiss, maybe he'd have been able to walk away after his duty here was done, leave it at that. Instead, it fueled his desire to keep her, to get her horizontal, or any which way he could get her. And damn himself for wanting to in the worst way.

"Fuck! Spike might've been in the vicinity the entire time, just waiting for an opportunity like this storm provided. No way would you have scented or even heard him above the raging storm."

"Had Vlad still been here—"

"We can 'what if' all night, but that's not finding India, Hawk." Alexander wanted to hit something, rip it to shreds, preferably Spike. He looked at Bobby, who had also entered the room with Anton. "Any ideas where we go from here?"

"I'm thinking the little SOB will want to get out of Dodge and fast. He's a coward in the worst way, and he ain't gonna want to take on the Sons without backup."

"What about Raúl?" Kane asked.

Bobby shook his head. "You think the kingpin has time for Spike's petty scores? Raúl might be in the area, but with this, I'm betting Spike is on his own."

"I agree, Preacher. I don't think Raúl will want to involve himself. He has bigger fish to fry." Alexander ran his hands down his face and sighed. "So the question is what kind of vehicle are we looking for? No way he's out there with India on the back of his bike. He had to have either knocked her out or took her out of here kicking and screaming. He wouldn't chance the latter with you two so close. And she's not going down without a fight ... unless he threatened the unborn baby."

"Which is a possibility," Anton said. "Riding in this storm with no one on the back of a bike was treacherous enough. Preacher, can you get a description of the cage he drives? You still have friends in that MC, some that despise the new P. See what you can find out."

Bobby nodded, pulled the cell from his pocket, and left the room. Anton continued, "With any luck, he'll have a description of the vehicle. Preacher and I'll take the box truck. The rain is letting up. You three set out on bike. If any of us hears or sees a thing, we'll call the other."

"I'm thinking Spike will take the back roads and head south. He'll be more comfortable once he's off Sons of Sangue soil." Alexander could no longer stand still. He wanted back on the road before Spike had a chance to get to the California border. "If he has a flat in Santa Barbara, he won't take her there. Too risky. There has to be a place he'd take her that few know about. We need to intercept him before he hits Devil territory."

"You're probably right, Xander." Kane's irises rimmed black, telling of his own agitation over the situation. "As soon as Preacher hears word of a possible vehicle description, we'll all get on the road. Time's wasting."

"You can say that again." Every second felt like a ticking time bomb. "Let's hope he hears something that will aid us. Not finding her isn't an option.

CHAPTER THIRTEEN

India had yet to open her eyes, having no idea if she was alone, or if Spike was somewhere within the room. Her head pounded as if a symphony of drums played behind her frontal lobe. Taking slow deep breaths, she tried to calm the rising nausea. Every muscle in her body ached.

Where the hell has he taken me?

Turning her head to the side, she peeked through her lashes, not recognizing the crude surroundings. She blinked several times, attempting to focus her gaze. It was as though a light fog had settled in the room. All she could make out were a small table and two chairs, sitting in front of a tiny kitchen that had seen better days. A door to the left of the apartment-sized fridge stood open. Possibly a bathroom or bedroom.

"You're awake," came from somewhere in the room.

Her breathing quickened and her heart beat heavy against her sternum. "How long was I out?"

"About three hours." Spike walked into her field of vision, donning a smile that could only be described as pure evil. A shiver ran the length of her spine. "Cold?"

Misinterpreting her trembles, he retrieved a hole-ridden blanket and tossed it over her. India cringed as the rough wool settled atop her, wondering what had snuggled in the cover before her. Had she any energy in her limbs at all, she would've tossed aside the filthy thing. As it was, she was having a hard enough time just keeping her eyelids open.

"What did ... you give me?" Her tongue felt heavy, thick even, making speech difficult. "I can't ... remember a thing. Where ... are we?"

Spike crouched beside the cot. His face was mere inches from hers, and Lord help her, she couldn't even work up a good spit.

"Don't ... touch me."

"After the ether knocked you out, sweetheart, I gave you a little drug to help you sleep."

Her gaze widened and she sucked in a deep breath. "The baby."

Spike chuckled, the sound cruel, menacing. "Don't make the mistake of thinking I give a fuck about the baby. You were supposed to take care of that, as I recall."

"My ... baby," she said, barely above a whisper before her heavy eyelids closed and blackness once again consumed her.

A DOOR SLAMMED, STARTLING her. India had no idea how long she had been out this time. The nausea had thankfully subsided, but the pounding in her head remained. Sliding her feet to the side of the cot, she managed to get herself to an upright position. Spike sat at the small scarred kitchen table, eating a sandwich.

He held it out. "Hungry?"

India shook her head. "Where are we?"

"A cabin."

"I can see that, smart-ass." India scrubbed her face, trying to work away the fatigue and desire to close her eyes. "Are we even in Oregon?"

He nodded. "It's a little out-of-the-way cabin I confiscated from an old man up on the Bohemia Mountain a couple of years ago. It's a place where I can come in Oregon, keep an eye on the Sons of Sangue while they ware none the wiser."

"What happened to the old man?"

"He's buried out back. I could show you his grave."

India gasped. "You killed him?"

Spike's reply was nothing more than an easy smile. What the hell had she ever saw in the man? Christ, he was a one-man freak show.

"You're insane."

"Oh, I assure you, I am quite the opposite."

"Do any of the Devils know about this place?"

"Tank. But he's dead now, too, thanks to Rogue. You see, I trusted very few."

"The Devils are your brothers. I would think you could trust any of them."

He shrugged. "To a point. Man by nature isn't trustworthy. So, this place, I kept between Tank and me."

"What do you want with me, Spike?"

He chuckled. "It's simple. You belong to me until I say otherwise."

"I'm not a piece of property you can own. You can't just keep me."

Spike laid down his sandwich and crossed the floor, the old wood creaking beneath each step. India refused to show her unease. Spike thrived on the fear of others. She had seen it firsthand, time and time again.

He gripped the hair at her nape and yanked back her head, causing her to squeal. She had no choice but to glare up at him, hoping her distaste for him was evident. At one time, she had actually thought Spike rugged, but good-looking nonetheless. Now that she knew his true nature, he was as ugly outside as he was on the inside. The Spike she'd met months ago had been nothing more than a facade. But as much as she hated him in this moment, she couldn't regret the baby growing inside.

Never that.

"Let me go, Spike. What exactly do you have to gain from me?"

He shook his head, the smile growing. His fangs hung just beneath his upper lip as they emerged from his gums. "You don't get it, do you? Of course, you don't. You're a biker slut, trying to land yourself a free ride. Well, sweetheart, this ride ain't free anymore."

Her brows drew together. Seriously? What planet was he from? "If I were a slut looking for a biker, then I would've settled for anyone."

"Did you settle for me, India?"

"I thought—"

He gripped her chin so tightly it would no doubt leave a bruise. "You think I don't know about Xander? You practically reek of desire anytime he's near. And that boy will stop at nothing to get you back. That didn't start after California, sweetheart. Why the hell do you suppose I took you with me?"

"I…" Had she been so blind? "You didn't want anything to do with me, did you? You never did."

He released his hold on her and stepped back, shrugging. "I'll admit you were one hell of a trophy. My brothers thought I had scored a jackpot. Who doesn't want a beautiful bitch on his arm and in his bed? But truthfully, what I really wanted was to piss off that high and mighty Sons of Sangue pretty boy. Unfortunately, Xander never took the bait. He apparently didn't think you were worth the fight. All I got out of it was a pregnant bitch."

Spike tilted his face to the ground; his shoulders shook with mirth. "But you did me a favor, India."

"How?"

"When you left, you ran back to his arms. That boy will do anything to protect you. Any fool with a pair of eyes can see that."

"What are your plans for me, Spike?"

"I plan to lead Xander here."

"How?"

"It's simple. The good old-fashioned way." He held up a cell phone. "I'll tell him right where you are, but to come alone. Otherwise…" His finger crossed over his jugular.

"Then the joke is on you." India prayed she was correct. "Xander won't bother looking for me. He'll think I went back to you willingly and wash his hands of me. Your mistake is thinking he desires me. Xander is too arrogant to care for anyone other than himself. Why the hell do you think he's been single all of these years? Because he can't be bothered with a mate."

Spike studied her expression. She prayed she gave nothing away. "And yet he took you in."

"Because we're friends. That's what friends do. They take care of each other. Unlike you." She pointed at him. "The only thing you're good at is abusing women and using people for your own gain."

"Well then, you best pray you're still useful to Xander, sweetheart. Because if he's washed his hands of you, you'll be face down in the dirt beside the old man out back before sundown." His thumb indicated the rear door of the cabin. "I certainly don't plan to be saddled to a slut with a baby."

Her gaze widened. How the hell had she ever been so stupid and blind not to see him for the crazy-ass psycho he was? "It's your baby!"

"Perchance, sweetheart."

"I'm surprised you even know the meaning of that word."

Spike's features morphed into full vampire. His black gaze trained on her as he stalked forward, baring his fangs. "Never," he spat, "mistake me for being stupid."

Evil, yes ... stupid, no.

"I only meant to save you the trouble, Spike." Fear snaked up her spine, though she tried her damnedest not to show it. She would not give him the satisfaction. "Why not drive me back to town and we can all go on our merry way. I promise not to tell the Sons about this place or the fact you kidnapped me."

He gripped her chin again, causing her to flinch from the pain. "You aren't leaving here alive. Regardless of whether your boyfriend comes to the rescue. If he doesn't show up, you'll be fertilizer by nightfall. If he does, then we'll have some fun first. In the end, you'll both be feeding the earth from about three feet under."

Tears pooled in her eyes. India had no way of warning Alexander. She knew without a doubt he'd come for her. His honor demanded it.

"Please, just take me, then. End this cruel game and leave Xander out of it."

Spike released her, backed up, and pulled the cell out of his pocket again. He punched numbers onto the glass front, then held the phone to his ear. She could hear the ring and Alexander's gruff, "Speak, motherfucker," from where she sat.

"Xander," she yelled. "Don't listen to him—"

Spike backhanded her, sending her to the floor in front of the filthy cot.

"Listen, pretty boy."

India's ears rang from the blow to her head, keeping her from further hearing Alexander's side of the conversation, that and Spike increasing his distance from her. Had she known what awaited her beyond the door, she might've made a run for it. But with Spike's vampire DNA, she had no hope of outrunning him.

"You want to see India again, then you need to come alone."

Spike's smile told her Alexander had played right into his hand, causing her stomach to drop. Her only hope lay in the fact Alexander had been a vampire longer, rendering him much stronger. She supposed, though, Spike had already planned for that. The bastard wouldn't fight fair. India needed to find a way to help Alexander if they hoped to walk away from this fucked-up mess. Her biggest regret was involving him. Had she not run to Alexander for solace, Spike wouldn't have bothered to come after her at all.

After giving Alexander directions to the cabin, Spike tossed the phone on the table and placed his hands on his hips. He winked at her. Revulsion slithered through her.

"You're in luck, sweetheart. Turns out lover boy must care after all. He's coming to get you."

"Why Xander? I would think Rogue or even Draven would have been a more likely target for you. After all, weren't they the ones who infiltrated the Devils, killed some of your brothers? Caused others jail time? What the hell did Xander ever do to you?"

One of his brows rose. "You mean other than being a Sons of Sangue?"

"Yes, other than the obvious, jackass." India didn't care about stoking the fire. Obviously, Spike was already burning with fury. "Why target him?"

"He took someone that belonged to me."

"A woman?"

"I used to live here, in Oregon, long before I became a Devil." He paced the filthy wooden floor, his agitation evident. "I lived in Eugene, had the nine-to-five job, wore the dress shirt and tie. I was on my way up in the firm I worked for. My fiancée's father owned it and all I needed to do was pass the bar exam."

India didn't know what she had expected, but certainly not Spike in a normal life, on his way up to a prestigious job. "You were going to be a lawyer?"

"Surprise you? I'm not as simple-minded as you believed me to be. These"—he held out his tattooed arms—"haven't always been there."

"What happened to your fiancée?"

Spike stopped pacing and bared his fangs. "She met Xander."

"She left you for him?"

"Nothing that dramatic." He laughed. "After all, the biker would have never fit into her daddy's idea of the perfect life for her. Xander had been nothing more than her 'fantasy come to life.' Her words exactly. Which fit Xander perfectly, of course, because he wasn't looking for anything permanent. She was nothing more than a one-night stand, another notch on his bedpost. After that night in the bar, she thought she could go back to being daddy's perfect daughter and my devoted fiancée with no one being the wiser."

"She slept with Xander?"

He shook his head and smiled. "Let's call it what it is, sweetheart. He fucked her in the back alley of some dive bar. Up against the brick wall like a common whore, not the silver-spooned socialite she was. Certainly not the woman I asked to marry me."

India couldn't help but feel sorry for him. How horrible to find out your fiancée was stepping out with someone he likely thought beneath him. "How did you find out?"

"I saw them." He rubbed a hand over his sternum as though the admission cut him to the heart. She supposed, at the time, it had. "I was working late that night. She told me she was going out with the girls. I thought I'd surprise her on the way home, stop and have a drink with my favorite lady. The bar happened to be hopping for a Thursday night. The only place to park was at the back of the lot."

Spike walked to the window, moved the grimy threadbare curtain to the side, and looked out. "I had to walk by the alley on my way to the entrance. I saw movement. Two people were rutting like animals up against the wall. I chuckled, thinking nothing of it until the sound of my amusement caught the man's attention. When they both looked my way, I recognized the woman on sight."

Letting the curtain float closed, he turned around and stuffed his hands into his pockets. "I've never allowed myself to fall in love again. I left her daddy's firm and headed to California. While drinking away my sorrows in a dive bar, I met Tank and the rest is history."

"So, you blame Xander for what your fiancée did."

Although she could understand his anger, Xander was nothing more than his fiancée's fantasy. It could have been any biker who filled that bad-boy role for her.

"What happened to her?"

"She married some other schmuck. The man took over her daddy's law firm when he retired. They probably have a mansion on the hill with two to three kids by now."

"And it could have been you."

He did a sweep of the cabin with his outstretched hands. "And miss all this fun?"

"How long have you been carrying around this hatred for Xander?"

"Long enough." Spike laughed. "Years. The bastard never stayed with one woman long enough for me to make my point. Until now."

India couldn't help herself. She started to giggle. If Spike's expression was any indication, he wasn't any too happy about it.

"What the fuck in this amuses you?"

After her laughter subsided, India wiped forefingers beneath her eyes and dried the tears. "The fact you think Xander cares enough about me to finally exact your revenge. He didn't care enough when I followed you to California. What makes you think he cares now?"

One side of his mouth turned up. "Because he's coming after you."

"Only because he's honorable. You actually think he'd want to be stuck with me? I carry another man's baby ... *your* baby, for crying out loud. Xander can have his choice of any woman. He didn't want me before I met up with you. He certainly doesn't want me now. I played on Xander's good nature, his friendship, to take me in. Nothing more."

"Then why go to him?"

"Because I was afraid of what you would do."

"And you thought Xander would protect you from me?"

She folded her hands in her lap and nodded.

Spike shook his head and chuckled. "Then your faulty thinking will cost Xander his life because I'm not about to walk away from this until you both join the old man out back."

CHAPTER FOURTEEN

"Well, if it isn't the prodigal son coming home." Mircea raised a brow from where he sat in the lap of luxury. Vlad might have been holding him against his will, but his brother wanted for nothing. "What brings you here? Surely not to spring the butterfly."

"More like a puss caterpillar and just as venomous. You aren't going anywhere just yet, Mircea."

Vlad shut the door behind him, hearing the lock snick into place. He took a seat in the chair opposite his brother.

"Merlot?" Mircea held up a stemless wineglass before taking a sip.

"The question is, have you gone through my entire stock of wine yet?"

He chuckled. "With the cellar you have, it would take me years. I don't plan to stay that long."

"I should hope not." Vlad leaned forward, clasping his hands between his spread knees. "I do have something I need to discuss with you."

"What could I possibly help you with?" Mircea shifted in his seat, his eyes lighting with excitement. "I'm positively bored to tears. So please, anything you can entertain me with, you have my undivided attention."

"Women vampires have never been able to create a vampire through the years, not that I'm aware of anyway."

"If that were the case, then Rosalee most likely would've been responsible for quite a few vampires for every time she set her sights on a new prospect."

Vlad rubbed his short-bearded chin with his fingers. "Men turn females to mate so that new male true bloods can be born. That hasn't changed in all the years since I came into existence. And as far as I know, there are no other lineages of vampires, other than our family."

"I suppose it's possible there are other vampires out there that we aren't aware of. To think we are the only ones would not only be arrogant, but foolhardy."

"Anything is possible."

Mircea crossed an ankle over the opposite knee, draping his arm along the back of the sofa. "Is there a point to all of this?"

"Brea Gotti. Have you ever heard the name?"

Mircea shook his head. "Other than the obvious surname, no."

"One of the men from my grandsons' motorcycle club had secretly taken her as a mate, from what I was told. Her last name and her connection to the cartel kept Joseph Sala from telling the rest of the members about her."

"What does this have to do with a woman vampire turning a male?"

"The cartel assassinated Joseph, leaving Brea unmated."

"Go on." Mircea took another sip from his glass of wine.

"Brea approached a bar owner named Draven Smith. Apparently, Joseph had instructed her to do so should anything happen to him. Draven was a human."

Vlad stood and helped himself to a glass of the merlot. Turning, he leaned his backside against the wet bar and faced his brother again.

"When Draven and Brea went after the man who had taken out Joseph, Draven, apparently not knowing the impossibility of becoming a vampire via a female vampire's blood, took it upon himself to bite Brea, thinking he would become a vampire and gain strength to help her in her quest."

"Joke was on him." Mircea chuckled. "Imagine his surprise when he only received a mouthful of blood."

"If that were the case."

His brother leveled his gaze. "What are you saying, Vlad?"

"Draven turned."

"Impossible."

"So we thought," Vlad said. "As far as I know, Brea is the only female vampire in our history to change a human into a vampire with her blood. Why do you suppose that is?"

Mircea shrugged. "Hell, if I know. Damn interesting, is what it is."

"Rosalee was not a true descendant of yours, correct?"

"She belonged to her mother, not me." Mircea swirled the burgundy liquid in his glass. "I turned her. All of my true descendants were long since gone. As far as I know, the only ones left in the Tepes' lineage are your grandsons."

"What about Radu?"

"What about our dear younger brother?"

Vlad approached Mircea, stopping a few short feet away. "Do any of his descendants still live?"

"How should I know, and what does this have to do with the girl?"

"My grandsons are products of my sons and their sons. Any daughters I had passed long ago. The only vampires from my loins that survived through the years are Kane and Kaleb." Vlad retook his seat and placed his glass of wine on the side table. "You have no living descendants and none that were made into vampires. Leaving Radu's offspring."

"Even so, what does that have to do with the girl?"

"Here's what I'm thinking ... I turned simply by drinking human blood. I did not need to bite a vampire to do so. We never tested the theory with you because I turned you, and our dear brother Radu was already dead by then."

Mircea sighed. "I'm not following."

"Something in my DNA caused me to morph into a vampire by simply drinking human blood. What if that relates back to our father and he passed it along to the three of us? If that were the case, then any living relative of Radu could have the same DNA sleeping within him ... or her, for that matter."

Mircea sat forward, no longer looking bored. "You think a direct living descendant of our father, male or female, could become a vampire simply by drinking blood."

"Right, but I'm betting none of them are practicing in that particular habit." Vlad chuckled. "But let's say Brea carries the DNA, then it could be possible she could turn a human herself, by simply giving them our family's DNA. Think about it. Up to this point, all of the women who have been turned, were not related at all to the Tepes family."

"And you discussed this possibility with your grandsons?"

"No. Although, they are damn curious about Brea." He narrowed his gaze. "I wanted to run this by you first. See what your thoughts might be. And to see if it's possible if you had any bastard children running about."

Mircea waggled a long thin finger at him. "For that matter, dear brother, you could have a bastard child or two that you didn't know about as well."

"I do suppose that's true. One never knows." He leaned back and grabbed his stemless glass. "There's also the case of Ryder Kelley."

"One of Kane and Kaleb's men?"

Vlad nodded. "He turned in about a day's time, not taking the usual week."

"The last time that happened—"

"Was a true blood or with anyone in the Tepes family."

"FUCK!" ALEXANDER TOSSED his cell onto the wooden counter. His fist hit the surface, causing the cell and the dirty glasses littering it to jump.

Kane approached the bar, fastening the buckle of his black leather chaps, his lips set in a grim line. "Who was on the phone?"

"Spike. Bold motherfucker." Alexander jammed a hand through his hair. His jaw ached with fury. "Good news. You can now call off Preacher and Rogue. I know where the son of a bitch is hunkered down. Fucker never left Oregon. Also, he's made it clear he has India and isn't afraid to hurt her to get what he wants."

"What the fuck *does* he want?"

"Me."

Kane raised a brow. "What the hell did you do to that crazy motherfucker that has him so pissed?"

Alexander shrugged. "Other than being a Son? Who the fuck knows."

"Do I want to know what the bad news is?"

"I'm supposed to go alone."

"No fucking way." Kaleb strode over to the pair, shrugging on his MC cut. "We aren't letting you walk into some sort of trap, Xander. We all go. Motherfucker wants a party, we'll give him one."

Alexander shook his head. "Not an option I'm willing to take. I can't chance he'll hurt her or worse."

"Where's he hiding her?" Kane asked.

"A cabin up in the Bohemia Mountain. It's just shy of a three-hour ride from here, south of Eugene. I wouldn't put it past him to have someone hiding in the trees along the path, reporting to him if I have company. Sorry, P, this I have to do on my own."

"Fuck that shit." Kaleb jabbed a finger at the counter, the muscles in his neck tightening with his rising ire. Alexander knew Kaleb took Spike's actions personally. After all, Spike was a Devil, and any action done by a rival MC to any member of the Sons of Sangue was an action done to the entire club. "We're going with you. I'll call Preacher and Rogue and send them back to K&K Motorcycles with the box truck, then have them meet us on the road with their bikes."

Alexander chuckled, feeling zero of the humor. "And you think arriving on five Harley Davidsons would draw less attention? What's your plan, Hawk?"

"You'll arrive on your bike, go in the way he's expecting you. I'm betting there's only one road leading to that cabin. He's no fool." Kaleb smiled. "Fortunately, we aren't either. Me and Viper, we'll go up the left side of the mountain to the cabin on foot, while Preacher and Rogue take the right. No chance he'll get out of there without one of us intercepting him."

"And if he has the cabin surrounded with Devils?"

"Hell, from what Preacher says, most of his own men despise him." Kane pulled down a fifth of whiskey, pouring them each a shot. He held one out to Alexander, but he declined. Kane took the shot for him. "Not likely he'll get a lot of help from those bastards. He doesn't have their devotion the way Tank did."

"And the cartel?"

Kaleb quickly downed his shot of the amber liquid, then wiped the back of his hand across his lips. "You really think Raúl Trevino Caballero doesn't have better things to do than to get involved in Spike's petty squabbles?"

"I hope you're right, Hawk. We don't need Caballero's soldiers out there trying to pick us off, one-by-one." Alexander picked up his cell and shoved it into the inside breast pocket of his cut. "We ride together until we hit Eugene. From there, we split up. I'll take the obvious path up the mountain. You guys can work it out from there. I don't want to see or hear you. Knowing you're around will be good enough for me. I don't need Spike catching your scent."

Kane pulled out his cell and called Anton, quickly giving him a rundown of their plan. The two would meet them in Eugene in about an hour and a half. The four vampires would finalize their plan, making the trek to the cabin on foot—after all, with their vampire DNA, they could likely beat Alexander. He hoped to hell the scheme worked, because anything happening to India was not an option.

After tucking the phone into his jeans pocket, Kane shrugged into his leather cut. With a nod of his head, he said, "Let's ride, boys."

THE TRIP TO EUGENE HAD TAKEN far too long for Alexander's liking. Christ, it was hard telling what Spike might do to India in the meantime. Alexander wasn't about to call the son of a bitch and give him the courtesy of an arrival time. And after the three of them had met up with Anton and Bobby about an hour ago, they had gone their separate ways.

Now Alexander rode solo up the narrow dirt and gravel road, careful to maneuver around the treacherous larger rocks and holes, which prevented him from going a high rate of speed. From this far up the fall might not kill him, but it sure would hurt like hell. Thankfully, the rain had let up; had it continued, it would have made the ride even worse.

Thick evergreens and brush hedged both sides of the road, letting little sunshine through.

The views in the Bohemia Mountain were spectacular through most of the year, though summer and fall were his favorites. Alexander knew the area well, having grown up near Dorena Lake. The mountain had been a place of solace when his existence at times had been anything but comfortable. He loved to ride his motorcycle up the winding paths of Sharps Creek Road. Funny how his life had brought him back here, to his old stomping grounds.

Today, though, wasn't about getting closer to nature, or remembering a past left long behind. No, today was about rescuing a possible future.

His heart climbed up the back of his throat and fear inched up his spine the closer he came to the area to which Spike had directed him to, an old road leading to a worn-down shack. Christ, he hoped he hadn't arrived too late. If the son of a bitch so much as laid a hand on her, Alexander would make Spike rue the day he thought to piss with him and those he cared about.

Hell, he wouldn't simply put Spike out of his motherfucking misery. No, he'd make sure he suffered Alexander's wrath first.

Slowing his bike to a stop near the pre-described road—more like a dirt path—he cut the engine. He had to be within a few miles of his destination. Alexander kicked down the stand and stepped over the seat of his bike, listening intently to his surroundings. Other than the normal sounds of the forest—chirping birds, scurrying animals, slithering bugs—Alexander's amplified hearing picked up nothing that didn't belong. If Anton, Bobby, Kane, and Kaleb were out there, they were doing a damn good job at hiding their presence. He raised his nose and sniffed, not detecting the scent of another vampire either.

Alexander walked to the side of the road. There wasn't much of a ledge before it dropped off to a steep decline. Even so, he was sure his brothers would have no trouble navigating their way up the side. Alexander returned to his bike, straddled it, and restarted the engine. He kicked up the side stand and took off up the incline of the dirt path.

India is near.

He could feel it clear to the marrow of his bones.

A few miles up the ridge, an old shack came into view. It looked uninhabited and reminded him of those in the Ghost Town area, but Alexander knew better. He could now scent the son of a bitch as well as India's fear. The good news, it meant she was still alive. The bad news, Spike could now scent him as well. He'd need to get inside the cabin and distract him before his brothers came any where near.

Spike was a dead man; he just didn't know it yet.

CHAPTER FIFTEEN

Alexander alighted from his bike. After taking off his skull cap, he placed it on the black leather seat and did a quick check of his surroundings. He didn't detect any movement, friendly or otherwise. The forest was deathly still, other than a few birds flying overhead. The predator in him knew other animals lurked within the brush, leery of any human entering their habitat. The beast that had him worried, though, lurked inside the cabin. His gaze stopped on the run-down shack, catching the slight movement of the threadbare curtain over the rustic wood-framed window.

Spike was aware of his arrival.

Showtime.

After walking up the stone steps, he didn't bother with a knock. Instead, he strode in as if he belonged there. Before the afternoon was over, he'd prove so. The cocky son of a bitch who dared to challenge him was about to take his last breath. Alexander's gaze landed briefly on India, seemingly unharmed, then traveled to the object of his fury.

Spike stood in the kitchen nook, one hip leaning against the cracked tiled counter, arms crossed over his chest. "It's about fucking time, Xander. I was beginning to doubt the feelings you might have for my girl here."

"She's not *your* fucking girl," Xander growled. The thought of Spike's grimy hands touching India started a fire deep in his gut. "You have me, so let her go."

"She'd never make it back down the mountain on her own. And you"—the motherfucker smiled, followed by a chuckle—"aren't leaving here alive. So you see my dilemma?"

"That's where you're mistaken, you son of a bitch. You're right about one thing—one of us isn't leaving here alive." Alexander's gums ached as his fangs descended. "And that won't be me."

"You underestimate me, then."

Alexander worked his jaw and twisted his neck, hearing the cracks and pops from morphing into his vampire state. "I never underestimate anyone."

"Xander—" India whispered, her voice trembling. His black gaze darted to the old cot. "Please—"

Her distraction gave Spike time to react. The son of a bitch flew at Alexander, fangs bared, and knocked him against the roughhewn wall. The old shack shook from the force. Dust littered the air. They were damn lucky the structure didn't collapse around them. Spike sank his fangs deep into Alexander's neck, causing him to grunt from the sharp pain as Spike bit down, no doubt hoping to tear out his throat. India's muffled cry carried to his ears moments before he grabbed Spike by the shoulder and threw him across the room.

Spike landed on the old wooden table, the legs collapsing beneath the weight, sending him sprawling across the floor.

One splintered table leg punctured the Devil's side, air hissing from his lungs. An inhuman screech filled the room as Spike pulled the bloody makeshift-lance from his torso. He tossed it to the floor, where it clattered away.

Before Spike could get to his feet, Alexander leaped on top of him, his fist connecting with his elongated nose. Blood splattered across Spike's face and the back of his head thudded the table on which he lay, cracking the wood. Alexander gripped his shirt with both fists and pulled him to his feet.

"You'll never hurt another woman, Spike—"

Gunfire erupted outside, the noise deafening as Spike's laughter filled the room, blood dripping from his chin.

"What the fuck did you do?" Alexander asked.

"You seriously think I would trust you to come alone?"

Alexander wrapped his hand around Spike's throat, shoving him against the wall, damn near pushing him through the old boards. "Tell me why I shouldn't break your scrawny neck right now?"

"Because you have a choice, biker. Kill me now and let your friends die, or let me go and they live. You have seconds to choose."

"How the fuck do I know the gunmen won't continue if I let you walk? Your word means shit to me."

Spike attempted to clear his throat, a laugh gurgling out of him. Blood bubbled from his lips and ran down his neck. "I told them, if I don't walk out of here by the time your backup arrives, they are to kill anyone who comes near."

"Who did you give orders to?"

"Raúl Trevino Caballero's soldiers."

"Why do they care about you and your frivolous feuds?"

"What can I say, the fat bastard likes me." He laughed again, choking on more of his blood. "Besides, you idiot, it was never just about you."

India gasped. "The story… You told me—"

"Oh, it was all true, sweetheart, and why I chose Xander." When India didn't respond, he continued, "Raúl has his own reasons for hating the Sons of Sangue. My gift to him, one dead Sons, not to mention the others being gunned down outside. Puts me in his good favor. This was never about you, India, or the bastard baby."

"You son of a bitch."

Alexander's indecisiveness was costing him precious time. He couldn't allow his brothers to be slaughtered, not when they were there to help Alexander in his cause.

Spike took advantage of Alexander's hesitation and jerked free of his hold. In the blink of an eye, he moved across the room and yanked India in front of him, holding her to his chest by his forearm, a hunting knife to her throat.

"Last words?"

"You motherfucker! Hurt her and—"

The knife sliced her throat. Blood sprayed from her neck as India's eyes widened and her hand covered the gaping wound. The bloodied blade clattered to the floor as Spike disappeared through the open door. Gunfire continued, but Alexander could do nothing other than rush to India's side.

Tears filled his eyes.

"Fuck! Don't you die on me."

He picked her up and cradled her in his arms. He had minutes in which to act. Alexander knew he couldn't give her his blood. The baby would never survive the change and India would never forgive him for that.

Kaleb bounded through the door, bullet holes riddling his arms, legs, and torso. Thankfully, none of them kill shots. He'd heal.

"What the fuck … give her your blood, Xander. You have the Sons permission to turn her."

"The baby—"

Kaleb curled his lips and bared his fangs. "Fucking Spike knew he was giving you a choice. Then lick the fucking wound. Your saliva will help heal her and buy you time. Maybe enough so you can get her to the hospital before it's too late."

"Christ, we are in the middle of nowhere."

Alexander did as Kaleb had instructed, licking her shallow wound, the smoky flavor of her blood coating his mouth and throat. Thank goodness the cut wasn't deep. Even so, she had lost a lot of blood. Her head lulled back on his arm and she was losing responsiveness.

Decision made, he gathered her in his arms. "Viper, Rogue, and Preacher?"

"They're fine. Raúl's soldiers are all dead." It was only then Alexander realized the gunfire had ceased, as he'd been so worried about the woman in his arms. "Go. We'll clean up here."

Alexander nodded and headed for the door. She wouldn't be able to sit on the back of his motorcycle in her condition. Hell, she was barely conscious. Taking off at a dead run, he prayed he'd get her to the hospital in Eugene in time. It was at least an hour and a half by car.

He hoped to make it there in half that time.

THE WAY ALEXANDER SAW IT, he had two choices. He could either go to the little café on the first floor to get a cup of coffee, which would give him a few minutes rest from the monotonous beeping of the contraptions hooked up to India that measured her vitals, or he could rip the damn cords from the wall.

How the hell did the hospital staff endure the never-ending clamor?

It was a damn wonder patients got any rest.

Leaning back in the vinyl-covered highback chair, he blew out a steady stream of oxygen. Every fucking muscle ached from his scuffle with Spike. Even so, his pride had taken the biggest hit for allowing the son of a bitch to get away. The motherfucker was free to reign another day.

Next time, Spike won't be so lucky.

The beeps filtered through his musings as his gaze fell on India, lying prone in the bed, IV tubes and cords attached to her upper body. But it was the large white gauze covering her throat that gripped his heart like a vice. His mistake of not stopping Spike had almost cost India her life. Had there been any other outcome, the guilt might have nearly killed him.

Forgiving himself was going to be damn hard to come by.

While a cup of coffee would've hit the spot, until India awoke, he wasn't about to leave the room. He needed to be there for her when she came to. And although pulling the cords from the electrical outlets seemed like a way to cut the annoying beeps, it wasn't a viable option since she apparently needed the noisy devices. Not to mention the nurses would come running and no doubt force him from the room.

So here he sat, listening to the racket until India awakened.

To be by her constant side, Alexander had told a bit of a fib, a tiny white lie, if you will. By saying he was her fiancé, he could give the hospital permission for any procedure or care that she needed. Not a single person had questioned him when he'd announced their relationship status.

His own wounds had nearly healed and gone unnoticed, so the blood his clothes sported had been assumed as India's. Luckily, she had survived, considering the amount of shed blood. The doctor had informed him whatever Alexander had done to reduce the flow of blood had without a doubt saved her life. Most wouldn't have survived the neck wound, not to mention the amount of time she had gone without medical care.

It had taken Alexander considerable willpower to return to his human state before entering the hospital emergency room. After all, their clothes had been soaked with human blood, blood that called to his vampire DNA. Thankfully, the hospital had provided him with a clean pair of scrubs, even if he knew his clothes were to be confiscated as evidence once the authorities arrived. After washing up, the blood no longer tempted his vampire self into reappearing.

When the cops arrived to take his statement, he threw Spike under the bus. Not that he needed their help with the son of a bitch. Spike would most certainly die by his hand. But he couldn't have them thinking he might be responsible for attempting to murder India. They'd no doubt consider Alexander as a possible suspect to corroborate his story. Ridiculous considering the fact he brought her in. Alexander had given the officers Kane and Kaleb's names to bear witness to the deed, who would of course back up his account. Knowing the twins, they'd head over to the precinct in Eugene to make sure nothing would cause the Sons of Sangue backlash, even if they needed to use their hypnotic powers to do so.

Now, not only would Spike be running from his wrath, he'd have to go into hiding from the law as well. Alexander hoped it would keep the son of a bitch down for a few days, giving India a chance to heal before he tried to apprehend her a second time. Once she was back on her feet, all bets were off. Alexander wouldn't rest until Spike was dead and it was his blood on Alexander's hands.

One of the nurses walked through the door. The dry erase board on the wall said her name was Angie. Standing about five-foot-four and weighing probably no more than a hundred pounds soaking wet, she was a perky little thing. Alexander had yet to see her without a smile on her face, even after being ten hours into her shift. She approached one of the IV machines, looked at the numbers, punched a few buttons, then turned to Alexander.

Her bright blue eyes smiled right along with her. "Can I get you some water? Coffee? Anything? You've been sitting here a long time."

"Coffee would be great." The woman had read his mind. Now if she'd just stop the beeping. "I was about to go get some in the café, but I was afraid she'd wake up while I was gone."

"The sedative the doctor gave her wasn't strong, so she should be waking any minute." The nurse gripped India's wrist, her fingers resting on her pulse point as she looked at her watch. "Anything else I can get you?"

Alexander shook his head. "Just the coffee. Thank you. That would be great. She's going to be okay, right?"

"She's a lucky lady." The nurse glanced briefly at India. "Her vitals look pretty good. She's going to be fine."

Normally, Alexander wouldn't have missed the opportunity to engage in conversation with a pretty lady. Stunning even. But there was only one woman who held his interest as of late. His gaze followed the nurse's to where India lay deathly still in the bed. Her smooth chocolate-colored skin stood out in contrast to the white sheets. Her black hair fanned across the pillowcase, tangled and matted. Mascara smudged the dark circles beneath her eyes. He was pretty certain she wouldn't be happy should she be handed a mirror. But to Alexander, she had never been more beautiful.

His gaze dropped to her abdomen, covered by the thin hospital blanket. Damn if he didn't dread her hearing the bad news. She needed to be told. And it fucking sucked that he'd be the one to tell her. Alexander wasn't about to let her hear it first from a stranger, whether it be the doctor or nurse.

India had lost the baby.

She had lost a lot of blood and Spike had been the cause. The baby had meant everything to India, regardless of the baby-daddy or the fact the conception had been an accident.

Angie returned, her scrubs a much lighter hue of blue than his, and handed him a foam cup containing black coffee. Steam rose above the rim. "I forgot to ask if you took anything in your coffee."

"Black." He took the cup from her. "Angie, right?"

She smiled, her white teeth flashing behind a perfect set of red lips. "Yes."

"Thank you, Angie. I appreciate the coffee."

She attached a white cord with a red button to the bed sheet next to India's arm. "If you need anything, or India wakes up and needs something, just press this button. I'll be right outside the door working on my daily charts."

Alexander nodded and watched her exit with a gentle sway to her narrow hips. He leaned forward and braced his elbows on his knees, holding the hot cup of coffee between his palms. If he could will India awake, he would, just to know she was going to be all right. Sure, the doctors and nurses had said as much, but he needed to see the living proof, to hear her voice and see her warm brown eyes.

And until that happened, he'd sit right here.

"Hey, Xander," Draven said, gaining his attention as he entered. "Hawk said I would find you here."

Alexander straightened in his seat. "What's up?"

"Brea wanted me to let you know, if there is anything at all you need, please let her know." The barkeep scratched the spot behind his ear and grimaced. "Hawk said Spike told you this had something to do with Brea's godfather. I'm sorry India got caught up in his mess."

After lifting the foam cup to his lips, Alexander took a sip of the hot liquid, his gaze flitting to India. "Maybe it was about Spike pleasing Raúl, who the hell knows, but it started when India took up with Spike. He chose me for a reason when he could have focused on any of the Sons. And that's not on Brea's godfather. India made her choice and Spike used her to get to the Sons. India mentioned something about a story Spike had told her. We won't know what that is until she wakes up."

Draven pulled a chair toward Alexander, the metal legs screeching across the tiled floor. "It sucks he got away again, man."

"The guys managed to kill off Raúl's soldiers Spike had hidden amongst the trees, but yeah, Spike managed to get the hell out of there." Alexander sat back and took another sip of coffee, looking for peace and calm where there was none to be had. "The bastard will die at my hands. Mark my word, Draven. Raúl? We'll get him, too. His time is coming."

"He has a lot of foot soldiers."

"And the Sons of Sangue have a lot of strength and tenacity. I think Kaleb, Kane, Anton, and Preacher proved that on the mountain." Alexander chuckled, the humor lost to him. "I just wish I had been able to help. My brothers endured a lot of gunshot wounds, but in the end, Raúl's men paid the price. No tears were shed over their deaths."

"I don't suppose." Draven looked at the bed, his lips turning down. "How's she doing? I heard she lost—"

"A lot of blood." Alexander finished for him. The last thing he wanted spoken out loud was that India had lost the baby. If she could hear them, it would tear her up inside. "She'll be okay. I got her here in time."

Draven took the hint. "Good to hear, man. India's one of the good donors."

"About that, Draven"—Alexander ran a hand down his face, feeling the exhaustion—"I think it's time to retire her from donating. She won't be feeding any of the Sons from here on out."

Alexander stood and pulled the donor necklace from his pocket. The little blood vial and jewel dangled from the leather cord. He handed it to Draven.

The barkeep laughed, the gaiety reaching his eyes. "As if any of the Sons would think to use India. That goes without saying, man. She's yours."

"India belongs to no one, leastwise me. She can make her own decisions." Alexander glanced at India, her breathing slow but steady. Hell, he would just about sell his soul if he could turn back time, fix the wrongs done to her. Looking back at Draven, he said, "Make no mistake, though, if anyone thinks to ever harm her, they will answer to me. I'll always keep an eye on her, even if it's from afar."

"Sounds like that's coming from a man falling."

Alexander shrugged. "No matter. India doesn't need me. I wrestle plenty of demons and she doesn't need the baggage I come with."

"You don't think you're worthy of her love. Is that it?"

Alexander's right hand rested over the dog tags he wore beneath his scrub top. He'd never be worthy of her. Spike had done more than enough damage. She deserved so much better. "Something like that."

Draven smiled as he rose to his feet. "Knowing India, I'm sure she'll have something to say about what she wants. I've never known her to take shit from anyone, including you. I have to get back to the bar. Kaleb said he and the rest of the Sons will be coming by to talk to Brea. Something needs to be done about her godfather. It sucks for her, man. She loves him, but she also knows he's a bad man, guilty of a lot of bad deeds."

Alexander placed a hand on Draven's shoulder. "I don't envy you, bro. Can't be easy that Raúl, hated by the Sons, was obviously once well-loved by your mate."

"No truer words were ever spoken."

After a one-armed embrace, Draven left. Alexander curiously watched his retreating back. How the fuck had Draven turned? Up until Brea, no woman vampire had ever turned a human. Alexander was sure the rest of the Sons had also questioned it, but so far, the phenomenon had not been discussed, that he knew of, among the men. Most likely because, since their return, the Sons had plenty of other issues plaguing them. Once India awoke and she was out of the woods, he planned to question the twins about it.

A soft feminine sound washed over him like warm honey. He turned to see India's beautiful, chocolate gaze focusing on him, and his heart swelled.

CHAPTER SIXTEEN

INDIA OPENED HER EYES, THE SOUND OF BEEPING EASING HER from her dreamlike state. She had been on some exotic island with Alexander, swimming in the aquamarine waters and sipping drinks with little yellow umbrellas and maraschino cherries. Which, of course, was laughable at best. Alexander was far from the playful man in her fantasy. Nor would he likely be caught dead holding a glass sporting an umbrella.

No, the man standing before her was far more serious in nature.

Attempting to lift her arm, she found her limbs numb and unwilling to cooperate. No doubt the sedatives running through her system made them feel like two-ton bricks. An IV tube was attached to her forearm, clear tape holding the needle fixed. Her gaze traveled the sterile room, noting the machines that had roused her from sleep, before returning to Alexander.

She recalled Spike slipping the hunting knife across her throat before the blackness consumed her. Her fingers had covered the puckered wound as her blood gushed through her fingers. India recollected the terror of thinking she was about to die. Alexander's gasp and wide-eyed gaze told her he had feared as much. His handsome face was the last thing she saw before Spike released her and she began to fall weightlessly.

India cleared her throat, wanting to dismiss the horrible memories. Wetting her dry lips, she attempted to speak. Nothing more than a croak passed her lips. Not very ladylike, but then again, she felt as if she was on the losing end of the Running of the Bulls festival in Spain. Alexander placed a hand on her forearm, his gaze sympathetic, anxious even. She was awake, alive… So, what had Alexander so concerned?

India tried again. "Sp…ike?"

He pulled a chair closer to the bed and sat down. Taking her hand in his much-larger one, he laced fingers with hers. Warmth filled her. She got the impression he hadn't left her side.

"He got away, India. But not for long. I'll see the son of a bitch is dead if it takes my last breath." He brought the back of her hand to his mouth and placed a lingering kiss there. "You have my promise."

Her tongue darted out again, sweeping her lower lip. "Water?"

Alexander pushed the call button.

A moment later, a pretty nurse entered the room. "You're awake. I'm Angie, India. I'll be your nurse for the next couple of hours. What can I get for you?"

"Water … please."

"Absolutely. You might want to start with some ice chips first. I'll get you both for when you think you're ready for fluids.

You'll need to take them slowly at first. You had severe trauma to your neck. Luckily, the cut wasn't deep and your fiancé was able to get you here quickly. You had one of the best surgeons in Eugene. You were in the best of hands."

When the nurse quit the room, India glanced at Alexander and raised a brow. "Fiancé?"

His cheeks reddening slightly. "Someone needed to sign your admittance papers. And since we aren't related…"

"How … did I get here?"

"I brought you, which is why Spike is still breathing. The son of a bitch knew I wouldn't take after him. And since my brothers were busy with Raúl's goons, Spike got away." He smoothed the hair from her forehead with his free hand. The gesture moistened her eyes. "The doctor said you're going to be fine."

"How?" India touched the white gauze surrounding her throat. "Spike said we were up in the mountain. You had your motorcycle."

"I used my saliva to help heal the wound and staunch the flow of your blood. I carried you."

"The blood… Vampire…"

He chuckled. "Trust me, it took considerable willpower to beat back the beast so I could get you into the emergency room without scaring the hell out of them."

"Thank you … for everything." Had Alexander not done as much, she and her baby wouldn't have survived. "I'm sure the baby—"

Angie returned with a cup of ice and one of water, a white bent straw sticking from the lid. Not quite the cute umbrella she had envisioned from her dream. The nurse set them on the tray near Alexander. After helping India to some ice, she excused herself, pulling the curtain hanging from the ceiling and giving them privacy from the hallway where people milled about. The ice helped to soothe her sore throat. Angie had been correct. India wasn't quite ready for the water.

When India looked at Alexander, something had changed in his demeanor. Something was wrong. She could see it in his face and the way his lips turned down. The grip he had on her hand was no longer relaxed, but stiff.

"Xander?" Her heart beat heavy; her stomach plummeted. "What aren't you telling me? I'm going to be okay ... right?"

He nodded, his gaze solemn. "The doctor gave me no reason to believe otherwise."

"Then tell me."

"It can wait, India. You need to get your strength back."

She tried to sit, to no avail. Alexander was correct, she did need to regain some of her strength. But she didn't need to get out of bed to hear what was bothering him. "Tell me, Xander."

Alexander released her hand and sat back. He ran his palms down his face and growled. "I should be out there looking for that son of a bitch. I swear I'll rip his head clean off the next time I see him."

"Xander?"

He leaned forward again, gathered her hand, and held it to his chest. "There's no easy way to say this, *gattina*. You're going to be fine, in fact, more than fine. You won't have any lasting issues from the wound. The baby…"

Placing her free hand over her lips, she whispered as more moisture gathered in her eyes. "Tell me."

"You lost so much blood, *gattina*." He squeezed her hand. "The baby didn't make it."

The oxygen sucked right out of her. India had trouble drawing a breath. Her chest hurt, her eyes burned as the moisture turned to tears and rolled down her cheeks. Her lips quivered behind her hand. India drew her lower lip into her mouth and bit down, tasting her own blood.

I've lost the baby.

The baby Spike had given her.

And now the baby Spike had taken away.

Her tears turned into barely controlled sobs, causing a hiccough to escape. Her baby was gone. She had nothing and no one left. Her gaze fell on Alexander. Moisture clung to his lashes. His job with her was completed. He had promised to be there with her through the pregnancy, as a friend.

His duty had been fulfilled.

Grasping a tissue from the rolling table, she freed her hand from his and mopped her eyes, followed by blowing her nose. She needed to be strong when all she really wanted to do was curl into a ball and cry away her sorrow and pain. But she didn't want Alexander to see her like this. He'd never understand the grief threatening to do what Spike hadn't accomplished.

India looked away from him, unable to see the sorrow in his eyes a moment longer. Her own grief was threatening to swallow her whole. "You should go."

"You need me, *gattina*. I promised I would be here for you. And I will be."

"You promised"—she drew a shaking breath—"to see me through my pregnancy, and you did."

"India—"

"Why the hell can't you listen, Xander?"

India narrowed her gaze when she looked back at him, knew she was being unjustifiably mean, but couldn't stop herself. She was good and pissed. Angry at Spike ... hell, angry at the entire fucking situation. She had caused this, brought it on herself. But had she not gone to Alexander, then maybe Spike wouldn't have given two shits about her or the baby. No, she had been the sole cause of her misery. She was the reason her baby was dead.

"You need someone, gattina. I'm here for you."

When he reached out his hand, she batted it away. "Spike used me to get to you. You were his target, not me. And now? My baby is dead."

"Seriously?" He raised a dark brow, his face hardening. "You're going to throw blame my way? As if I had anything to do with you losing the baby? I'm the one that saved your fucking life, India."

She covered her face with her hands and let the sobs take over. Alexander stood so suddenly, he nearly knocking the chair from all fours. She had pushed him away, couldn't blame him for walking out. India felt his hesitation in her chest for a brief moment before she heard the soles of his shoes exit the room, taking her broken heart with him. India was to blame, not Alexander, and yet she had all but accused him...

The nurse called after him, but India was too far gone in her grief to hear what had been said. Instead, she pulled her legs to her chest and allowed the desolation and anguish to take over.

ALEXANDER HAD NEVER BEEN more pissed. Pissed at India, pissed at Spike, but mostly pissed at himself. He had been the one to put the timeline on their relationship, to put her in the "friend's zone." And now that she had followed his demands, his rules, he had never regretted anything more.

He had wanted to crawl into the hospital bed, gather her into the cocoon of his embrace, and make the hurt go away. Whatever he had felt for India, it had to be damn close to the L word. Because as he drove his motorcycle back to Pleasant, it felt as if his heart had been ripped from his chest, leaving him feeling exposed ... vulnerable. Something Alexander hadn't known since his screwed-up childhood.

Thankfully, Kaleb had the wherewithal to ride Alexander's bike down the mountain and bring him the keys. Even if a trek back up the steep terrain might have done him some good. The last thing he wanted, though, was to return to the cabin, scent India's blood that had soaked into the floorboards, or to relive the terror of almost losing her.

Now pulling back on the accelerator, he took the straightaway on Route 126 at over ninety-miles-per-hour. His tires ate up the tarmac, chewing up the distance before taking the next curve with ease. The open road had always been the serenity in an otherwise chaotic life. No better way to clear his mind and free him from the everyday quandaries that weighed heavily on his soul. Taking a deep breath, he tried like hell to ease the tension from his muscles.

Little good it did.

Alexander peered through an opening in the evergreens. Not a cloud in the sky. The sun might not be beating down on his back due to the cover of trees, but the elevated temperature caused sweat to roll down his spine and dampen his armpits. He welcomed the heat, making him feel anything other than the river of self-loathing sluicing through him. If he thought it would make a difference, he'd turn his bike around and return to India's bedside and beg for forgiveness, though he wasn't quite sure what the hell he had done to warrant her sending him away.

Hell, he couldn't control the actions of a psychopath.

And it certainly wasn't his fault Spike had targeted him, using India as a pawn in some fucked-up twisted game. Alexander had saved her life, even if he couldn't have done the same for her unborn child.

That is on Spike.

The sound of her sobs had followed him down the hall, killing him with each step that took him farther away. It had been all he could do to not turn around. India wasn't ready to deal with the truth that she had single-handedly fallen into Spike's trap. Alexander couldn't be faulted for any of this. So instead of doing as his heart desired, he'd raised his chin and squared his shoulders, heading down the long corridor and ignoring the nurse who had called after him. His pride had taken a blow, which is what carried him back to the clubhouse and his sedentary life.

Since Draven had informed him of the impromptu meeting at the Blood 'n' Rave, he knew the clubhouse would be empty, leaving him to his solitude and self-pity. He thought about his room and the fact the last couple of months India had occupied it, slept in his bed. Hell, her seductive scent was stamped over the entire damn room, not to mention her belongings littering about.

There was nowhere else he wanted to be.

The Sons of Sangue had been his brothers for so damn long, he hadn't bothered making friends outside of the club, nor was it necessary. Alexander would continue to lay his head on the new sofa for now, needing someplace that didn't smell like India and warm summer nights. Going elsewhere wasn't an option. He still had obligations. Spike, for one. The La Paz kingpin for two.

Regardless of what the Sons of Sangue discussed, he wasn't in the mood to hang with his brothers at the Rave tonight. He could go to the shop, work on some bikes at K&K

Motorcycles, but even a job he loved held little appeal at the moment. So instead, he'd head home, lick his wounds for a night, then hunt down Spike come tomorrow. His brothers could handle their plans for Raúl. Once Alexander took Spike's head, then he was all in to help take down the La Paz cartel and their fearless leader.

Too bad Vlad Tepes left behind the ancient practice of displaying heads on a pole, as Alexander was tempted to place Spike's head in front of the clubhouse for all to see. If for nothing else, it might send a message that the Sons of Sangue were not to be fucked with.

Regardless, Spike was a dead man.

Alexander was about to cut his immortal life short.

Now turning into the gravel parking lot of the clubhouse, he noted Ryder's bike sitting in front of the new window, telling him the ex-Devil had not followed the others to the Rave. Cutting the engine, he kicked down the side stand and stepped over the leather seat. He pocketed the key, tucked his skull cap beneath his arm, and headed for the door. Alexander couldn't help wondering why the vampire decided to stay at the clubhouse while the rest of the brothers met at Draven's nightclub.

He found the main room empty, which was just as well. Alexander detected Ryder's unique scent, telling him he was on the premises. If for some reason Ryder had already called it a night, all the better. The idea of chit-chat didn't appeal to him at all, not in his current mood.

He walked to the bar and set his skull cap down, then grabbed a bottle of Gentleman Jack from the cupboard behind. He placed it on the wooden surface, picked up a rocks glass, and poured himself two fingers, quickly knocking it back. The amber liquid burned his throat and warmed his gut. He may not have much use for the whiskey on most days, but it sure in the hell tasted good today.

"I thought you didn't drink that shit." Ryder's deep voice shook him from his reverie.

"I do now," Alexander grumbled, then poured himself another glass and downed it. "What are you doing here?"

Ryder retrieved the bottle of whiskey and helped himself to a tumbler of the amber liquid. He shrugged before lifting the glass to his lips and taking a sip. "Good whiskey is to be savored."

"Yeah? I doubt savoring the entire bottle would help my mood." Alexander leaned forward, bracing his elbows on the bar and palming his glass. "So why didn't P request your presence at the Rave?"

"I got the memo late. When I called him, he told me he'd fill me in." Ryder pulled out a stool and sat. "Look, man, sorry about your old lady."

"She ain't my old lady." Alexander shook his head, the whiskey churning in his gut at the mention of India. "She tossed me out on my ass. Guess that means she'll be moving out forthwith, huh?"

"P said you saved her life."

"I did, but the baby didn't make it. Guess that's my fault."

Ryder winced. "That sucks, man."

"It's her grief talking. She's taking it out on me. I get that." After pouring himself another glass of whiskey, he took a sip and welcomed the burn. "I have big shoulders. I can take it."

"You look like you're taking it well." Ryder chuckled. "What's got you bugged?"

"When she comes home, she'll be packing up and leaving."

"And that's what you don't want?" Ryder raised one dark brow. "You falling in love with her, Xander?"

He took another sip, his gaze going to the big window facing the parking lot. Was he? Hell, he'd never thought he'd ever be able to speak the four-letter-word, let alone feel the emotion. But if what he felt wasn't the L word, what the hell was it?

"Not sure I'm capable of falling for anyone. Didn't think it was a part of my DNA. Hell, my parents were the worst role models when it came to relationships. They didn't even know how to care for a kid dumped on them." He patted his chest where the dog tags lay, the clinking of the metal sounding loud in the otherwise quiet room. "Even while I served our country, I was a complete failure. Three of the men in my charge didn't make it out. I was supposed to protect them or go with them. They gave their lives for our country and yet, here I stand."

"The crosses you bear on your neck?"

Alexander nodded, looking down at his glass. "It was to be our final mission. The bomb went off and I was the only one who made it out."

"And you've never forgiven yourself because your men couldn't forgive you." When Alexander didn't reply, Ryder continued. "None of them would have faulted you. They signed up for the military, knowing full well what the circumstances could be. They are heroes. They died for their country."

Alexander looked up, his gaze landing on Ryder's. "So what does that make me?"

"A hero that survived the war."

CHAPTER SEVENTEEN

"Where's Ryder?" Anton sidled up to the bar at the Blood 'n' Rave, joining his brothers.

His dyed black hair was back to the original blond, looking more like his old self and moniker. But these days, the name "Blondie" was rarely tossed about since his preference was the nickname he took when going undercover.

Kaleb had called the meeting hours ago, requesting most of his men to attend, along with Draven and Brea. The latter would join them once the first topic was put to rest. Kaleb wanted as little ears on the discussion as possible and not have Brea Gotti privy to it until they figured out what the hell was going on. They had yet to hear back from his grandfather, but he was sure Vlad would report anything he had discovered from Mircea.

"I told him he could sit this one out, Rogue. He's back at the clubhouse," Kaleb said. "Xander won't be making this meeting either since he's playing nursemaid to India. I know most of you heard about the cabin and what went down. India lost the baby. It goes without saying that Spike's got a big old target in the center of his back. I doubt any of us will need to worry about him in the near future. Xander will make sure his days are numbered.

"The rest of us ... we need to worry about the La Paz cartel, more specifically Raúl Trevino Caballero. The motherfucker's getting bolder and no longer cares what the Sons of Sangue thinks. His henchmen were in the Bohemia Mountain. It's my belief his goal is to start picking off Sons of Sangue members. I think it goes without saying, I'm not ready to lose anymore members. We need numbers."

"We already patched over the prospects, Rocker and Lightning." Grigore looked down the bar at the two newer members. "I don't think any of the other prospects are ready to be patched over. They haven't been with us for much more than a few months, let alone a year. Not to mention, we could stand to bring in a few more."

"I agree,"Kaleb said. "We can take it to a vote on bringing in new prospects, but this does nothing to solve our current problem."

None of his men seemed opposed to the idea of bringing on new prospects since they needed to add more full-fledged members to the Sons. The problem was it usually took a year, of which they didn't have, for a prospect to be patched over. It was going to take more numbers than they already had if they were going to go after Brea's godfather. Raúl had a lot of foot soldiers. The Sons had already proven to be stronger and smarter than his men, but the Sons of Sangue numbers were far too small to take on the entire cartel, even if they did patch over their current prospects.

That's where Kane's idea came in.

His twin had been right all along.

Kaleb had been too damned stubborn to see the benefit.

Kane stepped beside Kaleb, the muscles in his cheeks taut. "Hawk and I have decided to patch over the Knights, bring them in as Sons of Sangue."

"Are you fucking serious?" Grigore's brows drew together. His gaze traveled around the bar. "Are you all on board with this? They're our fucking rivals. Letting them run guns in Oregon is one thing since we profit from the deal. But patch them over? I'm sorry, Hawk, but that will be the day when the Sons of Sangue needs the Knights' help. We'd be better off voting in our current prospects."

"Hear Viper out, Wolf," Kaleb said. "I felt much the same way as you, until now. We need numbers and I'm not about to see any of my brothers go down because of our age-old bad blood with Raúl and his fucking goonies. As I said, he's getting bolder. And we can't be assured he won't turn any of his men. We bring in the Knights, make them part of us. They already know the inner workings of an MC, not like our prospects who are still learning. Besides, being so newly with us, we can't say for sure they aren't plants from the cartel or the Devils. We can't take that chance. They haven't done their time. From here out, they aren't privy to our meetings."

"You intend to turn the Knights, then." It wasn't a question.

"We need their strength, Rogue." Kaleb looked at Anton, then at Bobby. "I think we, as vampires, proved up there on the mountain that Raúl's soldiers don't stand a chance against us. Not one-on-one, anyway, or even two-to-one. If we patch over the Knights and don't give them the benefit of our vampire strength and agility, it will be like leading sheep to a slaughter, especially should Raúl turn his men into bloodsuckers."

Grigore rubbed his short beard but said nothing. Kaleb could see he had yet to win him over.

"Think about it. We'll control both states." Kaleb paused, waiting for everyone to digest the idea. "Maybe with the cartel out of our business and Spike meeting his maker, we can even bring in California, patch over the remaining Devils. We could own the coast."

"Or eliminate them. The Knights are one thing," Grayson spoke up. "But the Devils? I say there isn't a damn man worth saving there."

One of Bobby's brows raised and his beard twitched, his lips all but disappearing within. "You saying I wasn't worth saving, Gypsy?"

"That's not what I meant, Preacher. And you damn well know it." Grayson nodded at Anton. "Rogue vouched for you. That was good enough for me. He's the reason you were saved and patched over. If you recall, I brought in Ryder. He was a former Devil."

"He was a snitch," Bobby added.

"A snitch for us. He wanted out of the Devils after what they did to him and his girlfriend." When Bobby didn't comment further, Grayson continued, "I'm speaking about the rest of the gang of twisted fucks still following Spike's lead."

"Not all of them are following his lead," Bobby added.

Grayson nodded slowly. "That may be true. But I say if we go after the Devils, it's on a person-to-person vote. The rest are eliminated or left to move on, and the Devils disbanded."

"I agree with Gypsy." Kaleb tapped his forefinger on the bar top. "None of this is without a vote. Including the Knights. We take this up back at the clubhouse where we'll call a church meeting. That way, Xander and Ryder will be in on the vote. Let's table the discussion on Raúl and our plans for the cartel until we have Draven and Brea join this conversation. It's only right she's here to weigh in on our plans. For now, I have another subject that needs to be addressed. A question I'm sure you've all asked yourselves."

"What's this about, Hawk, if it isn't dealing with Raúl?"

"Draven Smith and Ryder Kelley, Wolf."

"I was wondering why no one questioned Draven's turning before now," Grayson said. "Women can't turn men into vampires, so how the hell did that happen? And what's this have to do with Ryder?"

"Lightning is doing an ancestry check on them." Kane leaned against the back counter, crossing his arms over his chest. "Vlad's also checking into this as well. From past experience, no female has been able to turn a male, Rosalee included. So how Draven biting Brea worked, we have no idea. Which also brings up Ryder. He turned damned fast, which wasn't normal. Unless you're a true blood like me, Hawk, and Xander."

"And since Xander's parents found him in a trash can, dumped off by his real parents, we have no idea whose lineage he came from," Kaleb added. "There was no way to trace his ancestry. Not when his parents merely stumbled across him."

"Has anyone heard back from Vlad?"

"Not yet, Rogue. Once we do, we'll share the information." Kaleb grabbed a few bottles of Jack and placed them on the bar. "How about you go retrieve Draven and Brea and we'll continue our conversation about the cartel and our plans to take out Raúl and his lackeys. Anyone besides me want some whiskey? I'm fucking parched."

Kane chuckled. "That's because you never shut up, Hawk."

Grayson set some tumblers on the bar, while Kaleb poured the amber liquid. Glasses were passed around and the liquor began to flow. The men seemed to relax a bit, which was Kaleb's intention. They needed to see the benefit of bringing the Knights into the Sons of Sangue. Not only patching them over, but giving them their vampire DNA. The Sons had lost enough men. Kaleb wasn't about to lose any more, not if he could help it. Raúl, the murdering bastard, wasn't going to quit where the Sons were concerned, unless someone stopped him.

Anton, Draven, and Brea stepped through the curtained doorway that led from the private quarters upstairs. Many of the Sons had used the room over time to feed their many appetites. Brea glanced around the bar, her gaze taking in the Sons. Kaleb could tell she was apprehensive. Hell, she had only recently met most of them and they were plotting to take out her godfather. Kaleb couldn't blame her for being uneasy. He offered them each a glass of the whiskey, but they both declined.

"What's the plan?" Draven asked, wrapping his arms around Brea as he stood behind her.

Brea squared her shoulders, showing more bravado then Kaleb had seen most men possess. He admired that in a woman. Kaleb couldn't imagine what he'd think if someone planned to take out one of his loved ones.

"We need to locate Raúl," Kaleb said. "Take him by surprise. I doubt he's going to be easy to ferret out. From our experience, he moves around a lot."

"He does." Brea offered a slim smile, one Kaleb supposed she didn't feel. "Even for someone who knows him well, I doubt I'd be given his location by any of his men. He has a very loyal following. There were times my father didn't even know where he'd be, and they worked together. My godfather didn't get this far by being careless. You know the location of his beach house. I can give you the same for his main compound, but that doesn't mean he will be there."

Kane raised a brow. "You're on board with our desire to kill Raúl?"

"If I thought for a minute he could be rehabilitated, I'd say no. My godfather is a very bad man. I know that. He profits off the demise of others. He's guilty of the deaths of thousands. Now that he has vampire DNA, I fear that number will rise exponentially. He needs to be stopped."

"Ideas on how to find him?" Kaleb was open to any help Brea might offer. "Up to this point, it's been a cat-and-mouse game. We've had little luck finding the prick. No offense."

"None taken. I've put some thought into this, ever since Draven told me about the Sons coming up with a plan to take him down. He cares little about anyone, even tried to drown me when I wasn't willing to go with his crazy plan to be his bride." Brea rolled her eyes. "He actually thought I would go along with it and when I didn't—he tried to take me by force. Finding out I was already mated to Draven put a chink in those plans, thus his plan to drown me."

"If it makes you feel better, he had to have known he couldn't kill you that way," Grayson said. "He may have wanted to hurt you, and no doubt kill Draven in the process. But if he wanted you dead, vampires die only by a beheading or a shot that instantly stops the heart. His drowning you was likely nothing more than buying him time to escape."

"True." Brea shook her head, her lips thinning. "But given the chance, and he thought he'd benefit from it, no one near Raúl is safe, including me."

"What're your thoughts?" Kaleb asked.

"Raúl has a niece. She's the daughter of the man one of your people killed."

"Rosalee killed your godfather's brother," Kane supplied. "She's the one who started the feud. In return, Raúl took my son Ion's life."

"I'm so sorry for your loss, Viper. Did my godfather kill Rosalee?"

"No, my grandfather did. Raúl or I haven't forgotten. This feud won't end until he takes every one of our lives ... or I take his. That's why we need your help."

Brea leaned back into Draven's embrace. "Since this niece is Raúl's last remaining connection to his brother, he keeps her close. Where I wasn't technically family, she is. He'll guard her with his very life."

"You think we should go after his niece?" Grayson asked. "Will she be any easier to find?"

"Please don't hurt her. She's innocent in all of this, Gypsy."

"We wouldn't think to. If she gets hurt in this, I promise you it will be by your godfather's hand, not ours."

Brea bit her bottom lip thoughtfully. "You'll need to get someone inside, which may be impossible. It has to be someone from the club who Raúl doesn't know, one who doesn't wear a Sons of Sangue tattoo."

"Ryder Kelley," Grayson said. "I turned him. He was a surfing buddy of mine, turned snitch for me that damn near cost him his life. He still has the Devil's patch in the center of his back. He has yet to ink it over. When at the clubhouse, he wears a shirt because of it. We had planned to get new ink together but hadn't done so. Maybe Raúl will still think he's a Devil."

"It's worth a try," Brea said. "But you must know if Ryder is found out, my godfather will kill him. Ryder needs to know what he's getting himself into."

"I thought the cartel was responsible for the demise of Ryder's old lady," Kaleb brought up. "What if they recognize him?"'

"From what Ryder told me," Grayson said, "that was Raúl's brother. We can only hope the men working with him at the time are long gone as well. It's still worth a try. He's the only one of us who can pull this off, Hawk."

It was a huge risk. If Ryder didn't want in on the plan, Kaleb would understand. He couldn't in good conscience put one of his men into peril without them being in one hundred percent. Anything less could get him killed.

"What's his niece's name?"

"Gabriela Trevino Caballero." Brea looked at the ground. When she glanced up, moisture gathered in her gaze. "I don't want Gabby hurt. At one time, we were the best of friends. I looked up to her. She was gorgeous and two years older than me. She adored the father she lost."

"Did she know what he was capable of?"

"She was a child, Viper. She only knew what he wanted her to know."

"And her mother?"

Brea took in a deep breath, then let it out slowly. "Died in childbirth. Raúl is all she has. No siblings. And my godfather has no children of his own. The one thing money couldn't buy him. He was sterile."

"Then Gabriela is everything to Raúl."

"She is, Hawk. He'll stop at nothing to protect her."

"And probably why we have never heard of her until now," Grayson said. "Only insiders likely know about her to keep her from being targeted by his enemies. Smart move."

"If we choose to use Ryder, how do we get him on the inside?" Kaleb took a pull from his tumbler of whiskey. "And if we do manage to get him on the inside, what's the story if he's recognized?"

"I think we let Ryder fill in the blanks if he's recognized from when they killed his girlfriend," Grayson said. "No one knows that situation better than Ryder. The closer he sticks to the truth, the better off he'll be. As for getting inside, I have no clue. I believe that's where Brea comes in."

"My godfather is always recruiting soldiers for obvious reasons. He's in a dangerous business. His men are either killed or spending time in jail. The best way to get inside is through someone who already works for him. There's a bar along the coast in La Paz that's a known hang-out. Most people steer away from Salazar's. I can almost guarantee only locals go there. A stranger walks in that bar, they'll take notice."

"Sounds like our in." Kaleb looked at Kane. "What do you think, bro?"

Kane smiled. "I'm with you on this one. If Ryder thinks he can get in via the foot soldiers, I think it's a plan."

"And Gabby?" Brea placed her hands on Draven's forearms. He gave her a reassuring squeeze.

"We'll let Ryder know she's to be protected at all costs. I think if he can get in good with Gabby and romance her, it will give us a leg up on Raúl and his whereabouts." Kaleb rubbed his chin between forefinger and thumb. "Without her, we aren't going to come anywhere close to your godfather."

"And the Knights?" Grigore asked. "Where do they fit in?"

"We'll be sending them to Mexico to keep an eye on Ryder." Kane looked around the bar at each man. "Which is why we need them on board. Some of us will go to Mexico to back up Ryder, but we'll need to hang back or we might be recognized. The Knights haven't had any dealing with the La Paz cartel."

"True."

"Glad you finally agree, Wolf."

"Not agreeing yet, Viper, but you raise a valid point. Bring this up at the next church meeting. Although I have my reservations, I'm swaying your way."

"Great." Kaleb slapped the bar. "If Ryder agrees, then I'd say we have a solid plan to go after Raúl and his men. Time to put them out of business."

CHAPTER EIGHTEEN

India wasn't sure where she was going to go, but one thing was for sure, she could no longer stay at the clubhouse. After the way she had left things with Alexander, it was pretty doubtful he'd want to speak with her. Her parting words had hurt him. She had seen it in the set of his jaw, the square of his shoulders as he had turned and walked away. She had lashed out in pain. Once said, there was no taking the words back. Why the hell couldn't she have been struck dumb a second before?

"Spike used me to get to you. You were his target, not me. And now? My baby is dead."

She had all but blamed Alexander for the demise of her unborn child. India placed one of her hands over her abdomen, sorrow filling her once again from the loss. Tears sprung to her eyes, the anguish damn near crippling her. She had awakened in the hospital, seeing Alexander by her side … *the entire time*. The nurse had told her he hadn't left. That is, until she'd opened her mouth and chased him away. His parting words still stung, every one of which she deserved.

"You're going to throw blame my way? As if I had anything to do with you losing the baby? I'm the one that saved your fucking life, India."

She couldn't blame him if her bags were already packed and sitting by the front door. Maybe he wouldn't want to see her at all, not give her the chance to apologize. The thought of not seeing him again stung.

Way to pay him back for saving your life, India.

Shaking her head, she moved her hand to her throat, still covered with white gauze. Had she not harbored extreme hatred for Spike before, she certainly did now. The son of a bitch had tried to take her life, and would have, had Alexander not been there.

Spike was the sole reason for losing her baby.

She laid her head against the taxi seat and prayed Alexander would be at the clubhouse, give her the chance to make amends. Never had she been more sorry or sick to her stomach from simple words, words for which she could never make amends. If Alexander never wanted to speak with her again, she wouldn't fault him. She had pushed him away. Lush greenery rushed by the windows as the cab came closer to Pleasant. The closer they came, the more nausea set in.

Fear of losing him.

India had no idea what awaited her beyond the closed door of the clubhouse, a door she thought may no longer be open to her. The last few days at the hospital had been pure torture. Bile churned in her stomach. She touched the hollow of her throat where her missing donor necklace normally lay. She wasn't sure if it got lost in the scuffle, or what had happened to it. When she had called Draven to report it missing, he had informed her that it wasn't missing at all. Alexander had handed it over to him when he came to the hospital to see her. Apparently, Alexander had retired her from being a donor. Nothing she said would get Draven to go against Alexander's order.

While she should be pissed at Alexander for making that kind of decision for her, she couldn't get beyond the emptiness left inside her following his departure and the loss of her unborn child. In all honesty, being a donor had lost its appeal anyway. The only vampire she had any interest in had turned his back and walked away.

Alexander wouldn't have to kill Spike.

India would gladly do the honors.

Once she retrieved her things from the clubhouse and figured out where to go, then she'd track down Spike and put a bullet in the center of his dead heart. It was time for him to get up close and personal with her Ruger SR9. She'd make damn good and sure he'd never hurt another person.

The taxi pulled into the parking lot of the clubhouse, gravel crunching beneath the tires. Her stomach churned, causing her to swallow the bile wanting to crawl up her throat. She had said the words. Now she'd find the courage to make up for them if he'd give her half a chance. Hell, she'd spend the rest of her life trying to make up for them if Alexander would only listen.

India said a quick prayer of thanks beneath her breath when she spotted his bike sitting outside alone. No other MC member was present. What needed to be said between them didn't need an audience. Her orange VW Beetle was parked near the back of the lot where she had left it.

"If you'll wait," she told the cab driver, "I'll run in and get some cash. I'll just be a minute."

India exited the cab and approached the door. Her nerves were strung tight, not knowing what mood she'd catch Alexander in. She tested the knob and found it unlocked, then opened the door. Not seeing Alexander, she darted to his room, found her purse, and pulled some cash from her wallet. A quick look around told her Alexander had yet to boot her out on her ass. Everything was just as she had left it.

Upon leaving the room, she nearly ran into Alexander as he exited the bathroom, shirtless, with a pair of low-slung jeans hanging on his hips.

Their gazes met and held, but he said nothing. She waved the cash in her hand. "I need to pay for the taxi. I'll be right back. We need to talk."

He nodded, his eyes leaving hers and holding on the white gauze surrounding her neck. "We do."

India attempted to swallow the lump lodged in her throat, nearly choking the last breath from her. *Great.* She survives having her throat slit from ear to ear, only to be taken down by a set of jangled nerves.

Not waiting for further response lest he changed his mind and decided to toss her out on her ass instead, she jogged through the door and paid the driver. Taking a deep breath, she watched the white car circle the drive and head down the road. Squaring her shoulders, she reentered the main living area of the clubhouse.

Alexander had donned an old Pantera concert T-shirt and was now reclining on one of the new sofas, feet propped on the center coffee table and crossed at the ankles. He held a glass of water in one hand, while his other arm draped over the sofa back.

India flanked the empty sofa, earning her an "Uh-uh." His chin raised, indicating the empty seat next to him, and beneath his muscular arm. Her eyes moistened. Surely, he didn't hate her after all.

"I'm so sorry, Xander." India tried damn hard to contain the tears, drawing her lower lip between her teeth.

Alexander motioned again for her to sit, and this time she complied, crumbling onto the cushion. He tucked her into his side and wrapped her within his embrace, making her feel warm and safe. It had been so long since India had allowed anyone to care for her, other than when she had asked for Alexander's help.

Draven had given her a job years ago that afforded her to live on her own. She had left behind that job and her apartment to follow Spike to California, only to return pregnant, with no means to support herself, and nowhere else to go.

Alexander had been her savior.

"There's nothing to apologize for, *gattina*."

India chuckled miserably, the sound wet from her unshed tears. "I was so mean to you. It was uncalled for."

He set his glass of water on the side table. "You were hurting. I get that."

"I was, but that didn't give me the right to be a complete bitch. You saved my life and I repaid you by blaming you when I should have been thanking you." Tears rolled down her face unheeded. Alexander brushed away some of the wetness with the pad of his thumb. "Spike was ... is to blame. For that matter, I'm to blame. I'm the one who left and followed him to California, to get pregnant—"

Alexander gripped her chin and stopped her from heaping on more guilt. His touch seared her flesh, heating her in places she had no right thinking about at the moment. Desire she had no right to.

"You made a mistake, *gattina*. We all make them. We learn from them and move on. Unfortunately, you paid the ultimate price. You lost your baby."

India told herself she wasn't going to do this, to sob uncontrollably. She had thought she'd left behind the hurt at the hospital. And yet the tears couldn't be stopped. She turned into his chest and released the ache bubbling to the surface. Alexander's hand smoothed down her spine and he kissed the top of her head, whispering to her that everything would be okay.

And damn if, somehow, he didn't make her believe it.

INDIA'S SOBS CUT STRAIGHT to his heart. Christ, no woman had ever affected him the way she did. Her pain sliced through him, damn near crippling him as if it were his own.

He would give anything to turn back time, to give her back the impossible. Her baby had been taken ... stolen from her womb. Something that, once taken could not be given back. And even though he could feel her anguish, he couldn't pretend to know how she felt. All Alexander knew was India agonized and no amount of comfort he offered would make that go away. So, he held her and rubbed her back, whispering to her that everything would be okay.

Empty promises.

Hell, no one could set someone else's world right. And yet, he knew he'd die trying. India didn't deserve the pile of shit heaped on her. He had been Spike's target, even if she had initiated the turn of events by taking up with the bastard.

Spike was a dead man.

India sat back, scrubbing her face with her hands. Her puffy eyes held a sadness he wished he could erase. Her lower lip trembled. He used his knuckle to smooth over the silky flesh, easing the tremor. Her gaze dropped to his lips and damn if he didn't want to kiss her. But it would be beyond callous to take advantage of the broken woman beside him. Oh, he wanted her. There was no doubt in that. And scenting her newly arrived desire, he knew she was of the same mind.

Making love to her, though, wasn't going to happen.

Not today.

Not like this.

India deserved his respect and time to heal. Not some rutting animal needing to assuage his baser needs. When he finally allowed himself to make love to India, it would mean far more to him than just another romp in the sack, another notch on his bed post.

India palmed his stubbled cheek. "Thank you."

"For?"

"For saving my life, for sitting by my hospital bed endlessly and tirelessly. Thank you for not turning your back on me when I was a complete bitch. And thank you for not throwing me out on my ass, which I no doubt deserve."

"I didn't tell you that you have to look for a new place"—he winked—"first thing come morning?"

She slapped his shoulder, blessing him with a slight smile, the first genuine one since waking up in the hospital. He was making progress. Even fresh from her sobs, she had never looked more beautiful. Her smooth skin, her deep brown eyes, her silky black hair. Everything about her not only kicked up his desire but damn near overloaded his heart. In truth, Alexander never wanted to do without this woman. The fear he had experienced when he thought he might lose her, he never wanted to encounter again. Once they put this whole ordeal behind them, he'd make sure India stayed by his side forever, even if he had to beg.

Never had he wanted to protect someone with his very life, to cherish them with his entire being. And yes, never had he loved someone so much it hurt. He'd earn her love, show her he was worthy of it, and prove so by killing the man who robbed her of her first born.

"Seriously, India," he said and chuckled, "you can stay here for as long as you need."

"I don't want to be a burden to you or the others. I can see if Draven will give me back my old job, then find a place of my own."

Alexander threaded his fingers through the hair at the side of her head, smoothing through the silken strands and cupping the back of her head. "You, *gattina*, can do whatever makes you happy. If staying here is it, then you're welcome as my guest. No one here would ever question that."

"You know what makes me happy, Xander?"

"What's that?"

"You."

Warmth spread through him from her declaration. He might not be ready to put into word vows of love, or happy-ever-afters, but her avowal warmed him just the same. Their lives were too twisted from the pain Spike had brought to think about what tomorrow might bring. Alexander wanted to be free of the bastard who had already caused them so much pain before making any admissions of his own. Then and only then would he think about taking her as a mate, taking their relationship to the "forever" status.

Mate.

Never in his godforsaken life did he ever think he'd use that word regarding another living soul. And yet, here he sat thinking about life with India, babies, and the whole nine yards.

To keep himself from professing anything prematurely, Alexander lowered his head and settled his lips over hers, telling her everything he refused to voice.

Christ, he wanted her, more than wanted.

I crave.

Her hands slipped up his chest and snaked around his neck, returning his heated kiss with fervor. Her fingers splayed across the short-cropped hair of his skull. His cock stood and took notice, already plaguing him. India broke the kiss long enough to slip onto his lap, her long slender thighs cradling his. Surely, she felt the evidence of his desire resting against her. The scent of her own desire grew, the sweet aroma wafting to his nose. His nostrils flared. Lord, he had never smelled a more powerful aphrodisiac. It was all he could do to keep from tossing her onto her back, ripping off the scrubs, and burying himself to the hilt.

India slowly rocked against his erection, the roughness of the jeans between them deliciously abrading. Much more and he feared he'd come in his fucking jeans. Talk about premature. And yet, he couldn't stop her, not ready for the painfully exquisite ache to end. He'd no doubt have to finish himself off later as he wasn't about to take advantage of her.

Not like this.

Hell, she had just lost the baby a mere week ago.

He thrust his tongue past her lips, deepening the kiss, possessing her the way no other man would have a right to. He'd kill the first one who tried. India belonged to him and he'd be damned before he allowed another man or vampire to touch her. Alexander swallowed her moan, loving the essence of her hunger. He wanted to watch her come apart, know that he was the reason ... erase away any reminiscence of Spike and their illicit affair. He wanted to be the face India called upon when she fantasized.

Alexander eased back, breaking their kiss long enough to undo the tie of the scrubs she'd worn home ... *their* home.

India stilled his hands. "I may still be spotting."

A grin lifted his lips. "And you think a little blood bothers me?"

She moaned again, biting her lip, and closing her eyes. Heat flared white hot, further hardening his groin. He slid a hand beneath the cotton material, to her soft underwear and beneath to her satin flesh. Her breath hitched as he slipped a couple fingers between her thighs, separating her folds, finding her already wet.

When India opened her eyes again, Alexander held her gaze, watching as her pupils dilated, her lids grew heavy. The pulse point at the hollow of her throat quickened, visible just beneath the white gauze, drawing forth his fangs, aching with the need to sink into the side of her neck. It had been a few days since he had last fed. Abstaining wasn't his norm, but feeding from her after so much blood loss wasn't about to happen. Ignoring his gnawing hunger, he slid first one finger, then two into her hot center. India rocked against his palm, her walls gripping his fingers. Euphoria shot through him, straight to his penis, further paining him.

Using his free hand, he cupped her head and brought her back for a deep, searing kiss, making love to her tongue the way his erection was being denied. Increasing the rhythm, her wetness coated his fingers. Alexander could tell she was close to falling over the edge.

Breaking the kiss, he withdrew his fingers and forced her to open her eyes. Her lips were red and slightly swollen from his kiss. Fuck, she had never looked so hot or doable. But the white bandage reminded him it was not the time.

This is for her.

"Look at me, *gattina*."

"I am," she whispered, breathless.

"No." He licked his lips. "Look at me when I make you come."

Reinserting his fingers, he increased the rhythm as his thumb found the little knot of nerves, circling it and adding pressure. Her eyes closed, and her lips parted. "Oh, God."

"Look at me, India."

Her eyelids popped back open. Her walls trembled and tightened around his fingers. Her mouth rounded as she sucked in oxygen.

"Oh…" Her breath hitched. "Oh my … Xander…"

And her climax washed over her, her gaze hooded as she collapsed against his chest. Her cheek rested over the heavy beat of his heart. Alexander removed his hand from the scrubs, suckled them clean, only to further plague his hunger.

"Fuck," slipped past his fangs.

India raised her head, brushing her long black hair from her face, and looked at him. Alexander toyed with one long strand of dyed red hair. He loved the funkiness, found it sexy as hell and hoped she continued the style.

Her hand drifted down his T-shirt, over his abs, and headed for the erection still hidden by his jeans. He placed his hands over hers to stop her from reaching her goal. She raised a brow.

"Not today, *gattina*. Not until you have fully recovered." His hand indicated the gauze first, then tapped her sternum. "Today was about you."

"Xander—"

He shook his head, not to be swayed. "You need to rest."

After slipping from beneath her, he picked her up and cradled her against his chest, heading for his room.

"Then where are you taking me?"

"To your bed." He smiled. "Where you will get some sleep."

"Will you lay with me?"

"Only until you fall asleep. I need to feed, and before you even think it, the answer is 'no.' You've lost enough blood."

"Xander?"

He looked at her, nudging open the bedroom door with his bare foot and carried her to the mattress. With all the care he might give a child, he laid her upon the comforter.

"Stay until I wake up. Then—"

Lord, if he stayed, would he be able to resist? "Yes?"

"We're going to talk about you retiring me from being a donor."

His face heated. Something told him, he was about to get an ass-chewing. Alexander chuckled, looking forward to the argument. It would be good to have her back. Not that he didn't like this softer side, but he'd much rather spar with her feisty side.

"We'll talk," he said, then crawled onto the bed with her and gathered her into a spoon, cursing the damn erection still plaguing him.

CHAPTER NINETEEN

RYDER BRUSHED HIS OVERLONG BANGS FROM HIS FACE AND stared into the tumbler of whiskey he held between his palms. When he had arrived at the Blood 'n' Rave, all of his brothers had already gone home, leaving him to drink alone. He glanced around the establishment, watching several women gyrate about the large tiled dance floor.

Women of all sizes.

He wasn't picky, he loved them all.

Knocking back the rest of his Jack, Ryder considered hitting the road. There wasn't much appeal in staying since he had already fed unless he considered getting a piece of ass. For some reason that he couldn't name, even getting laid wasn't a high priority at the moment.

The bartender approached and asked if he needed a refill. Ryder nodded, then pulled a few bills from his pocket and laid them on the counter.

"Sons drink free." The bald man ignored the cash. "Boss's rules."

Ryder tipped his chin. "Then keep it as a tip. I pay for what I drink."

The man took the money and shoved it into the pocket of his worn jeans. He looked like he could use the extra cash. "Suit yourself."

The man went to serve another customer when a short-haired blonde with black-rimmed glasses sidled up beside him. Cathy was one of the donors with whom he didn't mind chatting. As a matter of fact, she was one of his favorite donors, the one he had most recently tapped. She never pressured him or his brothers for more. Being in her company was like talking to a buddy and not a donor looking to mate up.

She bumped hips with him. "What's up, sweet cheeks?"

Ryder chuckled. "Careful, Cathy, or I might think you have a thing for me."

"No worries. I only have eyes for Draven, and well"—she waved a hand in the air—"he's already taken."

"Too bad, you might have made me a good mate one day."

It was her turn to laugh. "No, thank you. I'll share my blood with you, but I'm not about to go down that road. I'm not becoming anyone's bloodsucker for eternity."

"Never considered it?"

"Nope. I'm fine with sharing my blood." She shivered. "But no way in hell I'm drinking anyone else's."

Ryder turned up his nose and scented Grayson long before he joined them at the bar. He draped an arm over Cathy's shoulder and placed a noisy kiss upon her cheek, which she wiped off.

"I'm wounded." Grayson bestowed Cathy with a smile and a wink. With his enhanced hearing, he had no doubt heard Cathy's confession. "Not even for me?"

"Not even for you, big guy." Cathy blew an air-kiss at him. "Besides, Tamara would suck my ass dry next time she decided to tap my artery. Although, I've got to say you are my favorite Son."

"Hey."

She smiled. "No offense, Ryder. But Gypsy's a sexy man-beast."

Ryder snickered. "None taken. Besides, I can see that about Gypsy. I think I might have a wee little man crush—"

"Don't even fucking say it, Ryder." He raised one of his dark brows.

Grayson turned to the bartender and tapped his hand on the wood surface, earning him a tumbler of whiskey. He quickly downed the contents, set the glass on the bar for the bald man to refill it, then turned back to Ryder.

"We need to talk, bro."

"Sure, man. Upstairs?"

Grayson nodded, then asked Cathy to excuse them. She gave Grayson's beard a quick tug, then headed for the front of the establishment. Ryder followed the man who had turned him through the curtained doorway and up the stairs, leading to the room reserved for the Sons. Once inside, Ryder shut the door behind them.

"What's this about?" Ryder sat on the leather sofa and crossed one booted foot over his knee. His arm, holding his tumbler of Jack in his hand, draped the back.

Grayson sat on a leather armchair facing him. "We need your help."

"Mine?" Ryder's gaze narrowed. "You saved my life, Gypsy. The Sons gave me a home. Whatever you need, you know I'll do."

Grayson took a sip of his whiskey. He rubbed his whiskers with his free hand. He wore his beard longer than Ryder's, who preferred his closer to his face.

"The meeting you weren't at tonight, we discussed the cartel and our need to bring down Raúl."

"No secret there."

"No, but we haven't had any luck finding the cagey little bastard. We enlisted Brea's help. Even she doesn't know her godfather's whereabouts. And following her and Draven's altercation with the man, she supposed it would be even harder to learn the details of his latest location."

"What about Spike?"

"Xander will take care of that piece of shit. He may somehow be a pawn in Raúl's games, but we seriously doubt the kingpin puts much trust in him. I'm willing to bet Spike only knows his location on a need-to-know basis."

Ryder nodded. "You're probably correct. So, where do I come in?"

Grayson set his glass on the side table and leaned forward, bracing his forearms on his knees and clasping his hands. "We want you to infiltrate his cartel."

The man was off his rocker. Certainly, Ryder would be signing his own death certificate if he said yes. "What if they find out I'm a member of the Sons?"

"You'll most likely be killed."

Ryder chuckled with a shake of his head. "At least I know where I sit with my brothers."

"It's not like that, Ryder, and you fucking know it. You're my bro from another mother. Besides, you're the only one without a Sons of Sangue tattoo."

He couldn't very well say no, not after the man, his *brother*, had saved him once before. Like Grayson had said, they couldn't be closer if the two were born of the same mother. Had it not been for him, Ryder would've already been eating dirt from six-feet-under.

"And I still wear the Devils' one. If you aren't sending me in to get killed, then tell me your plan."

"You know I love you, bro. If I didn't think this was a solid plan, I wouldn't even ask it of you."

Ryder hoped to hell it was a fucking solid plan. Anything else and he'd be meeting his maker. "And if I say no?"

Grayson's lips thinned. "Then I tell the Sons we need to come up with another plan. We won't force you to do anything you aren't comfortable with, Ryder. This is on a voluntary basis."

He rubbed the back of his neck and grimaced. "Because you don't want my death on your hands."

"Because we wouldn't ask you to do anything you didn't think you could walk away from, bro. You come back from this and I'll gladly pay to have your fucking Devils' tat inked over."

"It's a deal." Ryder laughed, hoping to hell he could collect. "You definitely know how to talk my language. Now, tell me about this fucked-up plan, because I have no doubt it is."

Grayson gave him the details, the fact he'd be heading for La Paz, where according to Bobby, most of his old MC members were never invited, right down to romancing the kingpin's niece. Were they fucking nuts? If he messed this up, Raúl wouldn't simply take his head, he'd want Ryder castrated, making him wish for death.

"What's her name?"

"Gabriela Trevino Caballero. Brea said she goes by Gabby."

"Knowing Raúl, she probably looks like a troll."

Grayson grinned, his eyes full of mischief. "You think I'd send you in there if she was ugly?"

"In a heartbeat," Ryder said, earning him a laugh from Grayson.

"From what Brea said, bro, she's gorgeous."

"Yeah, well, I'll be the deciding factor on that. You know how women are. They all think their best friends are beautiful. Hard to believe someone as ugly as Raúl would have a living relative winning any beauty contests." Both men stood. Ryder took Grayson's hand and gave him a one-armed hug. "Tell Hawk I'm in."

MOONLIGHT FILTERED THROUGH the mini blinds into the room, casting stark white lines across the dark comforter. Her back was toasty, telling India that Alexander had either stayed put or had returned following his feeding.

"You're awake," came the deep timbre of his voice.

India snuggled into his warmth, feeling the delicious evidence of his desire against her backside. Oh, what she wouldn't do to roll over, remove her bottoms, and slide it on in. But she had a hunch Alexander would stop her from doing so.

Yes, she had lost her baby. Yes, she was an emotional basket case. Yes, she was recovering from a severe cut to her throat, though, she bet it was healing quicker than normal thanks to Alexander's saliva. All that said, she still wanted Alexander, always had, and she'd be damned before she let him crawl out of bed until she got her way this time.

He wanted her, couldn't dispute the fact with the impressive erection nestled in the cleft of her butt cheeks. India had no clue how to successfully seduce a vampire and she was pretty certain Google wouldn't be of any help. Being that she was already halfway there, and getting him hard wasn't going to be a problem since he already took care of that little … er … big problem, India knew it was more of a mind-over-matter issue. A smile slipped up her cheeks as she again snuggled against said large object.

"*Gattina*…"

"Hmmm … Xander?"

"Could you do a vampire a huge favor and lie still?"

She wiggled against him, earning her a groan. "Why, Xander, whatever for? Aren't you tired?"

His chuckle rumbled against her back. "You are a little minx."

"Not sure what you mean."

It was easy to contain her smile since he couldn't see her face. Her mirth was a whole different matter.

"Oh, I'm sure you do," he whispered against the shell of her ear, his breath fanning delightfully over her flesh. "A vampire only has so much willpower."

Alexander dragged his fangs over the soft skin of her neck as if proving his point—or should she say *points*? India knew he wouldn't bite, not when she had already lost so much blood. The feel of his fangs against her throat was a huge turn-on. If it wasn't for her accident she might entice him to bite. Instead, she'd have to appeal to his sexual nature, one from which she was pretty sure he was used to abstaining if there was any truth at all to the rumors within the donor society. Which reminded her, she needed to talk to Alexander about his overbearing ways.

Sex first. Talk later.

No way in hell was she going to miss a golden opportunity. Alexander might not crawl between the sheets with her again. Knowing this, she wasn't about to give up, not this time.

"Did you feed?"

"I did." His breath fanned over her shoulder, just before he placed a tiny kiss upon her flesh.

The ache between her thighs grew. There would be no need for a condom since vampires couldn't impregnate humans, nor could they contract diseases. They were about as close to safe sex as abstinence.

"I shouldn't be jealous."

India felt his slight withdrawal, making her curse her loose lips. He was quiet for a long moment before he whispered, "Are you?"

"If you're setting me up with this question, Xander, fair warning, I'll fail."

"I'm not sure what you mean."

"Meaning, if you want zero emotional attachment from me, it isn't going to happen. It's too late for that. I don't want a friend with benefits." Alexander tightened the arms wrapped around her, bringing back his warmth. She sure hoped to hell that meant he was leaning in her favor. "I'm not asking for forever. I know you don't want that, you've made it perfectly clear to everyone you aren't looking to mate. But is 'happy for the time being' too much to ask for?"

He chuckled. *Great.* She was holding a serious conversation, and he's finding humor. India sighed. "Just forget I said anything. I'll take what comfort you have to offer tonight and find a new place to live as soon as possible. I don't want to be—"

Alexander placed a callused hand over her lips. "Would you shut it long enough to allow me a reply? Fuck, if you aren't the most maddening woman. You said that I make you happy. Well, guess what? You, *gattina*, make me happy. I can't tell you what that means for the future, but I can tell you I don't want a friend with benefits either. As a matter of fact"—the hand that covered her lips now smoothed over her shoulder and down to the curve of her waist—"I'm pretty sure I might drain any man who thinks he can touch you … starting with Spike."

"I don't want to talk about him."

"That's good, because that makes two of us."

Her breath drew in as his hand slipped under the edge of the scrub top she still wore. Real sexy. Alexander ghosted his palm up her ribs, stopping at the curve of one of her breasts. He cupped it as if testing the weight, no doubt purposely avoiding her pebbled nipple. She arched into his hand, hoping to encourage him to explore just a bit further.

"As a matter of fact"—Alexander placed another kiss in the crook of her neck and guided his other hand south—"I don't want to talk at all."

India sucked in oxygen as his fingers breached the tie of the scrubs, loosening the ends. As he skimmed over her lower abdomen, the sweet spot between her legs ached, begging for his touch. One of his fingers slipped between her folds, smoothing over her. India tilted her head onto his shoulder and moaned. His touch was magic, no other way to describe it. She swore, had she not been biting her lower lip, she would have come with one mere touch from him.

How the hell did one man wield so much power over her?

Never had an orgasm been so easy.

As if sensing her oncoming release, he said, "Hold on, *gattina*, not yet. This time I want you to come on my cock."

Withdrawing his hand, he pushed down her scrubs, over her hips and legs, where she could kick the cotton free. Alexander wasted little time divesting her of the top until she lay spooned against him sans clothes. Damn if the feel of him fully clothed against her naked body wasn't even more of a turn-on.

In fact, India couldn't remember ever being as turned on. Her heart hammered against her ribs, her nipples hardened almost painfully, and her sex ached for his touch. If he didn't comply soon, she was ready to take matters into her own hands. As if he had read her mind, which she was pretty sure wasn't one of his enhanced abilities, he cupped both of her breasts, lightly tugging on her nipples between forefinger and thumb.

India moaned, her hands covering his. Maybe if she held them there, he couldn't withdraw. Alexander was setting her on fire. She was attracted to his heat like a moth to a flame. With each tug and pull, it was as though she could feel the sensation clear to her womb.

Empty womb.

Damn it, she would not think about what had happened or of the bastard guilty for her loss. Instead, she snuggled more fully into Alexander and whispered, "Fuck me."

"No, *gattina*."

India gasped. Please, for the love of everything that is holy...

He pulled his hands free of her hold and cupped her chin, forcing her to turn her head and look at him. Her cheeks heated.

"But I will make love to you."

CHAPTER TWENTY

"Fuck me."

Seriously? He might feel that way about the many nameless faces he had slept with over the past many years, but not India. While hearing the words tumble from her lips was smokin' hot, she wasn't a nameless fuck. Truth of it, she was probably the first woman he—since turning vampire—hadn't wanted to just fuck. Like it or not, there was no way he was going to have sex with her and not have his emotions get tangled up.

She had been through so much, the white gauze covering her throat a blinding reminder. Rolling from behind her and tucking her next to his side, Alexander gripped the edge of the tape and slowly lifted the bandage, tossing it to the floor. The wound still looked angry in the darkened moonlit room, puckered where the sutures held the flesh together. The DNA in his saliva had aided the healing, the tiny threads likely no longer needed. Once removed, she'd be left with a scar.

India's large chocolate eyes stared up at him, clearly nervous, her lower lip tucked between her teeth. It was her desire wafting to his nose that spurred him forward. His hunger grew exponentially. Christ, he should run as far and fast as he could. For once he made love to her, there would be no turning back. India might not realize it, but she was his ... for all eternity.

But it was already too late for second thoughts.

He may not have wanted to mate in the past, but it only took this woman to come crashing into his life to change his mind. He wanted what the twins had, what Grayson had. He craved to join the ranks of Draven and Bobby. And if Anton was smart, he'd help Kimber make up her mind already, not chance her turning her back on his vampire world.

The Sons of Sangue were quickly losing their single status, leaving few unmated originals.

India licked her lips, drawing his attention back to the naked beauty beside him. All clear thought quickly fled his befuddled brain. He had a willing woman in his bed and he was contemplating his single status? He needed his damn head checked.

Tangling his fingers in her black hair fanning his white pillow, the silky threads were like a balm to his callused hands. He ran a knuckle down her downy-soft cheek. Never had he wanted to protect someone more. The thought of almost losing her he couldn't begin to contemplate.

Alexander lowered his head and drew her lower lip into his mouth, pulling gently on the soft flesh, careful not to nick it with his fangs. One taste of her blood and he knew he'd want more. India slipped her hands up his chest, palming the back of his skull, anchoring him as if she feared he'd change his mind.

Not this time.

No fucking way.

He deepened the kiss, wanting to possess her body and soul so that she'd never question who she belonged to. Not that he was the Neanderthal she had accused him of being. He was all about women's rights and all that. But India had already made it quite clear she was of the same mind.

He belonged to her.

Her tongue sparred with his, giving him everything she had and then some. His groin ached and his jeans were way too fucking tight. Hell, he had wanted to take his time, show her what it was like to be cherished, but as hard as his cock was even a vampire had his limits.

He tilted his head, giving him better access, careful not to disturb the wound on her throat. He gripped her tiny waist, holding her fast to the mattress. Alexander made love to her mouth, the way his body ached to. India's breath hitched; her hips squirmed beneath his hold. She tasted of warm honey and hot summer nights. Melting beneath his touch, she gave all of herself to him, a gift to be sure.

Spike unwittingly filtered through his thoughts. It galled him to think of the bastard lying with her, taking what Alexander hadn't had the courage to claim months ago. He'd wipe Spike from her memory, show her what being adored felt like.

India turned into him, deepened the kiss and strengthened her hold, depleting his brain from any further thoughts of his nemesis. He smoothed his palm from her waist, down her abdomen to her trimmed curls. He slipped a finger between her thighs, finding her clit and circling the tiny nub. India moaned, her thighs parting, begging him silently for more. He slid a finger inside her, then two, moving them slowly. Her walls gripped his digits, looking for the climax he wasn't about to give.

Not yet.

He wanted to be buried to the hilt, feeling the tremors when she came. Removing his fingers, earning him a protest from her lips as he ended the kiss, Alexander licked a path from her ear down her jaw, to the hollow point of her neck. Her pulse beat heavy against the pad of his tongue, and damn if he didn't want to drink from her, recalling the smooth smoky tang of her blood.

"You're killing me." India wiggled beside him, his hands back to holding her in place. "Please, Xander."

He raised his head, a grin upon his lips. "Please what, *gattina*?"

"Let me come."

"All in good time." He lowered his head again, capturing with his mouth one of the taut buds of her breasts, his fingers toying with the other.

India tilted her head into the pillow, pressing her chest more fully into him. "Oh ... my ... if you would just…"

"Just what?" He nipped the taut bud, then soothed it with his tongue. "Ask and it's yours."

India looked at him. "Then take off your damn clothes already, Xander. Let me touch you."

He laughed again, but stood and did as instructed. He peeled his T-shirt over his head; her gaze traveled the sparse hair on his chest, following the line to his jeans. Alexander took his time, undoing the button and slowly lowering the zipper. India's tongue wet her lips. Fuck, she hardly had to move to make his cock jump.

He shoved the rough material from his hips, leaving his erection tenting his boxer briefs. India sat, slipped to the side of the bed, and grasped the waistband.

Alexander smiled. "You are a greedy little minx."

India looked up at him and pulled down the front of his briefs, encircling his erection with her hand. Alexander hissed. Using her free hand, she shoved the cotton over his ass and allowed it to pool at his ankles with his jeans. All he could think about was getting her to wrap her bow-shaped lips around his cock. He wasn't sure he could abide by the "no come" rule if she did.

Her tongue touched the tip of his cock, licking off the drop of pre-come that had come to the surface. With one hand she cupped his balls, while the other slid up and down his erection, paining him as he tried to think of anything other than what she was doing. Unfortunately, it wasn't working. About the time he fisted her hair and was about to pull her to her feet, she sucked him into her mouth, damn near taking him fully. As her mouth retreated, her hand followed it up the shaft. Fuck, she knew what the hell she was doing and he refused to examine that thought further. Best he be happy with the idea his cock would be the only one getting her wicked talents from here on out.

India ran her tongue along the heavy vein on the underside before taking him back into her mouth. Much more and he wouldn't have to worry about his hasty rule. She'd get the job done, making him one happy motherfucker. Instead, he pulled her to his feet and kissed her soundly, his erection now throbbing between them. He still wanted to be buried deep when they both reached their release.

"Fast and furious, *gattina*."

She blinked at him. "What?"

"I wanted to take you slowly, give you time, but man, you have me ready to blow. I need you now ... and I need it to be furious."

She laughed, the sound pleasing to his ear. "Then what are you waiting for?"

Alexander turned her around. He gently nudged her forward so her hands braced the mattress and her backside pointed at him, and what a great ass it was. He gripped her waist with one hand, then ran his erection along her slick folds.

"Tell me now if this isn't what you want, *gattina*. It will be your last chance."

Her body went stock-still in his hold. "Last chance?"

"If I make love to you, you'll fuck only me. Understood?"

India glanced at him over her shoulder. "And you?"

"I promise you, I want no other."

"Then take me."

Alexander didn't need to be told twice. He guided the head of his erection to her opening and slid in. Damn, she was seriously wet. Alexander didn't think he had ever felt anything closer to ecstasy. He stilled, giving his cock time to recover or it would be over before he even began. Using his free hand, he twisted her hair into a ponytail and gently pulled her head back, careful not to put a strain on her wound.

With all of the control he could muster, he began moving within her, urged on by her backside meeting him, thrust for thrust. When he was confident she was taking him, no pain involved, he dropped his hold on her hair, grabbed her waist with both hands, then began slamming into her. The only sound in the room was the meeting of their flesh and the tiny moans escaping India's lips.

Her hands fisted the comforter, her appetite matching his with every exertion. Never had he met a woman hungrier than India. The way she moved, the way her walls gripped him like a vice, everything making her his equal.

"*Shit*..." He growled. "You need to come now, *gattina*, or I might just selfishly beat you to it."

One of her hands released the bedspread, reached between her spread thighs, and circled her clit. Her moans increased. Her breaths quickened; her walls quaked. India arched her back, crying out his name. His cock felt her hold as if it had been her hand.

"*Fuck*," he said, drawing out the word as if it were the most beautiful sight he had ever seen.

His muscles contracted, his ass cheeks tightened, and his release came just seconds after. He held fixed for a moment, allowing the euphoria to subside. India stayed her position, her head tilted downward, her breathing slowing. Withdrawing from her, he wrapped a forearm around her waist and pulled her against him. He placed a tender kiss in the crook of her shoulder.

"Are you okay?"

She shuddered. "More than."

"Mine," he whispered.

"Yours."

Before he could make that happen for eternity, before confessing his undying love, there was one person he needed to deal with. The one person now unspoken between them. Once Spike personally met the Grim Reaper, Alexander planned on making his relationship with India a permanent one.

Until then, he'd refrain from using the word "mate."

ALEXANDER STEPPED INTO HIS discarded jeans, pulled them over his hips, and slipped quietly from the room. The door closed with a soft snick behind him. India had fallen asleep about a half hour ago but he was too keyed up to sleep. He could've easily flipped her onto her back for round two. Now that he had made love to her, he wanted more. Since India was still recovering from her wound, Alexander thought it best to give her time to heal, which meant sleep, not dealing with a vampire's overactive libido.

Entering the living area, he spotted Grigore and Ryder watching the clubhouse's new seventy-five-inch screen, laughing at some old reruns of *Seinfeld*. He grabbed an empty glass, filled it with water, then joined them. He sat next to Ryder on one of the sofas and kicked up his bare feet onto the center table.

"You could've at least threw on a shirt, GQ," Grigore said, taking a sip out of the glass of whiskey he held. "Save us from all that excessive manliness going on."

It had been some time since he had heard the earned moniker coined a while ago after shoring up his long hair. "Fuck you, Wolf. You're just jealous."

"Hey, chicks dig a dad-bod."

"You keep telling yourself that, buddy."

Grigore lifted his shirt and patted what was far from a large belly. Though it did have a good sprinkling of hair, which had earned him the nickname "Wolf."

"Cover that shit up. You'll get fur in my water."

Grigore laughed and pulled his shirt over the pelt. Maybe calling it a "hide" might have been a bit of an exaggeration.

Ryder raised a brow, a crooked smile curling his lips. "Having a little fun in there? About fucking time."

"What the hell is with you guys? You have nothing better to do? It's not like I haven't had to put up with your night-long escapades. Making love to someone isn't something new we've done around here."

"No, but *you* don't usually bring them home," Grigore said. There was a lot of truth to his statement.

"She's temporarily living here, for crying out loud. Was I supposed to take her elsewhere?"

"Lighten up, Xander." Ryder laughed. "We're only having fun with you, not to mention pointing out the obvious. You should've hooked up with that hot little donor long ago."

Grigore aimed the remote at the television and muted the sound. Apparently, the conversation was about to take a more serious tone. "Meeting at the Rave got over early."

"How'd that go? Hawk said he'd catch me up later."

Grigore gave Alexander the short version of their plans to send Ryder into Mexico. He had never been one to go into great detail, instead giving Alexander the extremely condensed version. Alexander was sure Kaleb would finish filling him in on the Sons' plans to infiltrate at another time.

"You okay with that, man?" Alexander looked at Ryder.

"I drew the short stick." Ryder shrugged. "Who else could do it? I'm a former Devil."

"So is Preacher."

"Preacher's mated. Besides, I still sport the Devil tattoo." Ryder tipped up his glass and swallowed the remaining whiskey. "And when I do ink it over, Grayson promised to pay for it. Can't beat free ink."

Alexander knew Ryder made light of the situation, but this was some serious shit. He was about to get mixed up with a compound of dangerous men. While Alexander was positive the twins wouldn't send Ryder in without someone having his back, he'd bet there wouldn't be many of the Sons following him south. After all, with the kingpin having enhanced abilities from his vampire DNA, he would be able to scent any vamps in his camp. What the hell would they tell Raúl about Ryder being a vampire?

"Viper and Hawk come up with a story for you yet? Not like Raúl won't know you're a vampire, man." He kicked down his feet and set his glass of water on the center stand, turning toward Ryder. "None of the Devils are vampires that we know of, other than Spike. I got to believe he's too damn selfish to turn any of his men. He'd rather hold his powers over them."

"Preacher said when he and Anton went south, they weren't able to detect any of the Devils being turned," Grigore said, backing up Alexander's belief.

"You're taking out Spike, right?" Ryder asked.

"First chance I get."

Ryder shrugged again. "I'll tell him Spike turned me. That we were plotting to take out the VP of the Devils because he wasn't following Spike's lead. I was Spike's choice for next in line. I'll say that with Spike dead, I'm no longer in the Devils' good graces, so I left them and came south for work."

Alexander thought about Ryder's plan. It could work, but there was still one little hole to fill in their story. "That might work. Except for the fact, the Devils still think you're dead, Ryder."

"First, we need to make sure Spike's dead before we put this plan into action," Grigore said. "Then 'Ryder' can return from the dead."

"Fuck, what a mess. Sure we still can't send in Preacher?"

"No can do, GQ." Grigore shook his head. "I forgot to mention Ryder needs to get inside and woo Raúl's niece. Tena would never go for Preacher down there trying to get it on with Gabriela Trevino Caballero. From what Brea says, she's smokin' hot."

Alexander rubbed his stubble. Grigore was correct, no way in hell Tena would give Bobby the okay, even for the sake of a Son's mission. "So, how the hell does one rise from the dead?"

"The Devils know he was a Son's snitch and Tank ordered him dead," Grigore said. "Once Spike's gone, Ryder tells someone from the Devils that he never snitched to the Sons. Tank lied. Hopefully, he can convince them it was because he had wanted to leave the Devils, which we already know that much was true. The sons of bitches left him for dead, but he had survived the attack. That will cover his tracks if anyone from the Devils sees him with the La Paz crew. Once Spike's gone and the Devils' never really having his back, he wants a piece of the cartel action."

"What about the cartel killing your girlfriend, Ryder?" Alexander couldn't leave any stones unturned. They had to go in with a believable story or Ryder would be toast. "Raúl didn't know anything about that?"

Ryder shook his head, rubbing the scar on his chest and shoulder, left as a reminder. "It was all his brother's doing. Raúl was never involved with the Devils until after his brother was killed. He pretty much stayed in Mexico. Handled that side of the business. I don't think I was ever on the man's radar. When Raúl hooked up with the Devils, it was not only to keep running drugs in the states, but to also target the Sons, since you guys are the ones responsible for his brother's demise."

"His brother took out Viper's son," Grigore growled.

Ryder flipped up his palm. "Doesn't matter. Raúl doesn't care the reason for his brother's death, only that someone took his life and that someone needs to pay. That being someone from the Sons, or as it seems now, all of the Sons."

"That asswipe is fucked in the noggin." Alexander took in a deep breath, leaned back, and crossed his arms behind his head. "This plan could work. At least we better hope it does. Anything less and, Ryder, you don't come back."

"It's the only way, Xander. Really, I don't mind." Ryder stretched his long legs in front of him and clasped his fingers over his abdomen. "I appreciate your concern. The truth is, the Sons saved my life. I wouldn't be sitting here if it wasn't for Grayson sharing his blood. He could've easily let me die on that boat. He owed me nothing. It's payback time. If that means going south to shake things up with the La Paz cartel and take out Raúl, then I'll do it. That motherfucker needs to go down. Just like his brother. We take enough of them out, the rest will scatter like flies."

"We best make sure we have a solid plan going in." Alexander sure hoped to hell Ryder was correct. "I don't want to lose any more of my brothers."

"I volunteered to follow him down." Grigore sat up, his large feet thumping the wooden floor. "I'm not mated either, so if anything happens to me, no loss."

Alexander creased his brow. "Fuck you say, Wolf. You would be a huge loss to the Sons."

Grigore winked. "That's good, then, because I don't plan on going down."

CHAPTER TWENTY-ONE

INDIA OPENED HER EYES, THE SCENT OF BACON WAFTING TO her nose. Her stomach growled. Food hadn't exactly been on her radar, so she hadn't eaten much of anything since her stay in the hospital. She was suddenly famished. Waking up to the smell of cooking food in a clubhouse of vampires who normally didn't eat people food, meant the concession was no doubt made with her in mind. The fact that Alexander had crawled out of bed and was cooking her breakfast warmed her to the marrow of her bones.

Rolling over to the empty side of the bed, India clasped the abandoned pillow and pulled it to her chest, inhaling the musk left behind by Alexander. A smile raised her cheeks, one she had no hope of displacing anytime soon. Her thoughts returned to the night before and the delicious way it had ended. Thankfully, Alexander hadn't over thought his actions and for once had acted on impulse.

Had she not been so tired and promptly fell fast asleep within his arms, India certainly wouldn't have minded a replay. But as it was, following their lovemaking, she had cuddled into his warm embrace, surrounded by his comfort.

"*Mine*," he had whispered. India knew Alexander would go to the ends of the earth to protect what belonged to him, which now included her. She'd never have to fear Spike again. The bastard had hurt her for the last time.

Bright sunlight filtered through the closed blinds, telling India she had slept well into the morning. A quick glance at the nightstand told her that dallying much longer and she'd miss the start of the day altogether. She swung her legs off the mattress and padded to the dresser, looking for something to put on since she had finished the night in her birthday suit.

India pulled open the top dresser drawer and withdrew a sports bra and a pair boy shorts, quickly donning them. From the next drawer, she took out a white tank and a pair of chambray shorts. If Grigore and Ryder were still about, she couldn't run around half-naked. Otherwise, she would've picked up Alexander's discarded T-shirt and slipped it on, wearing nothing beneath, hoping for a second seduction by her vampire.

Hers.

The thought widened her smile as she opened the door and walked to the small kitchen area behind the bar. Alexander stood at the stove, flipping scrambled eggs, while the other two clubhouse occupants were nowhere to be found. Stepping up behind him, shirtless, jeans hanging low on his lean hips, she wrapped her arms around his middle and placed a kiss on his shoulder blade.

India glanced around his body. "Is that for me?"

Alexander put down the spatula and turned, draping his arms over her shoulders. "I thought you might be hungry."

"You thought right." She patted her stomach. "I'm so hungry I could eat a horse. Thank you for thinking of me."

He kissed her forehead. "You're welcome."

India drew her lip between her teeth and looked up at him.

"What's wrong?" he asked.

"That's how you greet me after last night? A chaste kiss on the forehead?"

Alexander's laughter bubbled up from his gut, his smile a warm balm to her soul. "No, *gattina*, this is how I greet you following last night."

He framed her face within his palms, dipped his head, and sealed his lips to hers. What started out warm and welcoming, quickly turned into deep and all-consuming. Screw the breakfast, India had an entirely different type of hunger on her mind now.

Alexander set her apart from him, giving a quick slap to her backside. "In due time, *gattina*. Remember, I can scent what's really on your mind. But food first. You need your strength to finish healing."

Her cheeks heated. Damn vampire enhanced sensory anyway. "Of course. You worked hard on breakfast. It smells delicious."

Alexander plated up her scrambled eggs with peppers and cheese, a couple slices of Texas toast, some fresh melon, and several pieces of bacon. Her stomach growled once more, making heat rise up her neck all over again.

"See? You are hungry. Eat."

India grabbed the salt and pepper and seasoned the food before picking up her fork. She scooped eggs into her mouth, then washed down the bite with a swig of orange juice that Alexander had set in front of her.

"Aren't you going to have any?"

His grin reached his dark eyes. "You know I don't need it."

"No, but surely you can enjoy a good meal. I can't eat all that you made."

Alexander tucked a few wayward strands of her black hair behind one of her ears as though he couldn't help but touch her. "I do when the moment calls for it, but I prefer a good rare steak over eggs and bacon any day. Beef would be my preference. For the most part, I don't eat people food. There is no reason to pretend I'm enjoying breakfast with you when I'd much rather tap your carotid."

She swallowed another mouthful and looked at Alexander. Her heart dropped to her stomach. "I wish I could—"

He smiled, running a knuckle down her cheek to the side of her neck. "Oh, you will, *gattina*. Just not today. When you get strong enough, you'll be my personal donor … *for now*."

India searched his eyes, looking for the meaning of his added "for now." Surely, he didn't mean that he'd partake from her for the time being, only to dump her if someone prettier came along. Her heart couldn't take watching Alexander move on. No, she wanted him to be her forever, for all eternity. India would do everything it took to convince him. Not that she had first chased him to seek immortality, never that. She had wanted Alexander because she thought him hot as hell, had been infatuated with him for some time. Now? She was in love with him and always would be. This kind of love never went away.

"Meaning?" she asked.

Alexander withdrew his touch and braced his arms on the counter in front of her, his expression unreadable. "Eat, *gattina*. Then I'll show you without words what you mean to me. You have no reason to fear my intentions."

India scooped up another bite of eggs, wanting to believe him, but his words "for now" rang through her brain. Instead of worrying sick about the implied meaning, India decided she would just have to change them from "for now" to "forever." Alexander Dumitru wouldn't know what hit him. After picking up a slice of bacon, she munched on it to hide her smile. He'd said that she made him happy and he had proven it by caring for her. Now she'd show him he possibly couldn't live life without her.

THE SCENT OF HER DESIRE was driving him fucking insane. If his jeans grew any tighter, he swore he'd split the seams. Alexander did his best to keep a hands-off approach while she finished her breakfast. Damn, if she wasn't taking her time, chewing each bite slowly, savoring it just to torture him. While it was great she enjoyed his cooking, he was hungry for an entirely different reason.

"How are you feeling this morning?"

Red infused her cheeks. "I'm fine, Xander."

"I can see you're *fine* from where I'm standing." He winked at her.

She laughed. "Cheesy pickup line."

"Yeah, well, I was never top of my class at picking up women." He shrugged, before thinning his lips. "I want to know what's going on in your head. You lost your baby."

India looked at her plate and took a deep breath before glancing back at him. Her warm brown eyes bore sadness. "I did. And I'm not done mourning the loss, trust me. It hurts my chest to even think of what I can never get back and makes me mad enough to want to kill Spike myself."

"I get those honors."

A tiny smile raised her lips. "Yes, you do. We already proved I'm no match for him. If you're asking how I'm feeling physically, then I'm fine. In fact, more than fine. I thought I confirmed that last night."

"You did." Alexander toyed with the dog tags around his neck, doing something, anything, to keep from reaching for her.

Grigore and Ryder had gone to bed long ago, so Alexander had free reign of the clubhouse living area. Neither would dare leave their room, knowing what was transpiring. It was a non-written rule, a "bro code" if you will. One to which he adhered several times for the sake of his roomies' antics. Once India was finished eating, he planned on savoring her, right where her plate sat.

"Why do you wear those?"

"Hmmm?" Alexander brought his gaze up from her perky breasts, straining against her white tank, nipples pebbling nicely against the fabric. He was beyond pathetic, ogling her while she ate. "What's what?"

India's grin told him she hadn't missed his perusal. She pulled the fork from her mouth, her lips wrapping the tines, maddeningly slow. "See something you like?"

"You're kidding, right?" Alexander wasn't the least embarrassed. "You got a great set of tits."

One of her dark brows raised. "Do I? I could say the same about you."

He laughed. "They're pectorals, not tits."

"Whatever. I like them."

"Men don't have breasts."

It was her time to chuckle. "I beg to differ. It's called 'breast tissue' whether it's a man or a woman. Pectoralis is actually the muscle that lies beneath the breasts. I aced biology."

Alexander skirted the counter, grabbed her fork and pushed her nearly empty plate across the surface. Her gaze widened as he gripped her tiny waist and lifted her to the countertop.

"So, I have an intelligent lady on my hands."

"Aced all the subjects, graduated top of my class."

He slipped his hands beneath her cotton tank and ghosted his fingertips up the flesh of her abdomen to the bra. His hands covered the soft material, reveling in the feel of her taut nipples against his palms. Alexander wanted flesh on flesh. Her sports bra was too damn thick for his liking.

"Did you go to college?"

"Uh-huh." She sucked in air as he shoved up the material, her breasts falling into his hands. "I did."

"What did you take?"

"Business. I wanted to open…" Pushing up the tank, he bared her breasts to his view. Taking one into his mouth, he sucked the tight bud before releasing it with a slight audible pop. "Oh … my."

"You wanted to open?"

"My own … business. You know it's hard to hold a … a conversation with you—"

"Talking is overrated anyway."

He took the other breast into his mouth, suckling it, nicking the flesh with his now-elongated fangs. Using the pad of his tongue, he soothed the tiny scrape, tasting of her smoky blood. Stepping back, he pulled her shirt and sports bra over her head, dropping them to the floor.

He palmed both naked breasts. "Now these … these are breasts. Clearly, you see the difference."

She chuckled until he sucked one of the globes back into his mouth while his fingers rolled and tweaked the other nipple. "Different, but a … a breast none the same."

Her breasts weren't overly large, but they certainly were a good handful. Placing his tongue between them and licking the length of her sternum, he slipped down her abdomen to the front of her shorts. If he wanted a lesson on anatomy, then he planned to take his time and study every part of her delicious curves. Gripping the band of her cute-as-hell short shorts, he lifted her hips and slid them off, letting them fall to the pile on the floor. She wore nothing but a pair of lacy boy shorts, that looked damn sexy on her. Screw thongs. These had quickly become his favorite thing on her. The white lace stood out beautifully against her darker skin. Did he say sexy as hell? Because there was no doubt she was.

Alexander bent at the knees, his fingers pulling the lace to one side, exposing her light sprinkling of curls and feminine folds. He glided a finger down her wet center, telling him "eat now, talk later." With his free hand, he adjusted the front of his jeans. His cock was just going to have to wait. Bringing up his hand and bracing her thighs open, he blew a slight puff of air. India moaned, tilting her head skyward.

Leaning in, he followed the path his finger had taken with his tongue. Damn, but she tasted sweet. India's back arched, her breasts tipping toward the ceiling. Her breathing quickened.

"Oh ... my... don't stop."

He chuckled. "I don't intend to, *gattina*."

India looked at him her eyes heavy lidded as she licked her lower lip, glistening it. Grabbing one of her breasts with her hand, she used the other to brace herself on the counter.

Fuck me!

His cock twitched in his pants and his groin ached as he watched her manual sexual play, tugging at her breast. Her breath drew in sharp when Alexander slipped two fingers into her. Shit, he wanted to see her come apart, have his name spill from her lips as she climaxed. He buried his fingers deep inside while his tongue circled her clit. Her hips rocked to the rhythm of his hand. She bit down on her lower lip, her walls tightening around his fingers. He knew she wasn't far from an orgasm. Oh, he'd get to his all right ... right after he took care of hers.

This woman undid him, laid his soul bare.

Never had he felt more exposed, raw.

Hell, never had he felt more alive.

India's thighs quivered, and both hands grabbed the edge of the counter as her legs tried to close. Alexander kept a hold on her thighs, not allowing the concession. Her back arched again, her lips rounded, as her walls gripped his fingers.

"Xander," she whispered, just before biting down on her lips, no doubt to keep from being loud.

Surely, she worried Grigore and Ryder might hear. Alexander nearly laughed at the thought. There was no privacy in a house full of vampires. Their enhanced hearing had certainly picked up her whispers, not to mention how their nostrils had definitely scented her desire. He'd bet it was a good chance they might even be doing a little solo action themselves. Alexander had done so a time or two when one of them had brought home a woman. Vampires were sexual beings and sometimes a little relief was absolutely necessary.

Withdrawing his fingers, he slipped the digits into his mouth to clean them. India's gaze dropped to his lips, her breath hitched. He pulled the boy shorts off her, discarding them with the rest of her garments. After undoing his jeans, he freed his cock. Alexander was no more ready to take it slow than he had been the night before.

His desire for this woman was fierce.

He grabbed her waist, allowing her to wrap her arms about his shoulder and pulled her from the counter. Holding on to her with one arm about her back, he positioned his erection and slid into her. India gasped as he seated himself to the hilt. She rocked against him, riding him hard and fast. His ass cheeks tightened with each intense thrust. Fuck, he wished he could sink his fangs into the crook of her neck.

Her blood roared through her veins. Her pulse throbbed. Alexander's nostrils flared as he scented the sweet smell of her blood calling to him. He leaned forward, licking the pulse point, torturing himself further. Damn, if he didn't have the restraint of a fucking saint.

He turned, backed her against the nearest wall, and thrust into her. Her brown gaze and tiny moans were his undoing. "You best be ready to come again, *gattina*. I think I'm fucking racing you to the finish line."

And with that, he sank his fangs into the soft flesh of her shoulder, careful not to draw fluid. Just the taste of her blood had him sliding over the edge, thrusting deep and releasing himself within her. India cried out, convulsing around his erection as he shoved in one final time. Her walls gripped him like a fist, holding him fast. Sweat beaded his brow. He released his fangs with a soft pop, his tongue sealing the tiny wounds.

India leaned forward, her forehead resting on his shoulder, her silky black hair a cape around her. When their breathing slowed, Alexander withdrew from her, allowing her to slide down the length of him.

"You still have on your jeans."

"I do." He chuckled. "If you want me out of them, then you'll have to race me to the bed. First one there calls the shots."

"No fair. I don't have your speed."

"I'll give you a head start, *gattina*. One, two…" He slapped her ass cheek. "You best get going. Three."

India took off with a squeal, running for the back bedroom. Once she cleared the door, he took off after her and jumped onto the mattress before her knee ever touched it. She never had a chance.

"Guess, I'm calling the shots."

India laughed. He loved the sound, could get used to hearing it daily. Hell, he wanted to make sure he heard it every damn day for the rest of their lives. India lay down, tucking herself against his side. She picked up the dog tags, reading the names.

"John Smith, Harold Jones, Walter Steele. Who are these men? You never did answer my question." She looked at him, her fingers now tracing the tattoos on his neck. "Three crosses. I always thought the crosses were related to your religion."

Alexander hated talking about his past and rarely did. Something in her gaze, the tone of her voice, had him wanting to be open with her. "The crosses have a double meaning, *gattina*. I was brought up to believe in God by parents who weren't fit to raise me. But yes, it also represents the three men, the dog tags I wear about my neck. I went to war with them. They were my men, my responsibility. And yet when it came time to protect them, I failed. I wear the crosses and dog tags as a reminder."

"I doubt you were responsible for their deaths. Did you personally kill them?"

He shook his head. "It was a bomb."

"Then you were no more responsible for them than you were for me losing my baby. That was Spike's doing. Just as these men died at the hands of your enemy. Not your hands."

He kissed the top of her head, knowing she was correct. Forgiving one's self was a hard thing to come by. Regardless, he'd never forget them or the fact he'd walked out of the hell without them.

"Where's yours?"

"My…?"

"Dog tags. You wear theirs, but not yours."

"I left the tags at the sight and carried theirs out. It was the only way to leave a piece of me there, while I took a piece of them home with me."

Alexander no longer wanted to talk about pasts, wars, or things that couldn't be changed. Tightening his arm around her, he whispered into her ear, "I'm about to call the shots."

Following his order, he proceeded to make love to her, slowly this time, showing her what he had yet to profess. They had all day and night for him to prove he was worthy of her love.

Come morning, though, he was going after Spike.

And this time, he wasn't about to fail anyone.

CHAPTER TWENTY-TWO

THE CELL PHONE SCREEN LIT UP LIKE A LIGHTHOUSE BEAcon in the middle of the night. Alexander blinked a few times, then grabbed his phone. When he and India had retired to the bedroom some time ago, he hadn't wanted to be disturbed, thus turning off the ringer and the vibration.

A quick peek told him it was five in the morning. What the hell was so important that Bobby would feel the need to call at this hour?

He slid his finger across the glass and placed it by his ear. "What the fuck, Preacher? This better be good."

"It is, trust me." Bobby's deep voice came across the speaker. "Spike's been located."

Alexander sat up, no longer sleepy as he jammed a hand through the hair at the top his head. India rolled over and raised up on an elbow, her gaze holding his. "What's up?" she mouthed.

He held up a finger, indicating to give him a minute, then returned to Bobby. "Where?"

"Santa Barbara, man. Apparently, he returned for a little par-tay with his men. Trouble is, not all are loyal to him. My good man, Sting, he's not a fan of the club P. Owes me a few favors. He remembered our trip south looking for Spike and called me. Said Spike's hiding out with a few of the Devils and laying low."

"How long?"

"Said he didn't know. Could be a day, could be a week, as far as he knew. We can't sit on this, man. We need to get down there if we want to catch his squirrelly ass. Know what I'm saying?"

Alexander blew out a steady breath. Oh, he had intended on looking for Spike today, that much was a given, and Bobby had just saved him a whole lot of trouble. His disappointment lay with the dark beauty beside him and wanting a little more private time with her. Not that he hadn't enjoyed every inch of her over the course of the previous day and into the night, but damn … another round would have been preferable over heading to Santa Barbra.

"I'll get dressed. Meet me at the clubhouse within the half hour."

"Sure thing, man. I'll bring Anton."

"I'll get Wolf. Ryder can stay here to look after India. We don't need those motherfuckers seeing him alive yet and ruining our well-laid plans."

"I'll call in Lightning and Rocker. Did Sting say how many men were in his camp?"

"At least ten of them, or so he thought, but not all of them bad."

"You text your man, tell him to get whoever the fuck is worth saving out of there. They don't want to be a part of the massacre coming to their door. Get the exact specs of the location. I don't want to be hunting these motherfuckers down, and I certainly don't want them forewarned of our arrival. You trust this dude?"

"I do, man. He's one of the good ones. Which is probably why he hates Spike."

"All right then, let's get on the road."

Alexander hit END, then quickly called Constantine "Lightning" Dalca and Peter "Rocker" Vasile. They were both hungry for some action. He then called Kaleb, letting him know what was about to go down. Thankfully, the club P had given them his blessing. He said he and Kane might've saddled up for the ride, but Vlad was due back in town any day. Alexander was happy to hear they were staying. More protection for India.

Tossing the cell to the bed, he turned to India, now wide awake. The apprehension in her eyes told him she had understood and was worried about his safety. Spike wouldn't get the upper hand ... not this time.

"Spike?"

Alexander nodded, then drew her into his embrace. He kissed her forehead before moving to her lips. Her hands slid around his neck and she kissed him, desperation evident. She had no need to worry. No way in hell would Spike cut his life short when he finally had someone to live for. He slipped his tongue between her lips, deepening the kiss. India belonged to him and he always took damn good care of his possessions.

To his chagrin, he didn't have time to explore things further, even if his cock was already hard and ready for a little more game. It would have to wait until he returned. When he did, it would be to ask her to be his mate.

Breaking the kiss, he smoothed a knuckle down her soft cheek. "I wish I didn't have to, *gattina*, but I must go."

"I know." She gazed at his chest, releasing the hold she had on his neck and threading the fingers of one hand through the sparse hair. "He needs to be dealt with."

Alexander didn't miss the fact she hadn't used Spike's name. He tipped up her chin with his thumb, wanting her full attention. "I have to ask, are you okay with me taking him out?"

Her gaze widened. "Of course. I didn't mean to make you think I was in the least bit worried about Spike. The bastard *deserves* to die. Left alive and he'll only wreak further havoc."

"Then what?"

The apprehension returned. "What if you don't come back?"

Alexander chuckled. "*Gattina*, I appreciate the worry, but he's no match for the Sons of Sangue. Spike's going down. As soon as the deed is done, I'll call you. Not until. Ryder will be here with you the entire time. Don't leave the clubhouse for any reason, just in case Preacher's informant isn't on the up-and-up. Are we clear?"

"Would it be okay if I invited the girls over?"

Alexander drew his brows together. "Like Cara, Suzy…"

Her smile warmed his heart. "Yes, and Tamera, Kimber, and Tena. I'd really like to get to know them better and they'll help keep my mind preoccupied."

"That's a great idea." He chuckled. "Ryder might not think so, but too fucking bad. What man in his right mind would complain about being in a houseful of beautiful women, right? Besides, the more vampires I have around you, the safer I feel leaving you."

Alexander patted her ass, then got out of bed. He grabbed a pair of boxer briefs, followed by his jeans, and pulled them on, then donned his socks and boots before searching for a fresh T-shirt. It killed him to leave India behind. On the bright side, though, once he made his way back they could finally put the past behind them.

"Xander?"

He turned, tugged a black, vintage Guns N' Roses concert shirt over his head. "Yes?"

"I'm sorry."

Alexander returned to the bed, framing her face with his palms and seeing the moisture in her eyes. "Stop apologizing, *gattina*. This is on Spike."

"But I made the mistake—"

He kissed her swiftly to keep her from saying any more. He had heard it enough. When he stood, he gave her wink. "We all make mistakes. Not another word about it."

Alexander the room and headed for the living area, calling out to Ryder and Grigore. Both men joined him by the bar,

Ryder still fastening his pants while Grigore elected to stand in his boxers.

"Really, Wolf? You couldn't have thrown on a pair of pants? We have a woman present."

He laughed, the sound deep and rumbling. "Just thought I'd let her see what she's missing."

Alexander shook his head, a smile creeping up his cheeks. "Fuck you, Wolf."

Grigore grabbed a pair of his pants hanging over one of the sofas and donned them.

"You really should pick up your shit."

"And since when do you care, Xander?" Grigore scratched the hair on his chest and yawned. "That little woman is going to get you all tied up in knots."

"I repeat … fuck you, Wolf," he said, earning him another guffaw.

"So what's this all about?" Ryder approached the crew surrounding the bar. "Mighty early breakfast meeting."

Alexander filled them in on Bobby's phone call. "The others should be here shortly, and then we get on the road. Ryder, you take good care of my woman."

One of Grigore's dark brows raised. "Whaaaat?" He drew out the word with feigned shock. "Mr. GQ takes a fall?"

India joined them. As she stepped beside Alexander, he draped an arm over her shoulder. "Like I said, Ryder, you keep a close eye on her. I'm holding you accountable for her wellbeing."

"You guys get all the fun and I get to play babysitter."

India tipped her head to the side. "I'm hardly a baby, Ryder."

His gaze raked over her, much to Alexander's dismay. "You can say *that* again."

"Hands off, Ryder."

It was his turn to chuckle. "Relax. I wouldn't think about it. But I must say you have great taste in women."

India placed a palm over Alexander's lips, keeping him from making a further ass of himself. "Thank you, Ryder."

The door opened and in walked the rest of the crew. They were a motley bunch, but he'd lay his life down for any of them. They were his brothers and the closest thing he had to family.

"Let's get this fucking show on the road," Bobby said. "We have about a thirteen-hour ride ahead of us."

Alexander pulled India into his embrace and kissed her soundly, ignoring the following catcalls. He used his middle finger to salute the men at his back.

Breaking the kiss, he tucked her hair behind one of her ears and whispered, "When I get back, *gattina*, we talk."

The last thing he saw as he headed out the door was her standing beside Ryder, wringing her hands in the front of one of his t-shirts that hung to her knees and a tear slipping down her cheek.

CARA SAT INDIAN STYLE ON the sofa with Suzi next to her. Little Stefan ran around the living room, chasing Ryder, who to India's surprise, was laughing and being a good sport.

Tamera sat on the opposite sofa, cradling a sleeping Lucian in her arms. India couldn't help but think about the baby she had lost, her hand automatically going to her abdomen. Her heart ached.

Kimber and Tena had also joined the group, sitting next to Tamera. Chad, Tena and Kimber's co-worker, sat in the adjacent chair. The living area flourished with activity, which was going a long way in helping India keep her mind off Santa Barbara and the massacre about to go down. She prayed the Sons of Sangue would be on the winning end. Anything less was not acceptable, nor did she think she could ever recover from the guilt that would come with it.

India sat next to Suzi and simply observed. She had always wanted to be a part of a large family and couldn't help desiring to be a more permanent part of this. While the guys were brothers in almost every sense of the word, the women had also bonded like sisters. These women would go to battle for one another. There was no mistaking the love in this room.

India glanced at Chad, whose gaze kept darting to Ryder as he lifted Stefan and tossed him into the air, catching him on the way back down. It was obvious that he appreciated Ryder's handsome physique. Who wouldn't? The biker was damn near stunning. To Chad's dismay, though, the man was one-hundred percent hetero.

"You're kidding, right?" Tena's words brought India's attention back to the conversations. The woman was smiling from ear to ear, pulling Kimber into a hug. "It's about time, girlfriend."

The women began tuning into the event unfolding between Tena and Kimber, whose cheeks were now rosy.

Shaking her head, Kimber laughed, proving she was anything but angry. "Why not announce it to everyone, Tena? Oh wait, you just did, loud mouth."

Tena shrugged, not offended in the least.

"What are we missing?" Cara asked. "Spill!"

"It's not that big of a deal." Kimber rolled her eyes, then sighed heavily. "I told Rogue this morning that I'd let him turn me. That is, if the Sons okay it."

"Squee!" Suzi jumped up, skirted the center table, and pulled Kimber into a hug. "You're kidding, right? I'd personally hurt any member who vetoed you becoming a mate. I'm with Tena, it's about damn time."

"We'll all be here for you, Kimber," Tamera added. "And I already know from personal experience that Rogue won't let you down or make you turn on your own. He'll take on some of the pain."

The women burst into laughter, knowing Tamera jested over the fact her man Grayson had skirted his responsibilities. It was water under the bridge and obviously no one bore hard feelings over an otherwise awkward situation. Anyone could see Tamera was head over heels in love with her man Grayson, and the same could be said for Kimber and Anton.

Apparently, Kimber was ready to face her fears.

India bet Anton was thrilled to finally be getting his way.

The women took turns hugging Kimber and welcoming her into the family, leaving India the odd woman out. Well, to be fair, Chad was also sitting in her corner.

"Great to hear." Ryder winked at Kimber, little Stefan now hanging from his pant leg. "Another brother off the market, leaving more women for the rest of us."

India hadn't missed Chad's sigh or look of disappointment; neither had Tena who slapped his shoulder.

"You can't have all the hot boys, Chad. You're such a dog."

He chuckled, and when Ryder glanced his way, he shrugged. "Can't blame a boy for trying."

Ryder smiled, obviously not bothered in the least. "If it makes you feel any better, Chad, for a guy, you're not so bad. I'm sure you do all right for yourself."

"Don't let him fool you, Ryder." Tena looked at Chad and rolled her eyes. "This guy got more dick than I did before I met Preacher. He has no shame."

Chad grinned. "Well, when you got it…"

Gaiety filled the room, and once again, several conversations started up again. It was India's eyes, though, that returned to Kimber. She couldn't help but be a little envious even if she was happy for the pair. India wouldn't mind joining their ranks if Alexander would ever open himself up to the idea.

Last night and the day before brought a smile to her lips. Alexander had not only been attentive and the consummate lover, he had also been a little naughty and hot as hell. She might not get his happily-ever-afters, but she'd make enough memories with him to last her a lifetime. India knew once Alexander tired of her and moved on, she wouldn't be able to. He was the only man for her. Hell, she might as well join a nunnery. And although she didn't look forward to the day that happened, India would never regret the time they spent together. She would forever be grateful for him helping her through the loss.

Cara slipped an arm around India's shoulder and gave her a slight squeeze. "Sweetheart, it's only a matter of time."

Suzi returned to the sofa, flopped down and kicked up her feet. "Cara's right. That boy doesn't know what hit him."

Had she been so obvious? India thought it best to feign ignorance. "I'm not following."

After picking up her wineglass, Cara clinked hers with Suzi's. "GQ is already gone, sweetheart. He may not realize it, but it won't be long before you join our ranks. I, for one, will be glad to welcome you into the family."

"Hear, hear," Suzi added. "It's obvious to me as well. He told all of the brothers they aren't allowed to tap your artery. Speaking of, where is your donor necklace?"

India's face heated. "Alexander gave it back to Draven."

"See?" Cara high-fived Suzi. "Only a matter of time."

"What has you three secretive about over there?" Tamera drew everyone else's attention to their hushed conversation.

Great.

The last thing India wanted was pity that would follow when Alexander failed to do what Cara and Suzi obviously thought he would.

"Who here thinks GQ is the next one off the market?" Suzi asked, humor lighting her eyes.

"So, that's what it's about. It's so obvious," Tamera agreed.

"We can turn together." Kimber smiled, nearly jumping from her seat. "That would be awesome since I really am a chicken about the pain. I hear it's fierce."

Tena gently elbowed Kimber in the side. "I told you before, when your man is holding you, you can endure anything. It's really not so bad."

Kimber's cheeks reddened. "But I kind of like it when Anton drinks from me, or the fact he doesn't need to go to a donor for sustenance."

"He still will tap your arteries, you little hussy." Tena picked up her glass of chardonnay and took a sip. Her gaze turned devilish. "He just won't get any nourishment from it. And it will be so much more pleasurable because you get to bite him back."

Laughter filled the room again. India was certainly glad she had invited the women over to help pass the time, but her thoughts weren't far from Alexander and her stomach was tied in knots. If anything happened to him, she'd never forgive herself.

This was her fault.

She had brought Spike down on the Sons.

India sure in the hell hoped Alexander was correct and Spike and the Devils were no match for the Sons of Sangue. Not only did she want Alexander back unharmed, but Anton and Bobby as well. Any other outcome and she would never be able to face the two women sitting across from her again. Thankfully, Kane, Kaleb, and Grayson were at the Blood 'n' Rave, waiting for the Vlad to return.

Three fewer Sons she had to worry about.

After picking up her own glass of wine, she downed its contents, then looked at the clock. The wait was nearly over. Two more hours and the Sons would come crashing in on Spike's siesta, hopefully putting him to sleep for good.

CHAPTER TWENTY-THREE

ALEXANDER USED THE BACK OF HIS FOREARM TO WIPE AWAY the sweat gathering on his brow. His skull cap was balanced on his lap. The trip south had taken a little less than thirteen hours as they had hauled ass down the coast. According to Bobby's directions, they were about ten minutes out from where Spike and his men were held up.

Adrenaline pulsed through his veins. It was all he could do to keep the vampire at bay for the window of time it would take to descend on the Devils. Waves crashed against the shore where they had pulled their bikes to await the call. Sting was instructed to get anyone worth saving out of the ranch style home on the edge of town. Once they were out of the way, then phone Bobby.

"How much longer, Preacher?"

Alexander sucked at the waiting game. He wanted action. Hell, he wanted Spike dead so he could get back on the road and get on with securing himself a mate. Although he was pretty sure India felt the same way, Alexander didn't want to give her time for second thoughts.

Bobby ran a hand down his long beard. "What the hell is your hurry, Xander? We're here. It's a matter of time, and the way I got it figured, we got all night."

"He's probably in a hurry to get back to his woman." Grigore guffawed, the only one finding humor in his remark. "The way those two have been going at it—"

"Fuck you, Wolf."

"You keep saying that, Xander, and I might start to think you got a crush on me."

"You really are an asshole."

"So, you and India, huh?" Anton asked. "You going to ask her to be your mate? If so, you got my vote, man. She's a good girl."

"Thanks, Rogue. I appreciate that."

"Seriously?" Grigore asked. "GQ is about to take the dive? For what it's worth and in all seriousness, I agree with Rogue. Get you off the market and there are more women for me," he added with a wink.

The consensus seemed from those present that no one would veto his union with India, meaning he wouldn't have to worry about how the church meeting would go. The Sons of Sangue approved of India. And although he was happy to hear his brothers liked her, they were beginning to sound like a bunch of chatty women, putting their two cents in about his fucking love life, thanks to Grigore. He was just about to tell them they needed to change the damn subject when Bobby's cell rang.

The large man pulled the phone from his pocket and answered. He swiped his finger across the glass and placed it next to his ear.

Showtime.

Bobby ended the call and shoved the cell back into his jeans pocket. "Sting says we have a small window. He's out, along with a few of the other men, leaving seven of them, including Spike. Sting said we might want to make tracks, though, since Spike's talking about hitting the road. Apparently, he knows he's got a big ol' target on his back. He's not willing to stay in one place for an extended period. There are six of us. Just so you know, I'm calling two. The rest of you each take out one."

"Spike is mine." Alexander's fangs elongated. "I think that goes without saying."

"Just keep in mind, he's conniving, a loose cannon. He won't fight fair."

"What are you saying, Wolf? I can't handle my own?" Alexander growled.

Grigore raised a brow in skepticism.

"Seriously? You're an ass. India was there. I had to save her life, otherwise the motherfucker would've never gotten away."

"Okay, then. Let's save this energy for those who deserve it," Anton spoke up. "We're wasting precious time. Let's go stomp some Devils."

"Does anyone get out alive?" Peter asked.

"No, Rocker." Bobby kicked up his stand and put on his helmet. "Sting assured me the ones surrounding Spike are the worst of the worst. Ain't a damn one of them worth saving. Let's ride."

The sound of the six Harleys rumbling to life was deafening, drawing the attention of those on the beach. They needed to get to the Devils before word got out the Sons of Sangue were in town. Even though none of them wore their colors, there was always a chance of being recognized. The men filed into line behind Bobby and Anton, then took off.

By the time they arrived, instead of men, there would be six menacing vampires descending upon the house. They would rid Santa Barbara of some of the worst criminals in their community, the kind not worth the oxygen they sucked ... including Spike.

He's going down.

No way in hell was Alexander returning to India without being able to tell her that Spike had paid his penance, that he would never be able to hurt her again. When he asked India to be his mate, there would be nothing standing between them. He was in love with her and he planned to tell her upon their return.

Moments later, the crew pulled up to the quiet, suburban street. Very few houses lined the road, leaving several overgrown empty lots. The ranch house was at the dead end. They couldn't risk driving their bikes, so Bobby led them into a field at the front end of the street. They'd take the rest of the way on foot, get in quick, and not give Spike a chance to split once he caught the scent of other vampires in the vicinity. No way could they mask their arrival. Any delay could mean losing their target. He was a wirier little fucker. No doubt about it.

"We hit the front door, no hesitation," Bobby said. "Xander, you take the back. From the point we leave this lot, Spike will have seconds in which to act. Since he has our speed and agility, he'll only need seconds. Are we ready?"

"Let's wipe the planet of these fuckers."

"Agreed, Lightning," Alexander said, then he looked at Bobby and nodded. "Let's rock."

No other word was needed. The six of them took off, their unnatural speed eating up the asphalt. Within no time, the front door lay flat against the scarred wooden flooring as Bobby didn't bother opening it. He'd knocked the fucker right off its hinges. Screams of death carried to Alexander's ears as he moved around to the back. Spike made it through the door, heading for the forest beyond. Alexander was on his heels, breathing down his back.

"Not this time, fucker." He leaped and tackled Spike to the grass, not giving him time to reach the forest, which would have afforded him cover.

Spike rolled, scattering leaves and vegetation. He used his foot to launch Alexander from on top of him. Alexander flew upside down into one of the trees. His back smacked against the large trunk, nearly knocking the breath from him before hitting the ground. After jumping to his feet, Alexander snagged the back of Spike's shirt and drew him up short from taking off again. The sound of his shirt ripping carried across the breeze.

Alexander threw him to the ground, leaping onto his back. Grabbing a fistful of dirty blond hair, he yanked back, exposing his neck and earning a hiss from Spike. "You ready to die, motherfucker?"

Spike chortled. His chest heaved. "You can't kill me. I'm fucking immortal."

"Apparently, your buddy Raúl left that part out of your vampire one-oh-one training. You aren't in the movies, you bastard. You may be harder to kill, but you can definitely bite it."

Alexander bared his teeth, sank them into the side of Spike's neck, and tore out a chunk of flesh, arteries, and muscle. Blood spurted from the large gaping hole, which began to heal almost immediately due to his vampire DNA.

"That was from India, you miserable fuck."

Spike barely managed to buck Alexander off this time, his strength weakened from the healing wound. He wobbled to his feet. Hunching down, his feet shoulder-width apart, he growled and rushed Alexander, knocking him to his back. Spike's gaze was wild. *Inhuman.* Alexander would bet there wasn't much humanity left inside of Spike.

And Alexander was about to do the world a favor.

In the blink of an eye, he flipped their positions so that he once again straddled Spike's chest. The grip he had on Spike's ribs with his thighs kept the vampire immobile. The blood-flow from the side of his neck staunched. Alexander's hand fisted over a broken branch within his reach, likely felled from when he'd hit the tree. He broke it in half, leaving one end sharp and aimed at Spike's soon-to-be-dead heart.

Alexander raised the branch. "This one is from me, motherfucker." He thrust it downward, straight through the man's heart, stopping its beat.

Spike screeched right before his eyes went blank. His facial features morphed back to his human state. Blood leaked from the corner of his mouth.

Satisfaction surged through his veins, remembering Spike's cruelty toward India, what he'd done to make her lose the baby, and all the hell he had caused for them as well as his MC brothers. He placed a bloodied hand over his dog tags, remembering the men he couldn't save during the war, knowing that by ridding the planet of this hateful fuck, he'd likely saved countless innocents who might have fallen victim to his madness had he lived. Finally, he was proud of himself for making things right for India, and for himself, and his future with her as a mate. He'd waste no more time glorifying over the fact the piece of crap was finally dead. He needed to make sure his brothers were okay.

He rose, wiped his bloodied hands on his jeans, then sprinted for the back of the house. Just as he reached the door, Anton stepped through.

"You guys okay?" Alexander asked.

"All dead. And Spike?"

"Dead."

"Good. Go gather his body. We're going to torch this place and get the hell out of Dodge."

Alexander retrieved the blackheart's body, tossed it into the living area with the remaining Devils, and walked out of the house via the back door. The authorities would likely call this massacre "gang related," for which it was. The smell of gasoline wafted to his nose, right before he heard the fire take hold. His five brothers met him in the back yard, watching as the flames quickly took hold and lit up the dark sky.

"Let's get back on the road, ladies," Bobby said.

Wasting no time, the five of them followed him back to their bikes.

HOURS LATER, THEY HAD PULLED into a rest stop just over the border of Oregon, having ridden through the night and into the morning. They had stopped long enough to stretch their legs and clean up, ditching their bloodied clothes for the clean ones they had packed in their saddle bags.

Alexander stood on the rocky shore, looking across the ocean and into the horizon when Grigore came up and draped a beefy arm across his shoulders.

"You going to be okay, man?"

Alexander smiled, feeling more lighthearted and free than he had in a long time, maybe even since the war. "Yeah. Thanks, Wolf. For the first time in what feels like forever, I can honestly say I'm great."

"You really do love her, don't you?"

Alexander would die for her. "Like no other. Let's hope she feels the same about my sorry ass."

———

KANE SAT AT THE LARGE TABLE in the center of the room, tapping the end of the pen against the surface. Vlad was due back any moment. The three of them had been waiting his return for the past hour. He hoped that his great-grandfather came bearing news on Brea and Ryder. Maybe even answers about Alexander's true blood nature.

Before Constantine had left with the others, he had reported to Kaleb his findings on Brea and Ryder's lineage. He had traced them both back to Romania. Kane would lay odds, by the looks of things, the two of them were somehow related, if not to him and Kaleb as well.

Grayson glanced at his wristwatch. "What time did the old man say he was coming?"

"Old man? Who are you calling old, Gypsy?" Vlad strode into the room. His presence always seemed to make any room grow smaller. His long black hair hung loosely about his fierce expression. "I can best you any day, son. You name the day and time and I'll be there."

Grayson chuckled with a roll of his eyes. "I'm no fool."

Vlad winked at him, then gave Kane and Kaleb hugs and solid slaps on the back. "Glad to be back, boys, but I'll need to make this trip brief. Although I had a better than usual visit with my brother, I can't help but think he's being nice for a reason."

"Mircea isn't nice without ulterior motives," Kane grumbled. The man was a menace to society. Kane would have taken Mircea's life when he had the chance had his great-grandfather not put his foot down.

"You ought to know, dear brother." Kaleb harrumphed. "You're the one who went to Mircea to get permission to mate with Cara while you were technically still mated to his stepdaughter."

"Don't remind me. I'm sure a day will come when he'll want something in return, even if Rosalee is no longer among the living."

"Thank goodness for that. No tears shed over her demise." Kaleb tipped his chin at Vlad. "We have you to thank for that little favor."

Vlad's lips turned down. "My brother wouldn't dare challenge my authority or decisions, regardless of his plans he had for the little bitch."

"If Mircea was smart." Grayson chuckled. "I'm thinking he's not too intelligent when it comes to handling you."

"There's a lot of truth to that." Vlad pulled out a chair and sat while the rest of them retook their seats around the table. His gaze searched out Kane and Kaleb. "Mircea and I had a talk about the anomalies here. Generally, true bloods turn quickly, such as Alexander. We can't help but think that it's quite possible this is the case for Ryder. If that's true, then I need to start seeing if my dear departed brother Radu has any living family members left."

"Why Radu and not you or Mircea?" Kaleb asked.

"Other than the two of you, I know of no other living relation. Mircea swears he's the last of his line as well."

"We were able to trace Ryder and Brea's lineage back to Romania." Kane rubbed his slight whisker growth on his jaw. "I don't think that's a coincidence. Any way we can tell?"

"I may be able to tell by the flavor of their blood. At least it's my hope there are similarities. I scented Ryder's presence. Can you have him come in here?"

Kaleb nodded, stood and opened the door. He called for Ryder to join them. Seconds later, the man entered the room.

Vlad stood. "Come here, boy. If you wouldn't mind, I'd like a small taste."

Ryder's brow furrowed. "Of?"

"Your blood."

"Can I ask why?"

Vlad ignored the disrespect. "We're attempting to determine your lineage. I may be able to tell by the distinct flavors or properties of your blood. It might tell me if you are a true blood, coming from the Tepes' bloodline."

Ryder offered his arm to the elder vampire without further question. Vlad brought Ryder's wrist to his lips and sank his fangs into the vein. After withdrawing a small amount, he licked the twin holes closed.

"Interesting." Vlad returned to the table. His hand indicated that Ryder should join them.

Vlad grasped Kane's wrist, repeating his actions. He traveled the perimeter of the table, sampling blood from all present before retaking his seat.

"Grandfather?" Kane asked.

"There is only one at this table who is not of the Tepes' lineage and that is Gypsy. His blood is missing the tang of the true bloods sitting here." Vlad looked at the Sons of Sangue VP. "You were turned, correct?"

"Yes. I was in a bad accident. Kane saved me."

"Which means Ryder is a true blood?" Kaleb shifted in his seat, his gaze narrowing. "One of your grandsons?"

Vlad shook his head. "Not mine. I had tasted Mircea's and my blood before I left my island. While Mircea and I had similar properties, we also had piquancy all of our own. You and Kane have the Tepes' blood, but you have an essence that is distinctly mine. Mircea has the Tepes' blood, but if you were born from his lineage you would have a flavor unique to him."

One of Kaleb's dark brows rose. "Are you saying Ryder is a direct descendant of Mircea?"

"Not at all." Vlad laid a hand on Ryder's shoulder. "You have Tepes' blood, son. You're a true blood for sure, but you don't belong to Mircea or me. What I believe is you're a descendant of my younger brother Radu, who was long ago deceased."

Kane sat back, blowing out a steady stream of air. "Well, if that isn't the fucking news of the day. Did you know your brother had any living descendants?"

"Not until now."

"And Brea?" Kaleb asked.

"She's on her way. I called the Blood 'n' Rave on my way here and asked that she meet us." Vlad stood and paced the floor. "If I'm correct, then Brea is also from my late brother's loins. If that's the case, then it was likely her direct descendant blood that allowed her to change Draven."

"I thought vampires could only have male babies," Grayson pointed out. "Brea is obviously not male."

Vlad raised a finger, waggling it. "You're correct, Kaleb. But 'vampire' is the key word here. Radu was never turned. Therefore, he could have children, both male and female. They still carried the Tepes' blood from my father. He died before his vampire DNA demanded he drink blood. And if my deductions are correct, the same could be said for his descendants. They would have awakened the vampire gene as I did had they drank human blood. But they hadn't ...until now."

The door to the clubhouse opened and Kane scented Brea and Draven's arrival. Seconds later, Brea entered the meeting room. Her short brown hair hung to her chin on one side, accenting her pixie-like features. She was tiny in stature but walked up to Vlad as if she were his equal, with no fear at all. Kane supposed it was her upbringing and her family history.

"You wanted to see me?" Brea asked. Draven stood behind her, his hands on her shoulders. "Draven said you requested my presence. Have I done something to displease you?"

Vlad chuckled, which Kane rarely heard. "I like this one."

"Thank you." Brea's blue eyes sparkled from the compliment. "You, sir, are charming."

Vlad motioned for Draven to take a seat, which he did only after Brea nodded for him to follow the directive. Draven was being protective of his mate, which was a noble gesture, but he'd never stand a chance against Vlad. None of them would. The primordial could, in truth, take what he wanted.

Vlad gripped her tiny wrist. "If I may."

She nodded, apprehension filling her gaze. Sinking his fangs into her tiny wrist, Vlad sipped from her vein before using his tongue to seal the bite. Vlad pulled out a chair next to her mate and she took her seat at the table. Vlad remained standing, bracing his hands on the surface.

"As you know the only two remaining primordials that we know of are Mircea and I. The term is reserved for the eldest of the lineage. In Mircea's case, that also encompassed Rosalee because he had given her his primordial blood to turn her. In Kane and Kaleb's case, they were not turned by my blood but rather born into it, making them true bloods. They will be primordials upon my death as the oldest living siblings remaining from my loins. Or should they drink from my blood. Had I used my blood to turn someone, as I did Mircea, then they, too, would be primordials. Over the years, I chose not to share my blood."

Vlad righted himself, walked around the table, and stood between Kane and Kaleb. "We know now, had my brother drank human blood as I did, he would have turned without my assistance. What I believe is my father had the vampire

DNA, passed on to us three brothers, and down to our descendants. Kane and Kaleb turned simply by ingesting human blood when they came of age. As do any true bloods."

"What are you saying, Grandpa? I'm not following." Kaleb looked up at Vlad. "What does this have to do with Ryder or Brea?"

"By the taste of their blood, I can confirm that Ryder and Brea belong to the Tepes' lineage. But they don't have the unique tang that belongs to me or my brother Mircea." Vlad continued around the table until he stood between Ryder and Brea. "What I am trying to tell you is that Mircea and I are no longer the only two primordials. Ryder and Brea are as well."

"Excuse me? I don't believe it." Grayson spoke, saying what they were all likely feeling. "How are they primordials?"

"My brother Radu died long ago, but not before siring children, none of which became vampires ... until now. Brea and Ryder are descendants of the same family line. Their blood has the same taste. You said yourself, Kane, that their lineage went back to Romania. I'm betting it goes back to my brother Radu. These two are the oldest descendants of my brother, which would be why Brea's blood was able to turn Draven. To my knowledge, she is the only living female descendant of the Tepes family."

"But I was turned by Kinky." Brea shook her head in obvious disbelief. "It was his blood that turned me."

"How many days did it take you to turn?"

"A little over a day."

"My little one"—Vlad placed a hand on her shoulder and knelt beside her—"had you simply drank any blood, vampire or human, you would have turned regardless."

He looked at Ryder. "Just as Ryder would have."

"And Alexander?" Kane asked. "He's a true blood—that we know as he drank blood to turn. His biological parents dumped him in a garbage can, where the parents who raised him found him. We have no way of knowing his lineage."

"Since I don't believe either I or Mircea have any other living descendants, I'm guessing he's of Radu's loins as well."

"And you'll know this by his taste?"

"Yes."

Outside the meeting room, the main door to the clubhouse burst open, followed by the return of the six brothers who had ridden south to take out Spike. Hoots and hollers were heard before Alexander walked into the meeting room, followed by the other five.

"What's going on?" Alexander's gaze traveled the room.

"Spike?" Kane asked.

"Dead." More celebrating traveled the room. Alexander looked at Vlad, who was studying him as the noise died down. "Why do I feel like I'm under a microscope? Everything okay here?"

Vlad gripped Alexander's wrist. "May I?"

Alexander's brow furrowed, but he nodded nonetheless. Vlad sank his teeth into Alexander's flesh and tasted his blood. Withdrawing his fangs, he once again sealed the holes. This time, Vlad paled and his breath hissed from him.

"What is it?" Kane asked.

"He's *not* from Radu's lineage."

"Then who? Mircea?" Kaleb stood and walked around the table. "What the fuck are you saying, Grandpa?"

Vlad looked at Alexander, his hand landing on his shoulder. "You, son, are one of mine."

Alexander's brows shot up, Kane wiped a hand down his mouth, and Kaleb shook his head in disbelief.

"He's our brother?" Kane asked.

Vlad shook his head, his gaze still on Alexander. "Half-brother. Your and Kaleb's lineage is proven. But apparently, I had a bastard child out there I did not know about. Alexander must be a descendant of that infidelity."

CHAPTER TWENTY-FOUR

THE CLUBHOUSE HAD FINALLY EMPTIED, LEAVING ALEXander to his thoughts. Christ, he was a distant relative to the man himself. Vlad Tepes had blindsided him. Hell, the only thing he'd been able to think about the entire ride home was seeing India ... telling her how he felt, asking her to be his mate.

Not that any of that had changed.

No, he still wanted her for all eternity, but it wasn't every day you found out you were related to the most powerful and eldest vampire. Not to mention the fact he was a half-sibling of the Tepes twins. His entire life had been spent wondering where he came from, or why his parents had felt the need to dispose of him. After all, isn't that what you do with garbage? Dispose of it? He may not ever get an answer to the latter, but he finally had an answer about where he'd come from.

Movement from behind caught his attention. Had he not been preoccupied, he would have scented her long before he heard her. Since everyone had gone to the Blood 'n' Rave to celebrate the demise of Spike, that left the two of them alone in the clubhouse. Alexander hadn't exactly been in the mood to party.

India stepped tentatively beside him. He stood by the bar, his hands wrapping an empty glass. "Whiskey?"

Alexander chuckled, covering her hand with one of his and entwining their fingers. "No. Even if the moment called for it. Just a lemon-lime soda."

Her deep brown eyes searched his. "Spike is gone?"

"More than gone, *gattina*. The fucker is never coming back. He's dead."

"Good," she said, though her facial expression didn't look too happy about the announcement.

Alexander bumped his shoulder with hers. "I thought you would be ecstatic."

She squeezed his hand. "Don't get me wrong. I'm happy he's gone and will never hurt another human being, but I can't celebrate the end of a life. Do you think he could've been redeemed?"

"If I thought that, *gattina*, I wouldn't have stabbed his black heart. Some people are incapable of being redeemed."

"I thought as much."

"He's the cause of your miscarriage."

"*And* the reason I had the baby to begin with."

"Can I ask you a question?" Her nod was his answer. "What story was Spike talking about up on that mountain?"

A wariness filled her gaze and she remained quiet so long he thought she might not want to answer.

"He told me how and why he became a Devil."

"And somehow has something to do with me?"

She wet her lips, drawing his gaze briefly to their perfect bow shape. "He was on his way up the corporate ladder of his fiancée's daddy's firm. Apparently, he caught you having sex with her in some dive bar back alley. He left the firm, met Tank, and the rest is history."

Alexander raised one of his brows. "I had sex with a lot of nameless females. So instead of blaming himself for not keeping her interest, he thought to blame me for his slut of a fiancée? I never had to beg to get laid."

"I don't suppose you did." India's smile grew. "You were her 'bad boy biker' fantasy come true."

"I sure to hell hope I'm *your* fantasy come true, because you're the only one who matters." Alexander turned, laying his forearms across her shoulders as they faced one another. "Would you do it all over again … with Spike, I mean?"

A smile inched up her cheeks. "If it meant having you in the end, yes."

Alexander couldn't help but ask. He was about to put it all out there on the line. "Does that mean you love me, *gattina*?"

She glanced down, her hands fiddling with the front of his T-shirt. "You want the truth? Or do you want me to say what I think you want to hear?"

He tipped up her chin with his thumb. "I want the truth, whatever that is. No more lies or half-truths."

India wet her lips with her tongue, drawing his gaze. Damn, if he didn't want to kiss her—and he would, right after he heard her confession.

"I think I always have, from the first day I saw you walk into the Blood 'n' Rave. You wore your Sons of Sangue cut and I so wanted to be your donor. I don't think I've ever seen a more handsome man."

His heart lightened. "And now?"

Tears welled in her eyes. "I will always love you, Xander, even when you don't want me anymore."

"*Gattina*, that's not even fucking possible."

India sucked in air; hope flared in her gaze. "What's not possible?"

"Not wanting you." Alexander ran a knuckle over her downy-soft cheek. "It may have taken a sledgehammer, but, babe—I'm all yours. Heart and soul."

She drew her bottom lip between her teeth to stop its trembling as a tear left her lashes. "You … you—"

"God, yes."

He leaned down and pulled that lower lip into his mouth, suckling it before deepening the kiss, sweeping his tongue into her mouth. She fisted his T-shirt and returned his kiss, tangling her tongue with his. His breathing deepened, his cock hardened. Alexander wanted to pick her up and carry her to his bed, make love to her properly. And he would, right after he asked her the one question still plaguing him.

He framed her face with his palms as he broke the kiss. "You have my promise, *gattina*. I will always love you."

Her smile filled her gaze. "For all eternity?"

"If you will have me."

India slid a hand south, cupping his jean-clad erection. "This is mine, too?" she asked playfully.

"Yours if you will be my mate."

India released him, gripped his nape, and brought him back for a soul-stealing kiss. Damn, but he loved this woman. He'd spend his lifetime showing her just how much.

Alexander broke the kiss and scooped her into his arms and started for the bedroom. "You know you haven't answered my question yet."

Her face glowed with love. "I've always wanted to be your mate, Xander. I just didn't know if you had it in you to ever take one."

"I didn't know it either ... until you." He nudged the open door aside with his booted foot and laid her upon the mattress. "Now, *gattina*, let me show you what you mean to me."

She laughed, scooting toward the headboard. "Close that door, big guy, because I'm about to give you the best sex you've ever had."

He did as he was told and stalked toward the bed. "Prove it." He chuckled. Kneeling on the mattress, it dipped beneath his weight. "Because we've got all the time in the world."

UPON DROPPING THE BOMBSHELL that Ryder and Brea were descendants of his younger brother Radu, Vlad had wasted little time heading back to his island near Belize. According to Vlad, Rosalee had been a primordial simply because Mircea had shared his blood with her, which meant Draven would also be primordial since he had taken Brea's blood.

Kaleb shook his head at the absurdity. From bar owner, all around fuck-up at times, to primordial. He couldn't help but chuckle at the outcome.

"What's so funny?" Kane asked, stepping off his bike.

"The fact that Draven Smith is primordial. How fucked up is that?"

Kane shared the humor. "He is a good guy. But yeah, I get it, Hawk. One day that fuck will be stronger than both of us if he isn't already, all because the blood he ingested came from one of the primordials. Good thing he's on our side, even if he isn't a Sons of Sangue member."

"Should we even tell him, Viper? I mean, it's not like Vlad came right out and said, 'Draven, you're a primordial.' I'm wondering if Draven even understood the significance of Vlad telling how Rosalee came to be primordial."

"He doesn't likely have a clue." Kane took off his skull cap and laid it on the seat of the bike and winked at Kaleb. "I say we wait to see if he figures it out on his own. He might even provide us with a little entertainment along the way as his strength grows. To think Ryder and Brea are actually distant cousins of ours. If Radu was still alive, they would be on our level, but since he's long passed, that makes them the head of the food-chain line."

"I know, right? I might just have to ask Grandpa for some of that blood of his so we can make primordial status, too."

Kane laughed. "You do that and see how far it gets us."

"You never know. And then there's Alexander, our half-brother." Kaleb stepped over his bike, unstrapped and grabbed the bag from the back, and followed Kane up to the Knights' clubhouse. "Crazy shit happening in our camp."

"It's about to get a whole lot crazier."

Kane knocked on the door. They had announced their visit, long before they made tracks north. Red had been told of their intentions, and thankfully with a little persuasion, the MC had been on board. Red would remain president of the Washington chapter, and the rest of the hierarchy would remain intact. After today, the Knights would be patched over and become the Washington chapter of the Sons of Sangue.

Red opened the door. A smile split his red beard as he took Kane's hand and pulled him in for a one-armed shoulder bump. "Good to see you, man."

He opened the door wider for Kane and Kaleb to enter. It appeared as though all the Knights were in attendance, per Kaleb's request. He didn't detect animosity from the men, which was a good start. The real trial would come after they found out about the vampire clause. Kaleb and Kane agreed it would be best to inform them in person. That way if any of the men decided to walk, they could use their hypnotic powers to get them to forget that part of the conversation and lead them to believe they'd simply refused to be patched over.

"Beer? Whiskey?" Red offered.

The twins both took the offered whiskey. After all, Kaleb wasn't about to be inhospitable. They took their seats at the large meeting room table, surrounded by the Knights.

Kaleb tossed his bag to the wooden surface. "Your patches."

Red's smile grew. Nice to see the man was onboard. "Never thought I'd see the day."

Kane chuckled. "Trust me, neither did we. But we see the benefit of growing the Sons and adding to our numbers. We'll eventually take over the West Coast."

"You'll all be asked to get a Sons of Sangue tattoo." Kaleb opened the bag and placed the center death skull on the table. "Make sure it includes this. The Knights' tattoo will need to be inked over. I think that goes without saying."

"It's part of our history, dude," one of the men spoke up. "I'd prefer to keep my tattoo, if you wouldn't mind."

Kaleb looked at Kane. "What do you say, Viper?"

"Honestly, I don't have a problem with it, if you don't." Kane glanced around the table. "Just make sure the Sons' tattoo is larger and more prominent. Any new member coming in, though, can only get a Sons' tattoo. The Knights are dead after today. Hawk?"

"I can consent to that." After all, they were asking to disband the Knights. "The old tattoos can stay on those of you grandfathered in."

Red sat back in his chair, his T-shirt stretching across his beefy chest. He laced his fingers over his rounded belly. "The Sons all voted us in? No arguments?"

"The vote was unanimous," Kaleb assured him. "This union is good for both clubs."

"I'm surprised, Hawk. I would've thought you, of all people, would've been against the idea."

"I was, Red. No doubt about it. Viper helped me see the benefit. I'm ready to put old prejudice behind for the good of the clubs."

"Same here," Red agreed.

Kane began outlining the union. He spoke of shutting down the running of guns and opening a new branch of K&K Motorcycles to be opened in Washington. Those who needed jobs could work there. Kane told them that his and Kaleb's business was flourishing and they needed more shops. K&K Motorcycles had received a lucrative offer to begin shipping their custom bikes overseas. If this all went through, they wouldn't need to run guns to make the chapter money.

Other than the motorcycle shop, their main goal was to assist the Sons' Oregon chapter in shutting down the cartel selling drugs in Oregon and Washington. The La Paz cartel and Raúl Trevino Caballero needed to be taken down. Red, along with the rest of the Knights, did not disagree with having to shut down the running of guns funding their club. After all, the twins were providing them with another way to earn income, one that wouldn't involve the law breathing down their backs.

"We have one more requirement." Kane stood, walked behind Red, and placed his hands on the man's shoulders. "This one is non-negotiable. Should any of you decide against the union after we disclose this, you'll be escorted from the clubhouse by myself or Kaleb. You will no longer have an MC."

The men began murmuring among themselves. Wary eyes traveled around the room. Red struck the mallet against the strike plate, earning back their attention.

Kaleb stood and pulled a top and bottom rocker, along with the center skull patch, from his bag. "One-by-one, you will each be called up here to get your patches. There is a catch. Upon doing so, you'll be asked to drink from either my or my brother's blood."

"What the fuck?" Red shrugged off Kane's hold and stood. "Why the hell would we want to do this? Some sort of weird cult? What's this about, Viper?"

Kane allowed his vampire features to take over his face, horrifying half the room, mystifying the others. To his credit, no one got up or fled.

Kaleb raised one brow and smiled. "Like my brother and I, along with the rest of the Sons of Sangue, you are about to become vampires."

The murmurs began again and grew in volume, though no one left their seats. Most likely out of fear. All eyes went to Red for direction.

Red glanced at Kane without fear. "You sure about this, man?"

"We'll give you strength and immortality, Red," Kane replied. "'Sangue' is Italian for 'blood.' Sons of Sangue to the end."

"Will we have to drink blood to survive?"

Kane nodded. "We'll see that Draven opens a nightclub here in Washington. It's a cover for his blood donors, women who willingly offer their blood to us. You don't require much. There is no need to drain or hurt them. This way there will always be a food source available to you."

Red ran a hand down the ponytail in his beard. "Who will teach us?"

"Kaleb and I feel it's best if I stay behind, see all of you through the change and teach you about being a vampire. Your lives won't be much different than they are now."

"Except we'll be drinking blood." A man from the back of the room jumped to his feet. "You guys are all a bunch of fucking looney tunes! Fuck this shit! I'm out of here."

Kane nodded at him. Kaleb laid down the patches and followed the man to the clubhouse door. By the time the man left, the only thing he remembered was he wasn't about to be a part of the merger with the Sons of Sangue.

Returning to the room, Kaleb asked, "Will there be anyone else?"

The rest of the men remained seated, no doubt waiting on direction from Red. He glanced around the room at each of his men, then back at Kane. "I'm ready."

Kane bit his wrist to start the flow of blood and held it out to Red. "Drink."

Red grasped Kane's wrist and, without hesitation, took it to his lips. When he was finished, Red turned and looked to the man next to him. "Gunner? As VP, I think you should go next."

The large man stood, raising to his six-foot-three inches of height. He out-bulked both of the twins, looking as if he worked out regularly in a gym. He'd make a formable opponent. Good thing he was patching over. Kaleb was more than happy to welcome one of his size on board. Gunner walked to Kane, grabbing his wrist, and took it to his lips. The rest of the men began filing into two lines, one in front of each of the twins. Within a short period of time, they had all retaken their seats, patches in hand.

"As mentioned, Kane has agreed to stay during the turning. It won't be easy, and there will be times you may even wish for death. No worries, you'll survive. You'll be stronger, faster, and with enhanced senses. I promise you, the agony will be worth it."

Kaleb stepped to the front of the room. "I'll see you all soon. I need to get back to Oregon. The first order of business will be sending some of you south of the border to protect one of ours. Viper will fill you in on all the details, once we have you all back on your feet."

Some of the men started to pale, sweat beading their brow. The change was starting. Kane took his seat next to Red, ready to settle in for the long haul. No one would be leaving the clubhouse for at least a week.

Walking to the doorway, Kaleb glanced back at the men. Some of them grabbed their abdomens, already in pain. He didn't envy them the agony, wishing he could have spared them but they needed to walk through the fires of hell to get their promise of immortality.

Kaleb said, "Welcome to the Sons of Sangue, boys," then left the building.

He was certainly glad Kane had offered to stay with them through the change. Kaleb had never been good with downtime. Stepping over the seat of his bike, he started the engine, did a half circle in the parking lot, and pulled back on the throttle. Kane was more than capable of finishing up here. The Sons of Sangue had just increased their numbers. His job now was to see Kane got his justice. Raúl was going down ... the six-feet-under kind of down.

KALEB TEPES SAT AT THE clubhouse meeting room table, the only other one present. That vampire was one scary motherfucker. No one in their right mind would cross him. He'd bet Kaleb would give any one of the Sons of Sangue a run for their money, except for Kane. If the two decided to ever fight it out, he'd put his money on Kane. He was the quieter of the two, but no less menacing.

Ryder had been summoned upon the president's return from Washington. Apparently, the trip north had gone well and the club past P was staying on to see the newly added Sons of Sangue through their change, some of those who would have his back in Mexico.

He sure as shit hoped P was correct and these were men of honor. After all, his back still labeled him as a Devil. He didn't need a Knight with an age-old ax to grind with a Devil and decide to take it out on him. Luckily, he wouldn't be sporting the tattoo for long, he thought with a smug smile. Grayson Gabor would be paying for his new ink. He'd be coming back to make sure that happened. Besides, the king of all vampires had just dropped the bomb that he had primordial strength, which would trump Raúl's strength any day.

"We don't need you to play hero, Ryder." Kaleb slugged back two fingers of whiskey. "We want you back alive."

"I got this, P. You don't have to worry about me."

"Gypsy didn't save your dumb ass only to be ashed at a later date."

Ryder chuckled. "I'll be back. The smart ass is paying for my ink."

"I don't doubt that. Make it happen." Kaleb smiled. "I think maybe you ought to take your time heading down there. Stay off the radar. Grow out your hair, maybe even sport more of a beard. We don't want to take the chance one of those fuckers saw you riding with the Sons."

"Good idea, P. Who knows, maybe I'll even catch the eye of Gabriela with the new look."

"I'm counting on it."

Kaleb grabbed the bottle of whiskey from the table and poured himself another glass before offering one to Ryder. He took the tumbler and quickly downed the contents, enjoying the burn all the way to his gut. He may not get much of a buzz from it any longer, but he still enjoyed the consumption.

"Brea gave us a description of the normal type Gabriela dated," Kaleb continued. "You ain't it. Another good reason to change up the appearance."

"She won't know what the hell hit her, P."

Ryder might not have been a lady killer, but he'd had his share of women nonetheless. He had little problem getting them out of their pants. Gabriela would be no different. Ryder wasn't cocky, just confident.

"Good. I'll expect you to head out in the next couple of days."

"And those following me?"

"They'll give you some time, then head south. Wolf, Lightning, and Rocker will be looking out for you from our camp. We'll also send a handful of Sons from the Washington chapter. We don't expect results overnight. We want you to go down and romance Gabriela. It's your only in with the kingpin."

"So, how do I explain my vampirism?"

"Blame it on Spike."

Ryder nodded, remembering his earlier instructions. "Good thing the fucker is dead. It'll help my cover for sure."

"We wouldn't have gotten away with the story without Xander ending his sorry ass." Kaleb leaned forward. "We'll get you a burner phone. The only numbers on there will go to our burner phones that Wolf, Viper, and I have. You get into any trouble at all, you call one of us and lay low. We'll bring the troops, get you the hell out of there."

"And what happens when I get in?"

"You keep us abreast of your progress. We'll decide further action by what's going on in La Paz. We have to play this by ear. There are too many variables to cement a solid plan. This isn't going to be completed overnight, Ryder."

"Yeah, I get that."

"You get your affairs in order and get ready to head south."

"Won't take long." Ryder chuckled. "I don't have many affairs to take care of. I'll be all yours."

He rose from his seat and headed for the door when Kaleb called out, stopping him. "You make sure you're careful. As I said, we want you back, man."

His smile grew. "Good to know, P. I'll be back. It's a fucking promise. And when I do, you tell Gypsy I'm collecting on that debt."

CHAPTER TWENTY-FIVE

Kaleb strode into the meeting room, shutting the door behind him. Any of the non-MC members left in the clubhouse living area would not be privy to the goings-on. Club P had called a church meeting and they were all to be present. No question. Alexander glanced around the room and the only two missing members were Kane Tepes and Ryder Kelley.

Alexander wasn't sure where the two men were but he was betting he was about to find out. Everyone's expressions told him they appeared to be just as much in the dark.

Kaleb took a seat at the head of the table and struck the hammer against the strike plate. All conversation ceased. "Let's get this show on the road, shall we?"

"I'll call the meeting to order." Anton, as club secretary, had his computer tablet in front of him. "What's on the agenda, P?"

"We have a couple items. It goes without saying that nothing leaves this room." Kaleb glanced around the table. Alexander knew this group of men. What the club P had to say wouldn't be discussed outside of this room, not even with their mates. "Ryder Kelley's life may depend on our silence."

"He's not here," Grayson pointed out the obvious. "I take it that's because he agreed to the plan laid out at the Rave."

"He did. Ryder's heading south as we speak and disassociating with us. He's taking some time off, then heading to Mexico when I give him the go-ahead. For now, his main focus is to change his appearance and lay low. You will not be able to get in touch with him, and should you run across him at some point, act as though you don't know him or treat him as you might a Devil. The only members he'll have contact with are Viper, Wolf, and I through burner phones. It's imperative when he gets to La Paz that they believe he's completely acting on his own. No ties to anyone."

"And Gabriela?" Anton asked. "Does he think he'll be able to attract her attention?"

"Honestly," Kaleb continued, "I believe it's our only hope of getting him inside. Raúl trusts no one. Ryder isn't going to be able to infiltrate the kingpin's camp without her. And even then, it's still a gamble."

"Which of us will be heading down there?" Grayson asked. Alexander knew the two men had been close since he had been the one to turn Ryder. "We can't hang him out to dry without backup."

"We wouldn't think of it, Gypsy. Wolf, Lightning, and Rocker will be heading down there when he gets closer to Raúl's home base. We're hoping to find him there. Brea will be providing us with the location."

"Only three?" Grayson arched one of his brows. "Forgive me for saying so, P, but I feel that leaves him at serious risk even with primordial strength. I volunteer to go along."

"Sorry, Gypsy. You're needed here." Kaleb tapped his forefinger on the table. "That goes without saying for the rest of you. You're mated. You'll stay here with the rest of us to run business as usual. K&K Motorcycles needs you. We'll be expanding and I'll need you to show the new hires the ropes. Besides, we aren't just sending in three Sons to keep an eye on Ryder. That brings us to the second topic of the meeting."

"Who's going with us?" Grigore asked. "I'd like to know who I'm traveling with. If they aren't Sons, can we fucking trust them?"

"Viper and I took a trip north yesterday, Wolf. Viper stayed behind to assist." Kaleb leaned back in his chair, crossing one leg over his knee. "The Knights are officially disbanded. We now have a Washington chapter of the Sons of Sangue. Some of them will be going with you."

"They aren't even vampires," Constantine weighed in. "Sending a human in makes us more vulnerable. I don't want to have to watch out for their weak human asses."

"I'd agree, Lightning, if that were the case." Kaleb smirked. "All but one of the Knights has agreed to be turned. That's why Viper stayed in Washington, to see them through the change and teach them the ropes. We not only increased our numbers but our strength. Once Ryder is in place, more of us will head to La Paz as needed. This operation will take time, and the Washington chapter will have plenty of time to gain their strength."

"K&K Motorcycles is expanding?" Alexander wondered about the business end of things. "Are we building a larger shop?"

"We're opening a new one in Washington. The new Sons of Sangue members will be working there. Time to keep them boys honest. No more running guns. Viper and I were working on a lucrative deal to send our customs overseas that recently went through, so we could use the help."

Kaleb outlined the rest of his plan, along with the details of his and Viper's trip north. "Are there any other questions before we adjourn?"

"What about more prospects?" Grigore asked.

"Anyone opposed to bringing new prospects on board, state your 'nay' now." No one vetoed the vote. "Then be wise choosing who you want to sponsor, boys. We can't have traitors among us."

Anton cleared his throat before Alexander had time to bring up wanting India as a mate. "If you don't mind, P, I have something I'd like to add to the meeting."

"Which is?"

"Kimber has finally agreed to be turned. I'd like your permission to take her as my mate."

"It's about damn time." Kaleb grinned, with a shake of his head. "I think that goes without saying for all of us, but yes, we can certainly put that to a vote."

"Before we do"—Alexander cleared his throat—"I was about to ask the same for India. I'd like permission to turn her as well."

Grigore chuckled. "Well, I'll be damned. You got my vote, GQ."

Alexander slapped him on the back. "You won't have to take my seconds any longer, Wolf."

"Very funny, Xander. Fuck you. I get plenty of women without having to saddle up with your throwaways." Grigore hadn't taken offense. Alexander enjoyed their good-natured ribbing. "Seriously, bro, never thought I'd see the day."

Alexander smiled. "Neither did I, Wolf. I don't think I even saw it coming."

"Well, then," Kaleb broke up the banter, "how about we put this to a vote and get the hell out of here?"

"I'll second that," Grayson said.

The "ayes" quickly traveled the table, no one opposing the two unions. Alexander's heartbeat quickened. He wasn't sure if he was more nervous or excited now that nothing stood in the way. Anton beamed, obviously having plenty of time to get used to the idea he was about to promise his forevers to Kimber. Not a doubt could be found in his big frame. The man's chest puffed like a peacock.

The men congratulated the both of them before filing out of the room as the meeting adjourned. A celebration was about to ensue, giving the men and women present a reason to hang out and congratulate the couples about to be mated.

Alexander, not one to party, would rather get India alone. The last thing he needed was to allow his nerves to get the better of him. Not that he didn't want to make India his, to be with her forever. He knew without a shadow of a doubt he loved her. His problem lay in his fear of disappointment. There was no turning back from a mating. No such thing as a divorce. Once mated, it was for eternity. What if India realized he wasn't who she thought him to be? What if he wound up falling short?

Before he turned her, he planned on making sure she damn well knew what she was getting into. Alexander wasn't about to lead her down a path of sorrow and desolation. Seeing her unhappy would damn near kill him. If he so much as saw the slightest hesitation, he'd set her free, no hard feelings. Alexander loved her too much to ever see her suffer for her hasty decision.

INDIA WATCHED ALEXANDER FROM across the room. He was speaking with Grigore and Kaleb, his face an unreadable mask. Her gaze had drifted to the clock well over a thousand times already. She swore the second hand ticked slower by the minute. Enough people came by and welcomed her to the family that she knew the vote had gone in her favor.

And yet, Alexander had hardly spoken two words to her.

She drew her lower lip between her teeth to keep the moisture from gathering in her eyes, refusing to cry. The last thing she wanted was everyone's sympathy or berating Alexander over his—what?—case of second-guessing?

Her gaze traveled the room. Thankfully, the party seemed to be winding down. Anton had his muscular arm around Kimber's neck, repeatedly whispering into her ear, causing her to giggle and her cheeks to redden. That's what India wanted. Every. Damn. Day. Not this Alexander, the one who would rather converse with everyone else in the room.

Finally, he glanced her way and smiled. Her heart damn near beat from her chest. She swore the entire room of vampires with enhanced hearing could pick up on it. He didn't look at her with regret. If anything, she saw the love she felt for him mirrored in his face. He quickly excused himself from his conversation and strode across the room, stopping just shy of touching her.

"Hey," he said, his tongue wetting his kissable lips.

"Hey, yourself." India wrapped an arm around her waist, her hand clasping her other arm to keep from touching him like she wanted. He had her more nervous than a virgin on her wedding night.

"Want to cut out of here?"

"And go where?"

Seriously? If the vote had gone in their favor, she thought he would've been more inclined to take their relationship to the next level. Not standing here discussing what? Some kind of a date?

His gaze heated, his dark irises swallowed by the blackness of his vampirism coming forth. "Quite honestly, I was hoping our bedroom."

India couldn't help the flutter in her chest or the elation that came with his confession. He hadn't been ignoring her. Alexander had been playing nice with the people who had given him permission to mate with her. Now, without a care as to who remained, he wanted to be done with the celebration as much as she did. India's desire rose exponentially and she didn't care how many in the room scented it. The only one that mattered, though, was the handsome man in front of her who was about to make her his mate.

"I thought you'd never ask."

He laughed, his fangs prominent beneath his upper lip. "If I could've escorted them out of here an hour ago, I would have. But they wouldn't have gone, even if I'd tried. What really matters to me is you."

The moisture she had been working damn hard to keep at bay broke loose. "You're all that's ever mattered to me, Xander. I love you more with each passing minute."

He wiped an escaped tear from her cheek. "Then meet me in our room in ten. I can't just up and disappear … well, I could. I'm sure they'd all understand. But I have a couple more people to talk to, then I'm all yours."

And he was. The thought made her heart soar. From this moment forward, Alexander Dumitru was hers, heart and soul, just as she was his. India said a few goodbyes herself to the women, telling them she was tired and ready to retire. The knowing smiles she received told her they all knew better. Not that she cared. Down the road, though, they might want to consider getting a place where the other occupants wouldn't scent what they were about to do.

INDIA LAY STRETCHED OUT ON the bed, waiting for Alexander. She wished he'd hurry the hell up. Not only was she ready to be his, but she wanted him deep inside her when she drank his blood to make her so.

The volume of the party had finally died down, telling her most had left the clubhouse. Not soon enough for her liking.

Soon, the door creaked open and a stream of light proceeded Alexander into the room. He had morphed into full vampire. After closing the door and stepping next to the bed, he leaned down and braced himself with his forearms. The mattress dipped beneath his weight. His smile grew, his teeth shining white from the dim bedside lamp. Alexander's gaze heated her flesh as it traveled over her already nude body. India had stripped the minute she'd passed through the door.

To say she was in a hurry was an understatement.

Was she nervous? Hell, yes. But her desire to love Alexander the rest of her life—no, for all eternity—trumped the pain she knew she was about to experience.

"I have to ask, India." Alexander's deep voice filled the room. "This is the only chance you'll be given to change your mind. I know I'm not easy to love and I sure in the hell am not deserving of you. Do you still want to be my mate? Or would you rather remain my girlfriend?"

India gripped a fistful of his tee and pulled him toward her. "Ask me again and I might just have to ash you."

Alexander chuckled as he stood up and stripped off his clothes, dropping them on the floor. Never had she seen anything more handsome or glorious. She had made a lot of mistakes in life, done enough to make him hate her, and yet he still stood here with nothing but love in his eyes.

Alexander crawled onto the bed, his gaze that of a predator. When he reached her, he dipped his head and kissed her long and hard. Her heated desire for him blew the head right off the mercury.

"Make love to me, Xander."

He didn't need to be asked twice. He spread her legs, moistened the tip of his cock with her arousal, and slid in. He filled her entirely, completing her. India wrapped her legs around his trim waist and held him firmly in place.

"You want to know what I want, vampire?"

His smile twinkled in his eyes. "Anything, *gattina*. All you have to do is ask and it's yours. I will always give you what you want, what you need. I promise to always protect you, even at the expense of my own life. I won't ever fail you. Heaven help me, but you make me whole again."

"Then give me your blood."

"Are you sure? Last chance."

She framed his whiskered jaw with her palms. "Keep it up and I'm going to bite you."

India felt his chuckle rumble through him as she dropped her hold. "Then Ms. Jackson, prepare to be mine just as I am yours. What is done cannot be undone."

He tore a hole in his left wrist with his fangs. Crimson blood flowed freely from the wound. Alexander held it to her mouth. She took his wrist without hesitation and drank, pushing her over the cliff. Never had she climaxed with barely a touch, nor had experienced one so strong. Releasing his wrist, his name tumbled from her lips. A conflagration begun in her belly, causing her eyes to roll back in her head.

At the expense of his own orgasm, Alexander rolled to his side, pulling her into his spoon, and kissed the soft spot beneath her ear. He whispered against the shell, "I'm sorry."

The pain began to engulf her, making her feel as if liquid fire ran through her veins. Alexander's arms wrapped tightly around her, hearing him groan in his own agony as he consumed some of her pain.

"I will never leave you, *gattina*," Alexander said. "My promise to you."

And she believed him, holding onto him as her affliction and pain became more manageable and his love empowered her through.

ABOUT THE AUTHOR

A daydreamer at heart, Patricia A. Rasey, resides in her native town in Northwest Ohio with her husband, Mark, and her two lovable Cavalier King Charles Spaniels, Todd and Buckeye. A graduate of Long Ridge Writer's School, Patricia has seen publication of some her short stories in magazines as well as several of her novels.

When not behind her computer, you can find Patricia working, reading, watching movies or MMA. She also enjoys spending her free time at the river camping and boating with her husband and two sons. Ms. Rasey is currently a third degree Black Belt in American Freestyle Karate.

Printed in Great Britain
by Amazon